Coup

Kit McKenna

McKenna Publishing, LLC

Other Books By Kit McKenna

THE OKLAHOMA SKIES SERIES

All Sorrows Are Less

https://mybook.to/AllSorrowsKitMcKenna

Paint the Earth Red

https://mybook.to/PaintEarthKitMcKenna

The Heart That Returns

https://mybook.to/HeartReturnsKitMcKenna

Perfect As You Are

https://mybook.to/PerfectKitMcKenna

The Art of Passion

https://mybook.to/ArtPassionKitMcKenna

A Matter of Trust

https://mybook.to/MatterTrustKitMcKenna

Get a FREE copy of the Valentine Short Mr. Wrong door

https://dl.bookfunnel.com/myptwbvjh0

THE BELLADONNA SOCIETY SERIES

A Pointed End

https://mybook.to/PointedKitMcKenna

A Murderous Intent

https://mybook.to/MurderousKitMcKenna

A Secret Revealed

https://mybook.to/RevealedKitMcKenna

A Devil's Snare

https://mybook.to/SnareKitMcKenna

A Predator's Threat

https://mybook.to/ThreatKitMcKenna

THE MORRIGAN MAFIA SERIES

Crossed

https://mybook.to/CrossedMcKenna

Coup

https://mybook.to/CoupKitMcKenna

Crashed

https://mybook.to/CrashedKitMcKenna

Prologue

FBI Agent Davis
"Crow" Jeffries

As soon as I touch down at Raleigh airport, I rent a car and drive to Stigler, North Carolina, a barely over the county line bedroom community on the outskirts of the metro.

I park in front of the county sheriff's office and survey the building. The office, along with the county jail, is in a separate annex from the courthouse. But I know I'm in the right place because it has the name of the office in large gold gilt lettering on the front window.

Just below that, in only slightly smaller letters, it reads, Sheriff Milo P. Stockton proudly serving you since 2000. So he's been in the office for a little over twenty years. He must be a professional glad hander to keep getting reelected.

When I step inside, I'm greeted by a round-faced, round-bodied man who appears to be in his early twenties. The name Huey comes to mind because of his shape and age and his overt unfitness for the job makes me wonder how he got it.

"May I help you?" Huey asks.

I flash my credentials. "Agent Davis Jeffries to see the Sheriff."

He blinks at me with owl eyes for five or six heartbeats, then shakes himself. "Yes sir. Wait right here and I'll see if he's available."

From his reaction, I take it they don't get many official visitors at their station. Rather than take a seat, I stand and peruse the bulletin board on one wall. Most of it is covered with business cards pinned to the cork, hauling services, housecleaning, something that might be candles for sale. There are also several missing person's flyers, mostly African American girls between the ages of eight and twelve.

"Agent Jeffries?" Huey's back and opening the secured door that separates the lobby from the office at large. "Right this way."

I follow Huey through the station as a half-dozen pairs of eyes follow me. It doesn't escape my notice that only one pair of eyes is surrounded by brown skin. By and large, unless all the non-Caucasians have the day off, the sheriff's department doesn't hold to the idea of a diverse team.

I cross the threshold into the head honcho's office and spot a confederate flag pinned to the wall behind his desk. Tamping down my initial reaction, I hold out my hand to the man. "Sheriff Stockton, I'm Agent Jeffries with the FBI."

"What can I do ya for, Agent?" The round-faced, round-bodied man drawls as he leans back in his chair, the furniture squeaking in protest at his shifting bulk. His middle and forefinger are stained from nicotine and the stench has permeated the walls in this office.

It would seem that the order for no smoking in public buildings took a long time to take hold in this one. Those same stained fingers make a scritching noise as they drag over his stubbled jowl. I instantly dislike him.

"I'd like to see the file on Cherish Monroe."

His eyebrows try to crawl up to his hairline. "Why?"

I don't want to give this asshole any information, but unless I'm willing to play nice, he's not going to cooperate. He might choose not to cooperate anyway, but I should do everything I can to smooth the way.

"We believe it could be tied to a larger case that crosses state lines."

"Is that so? In what way?"

Inwardly, I smile because he just gave me my out. "I am not at liberty to say. The connection is tenuous, but I had to come check it out anyway, to be sure."

"Tenuous," he echoes.

"Yes, sir."

He sits there, rocking in his chair just enough to make it screech and scream. After several moments, he leans forward and pushes a button on his phone, then picks up the handset. "Janice, bring me the Monroe file." Without ceremony, he drops the receiver back into place with a clatter.

A knock sounds at the door. "Come," the Sheriff calls out. The door opens to admit a petite harried looking mouse of a woman with hunched shoulders and her steel gray hair pulled back into a severe bun. She hands the file to the Sheriff then skitters back out the door, closing it behind her.

The Sheriff hands the file to me and just stares. Does he expect me to sit here in his office to read the file while he stares at me?

"Do you have a conference room or somewhere I can sit while I go through it?"

He shrugs. "Sure. There ain't much in it, though."

Another screech of the chair sees him gain his feet, and he maneuvers his bulk around the desk. Pausing at the open door, he points a finger at a closed door at the back of the office.

"Thank you," I say as I move around him to leave his office.

The room he sent me to is clearly an interrogation room. Part of me wonders if he's going to be standing on the other side of the glass, watching as I read through the file.

I flip it open, eager to get this over with and out of this office as quickly as possible. For a moment, I think I'm being punked. There is exactly one piece of paper in the file.

On the off chance that there might be someone watching, I don't react to the lack of information in the file. Instead, I pull out a notebook and make some notes.

The entire report boils down to receiving a call from Cherish's parents saying they've been told of the girl's location and are on their way there. No missing person's report, although I know for a fact one was made. No investigation notes by anyone looking into the girl's disappearance.

There's an arrival time for the officer on the scene following Cherish's parents there. Vague notes on the location, and a time when the child was released to her parents.

No photographs of where she was found or descriptive notes. There is mention of a flash drive that was found with the child along with the black feather, but no information as to what was on the flash drive. There are a lot of phrases using words like alleges and claims written with a deliberate slant that place the girl's veracity in question.

I copy down the address for Cherish's parents and close the folder. Returning to the Sheriff's office, I knock and he bids me come just as he did poor Janice. Handing the folder back to him, I ask, "There's a flash drive mentioned in the file, but nothing about what was on the drive."

His fingers scritch over his jowl again. "Well, that little drive thangy got lost somewhere between there and here and we weren't able to find it."

I want to ask if that's how they typically handle evidence, but there's no point. This guy probably has no qualms about losing evidence whenever it's convenient.

"So you don't know what was on it or who created it?"

"Nope."

"And there's no information about the suspects to be found."

"Nope. The house where the girl was found was empty 'cept for her, and the owners were long gone. Bank accounts were drained so they're probly in Mexico or some such."

I want to lean over the desk and smack this guy. Men like him are the reason law enforcement positions shouldn't be popularity contests. His fat ass has probably been sitting in that goddamn chair since he was elected, being a lazy, incompetent lawman.

Instead of flattening his nose, I drop the folder on his desk and turn to leave. "Thank you for your time, Sheriff."

"You bet. Anytime." The humor in his tone is clear.

Closing the door behind me, I stride out of the building and get into my rental car. While I sit there in front of the station, I call the number for Cherish's parents. Mrs. Monroe answers.

She's hesitant to let me come over and wants to discuss it with her husband first. I thank her for her time and give her my number. After talking with the Sheriff, I'm not surprised that she'd be leery of talking to another law enforcement officer.

I check into a hotel room and prepare to wait. The rest of the day goes by and I'm still waiting and growing impatient. However, I remind myself that they've been dealing with Stockton, who probably wasn't patient or even bothered to give them the time of day.

I find a restaurant for dinner, then go for a run. While I pound the pavement, I can't stop thinking about Stockton's irresponsibility in handling this case. Would he have even tried to arrest the suspects if they'd been found with the girl?

Based on the thin information collected by his department, the District Attorney wouldn't have had enough to take a case to court. From my vantage point, it seems deliberate and I wonder why.

Are the two offices in collusion? Does the Sheriff have a connection to the traffickers? Or worse, was he in league with them?

Is that why he supposedly lost the flash drive? I continue to stew over the questions raised today as I lay there in bed staring at the ceiling while sleep eludes me. At about half past four, my phone buzzes with a text.

When I see the message from Rae, everything in me relaxes. So, her uncle Max gave her the message. I wasn't sure he would, but I'm ecstatic he did.

The conversation between us ends abruptly when she says someone is at her door. My relaxed state evaporates as worry for her surges through me. I send her several messages but don't get a response. With a sigh, I give her my truth because it's all I can think to do before sleep finally pulls me under.

The next morning I'm wakened by the ringing of my phone. It's Cherish's parents' number. "Jeffries," I answer after clearing my throat. I can't believe I slept so late even though I didn't get much sleep. Usually, I'm up with the chickens regardless of what's going on, the result of growing up on a farm and life in the military.

We make arrangements to meet this evening after her husband gets home from work. I'm excited, glad they're willing to take a chance and talk to me.

Before I set my phone back on the nightstand, I see Rae's last response where she tells me to have a nice life, and yet again, I wonder why she's so adamant about the impossibility of our situation. From what she's said, she feels whatever this is between us, too.

In order to understand things from her viewpoint, I need to get her to give me more information. My father taught me to be a patient hunter. It's served me well in my careers, maybe it will serve me well with her, too.

Hunting is all about understanding your quarry's habits and behaviors. I can't go in guns blazing, but every time we talk, she reveals a little more. So, I'll just have to keep feeding that connection and tugging that thread that ties us together, hoping it will draw us closer. Setting my phone aside, I get ready for the day.

The Monroe family lives in a working-class neighborhood. Most of the houses are dated, but neat. With the sun high in the sky and mild temperatures, there should be laughter from kids playing. There are no children to be seen anywhere. Most likely, they're hidden behind their front doors, the parents afraid their child might be taken like Cherish was.

I park on the street, aware of the eyes on me from surrounding homes as curtains move and blinds are parted. The Monroe's front door opens as soon as I step onto the front porch.

The man filling the doorway has a stern demeanor and solid build. If I were meeting him in a dark alley, I might keep a hand on my weapon, but instead, I hold that hand out to him.

"Mr. Monroe?"

With a terse nod, he takes my offered hand and grips it firmly before stepping back to let me into his home. He leads me through the living room to the dining room where his wife and another man wait. I recognize the man from the sheriff's station.

"Mrs. Monroe," I say, holding out my hand to her. When she takes it, I introduce myself. "I'm Agent Davis Jeffries with the FBI."

The other man stands and offers his hand. "Deputy Samuel Bynum. I'm friends with the Monroes and they asked me to be here."

I take a seat across the table from the Deputy and Mrs. Monroe, with Mr. Monroe taking the seat at the head of the dining table. As soon as his rump hits the chair, he asks, "So, what does the FBI want with a closed case?"

"Well, there is a chance it could be tied to other cases."

"Those devils were doing this in other places, too?" Mrs. Monroe asks, her hand going to her throat to fiddle with the top button of her blouse. Mr. Monroe covers her other hand where it rests on the table with his meaty one and she calms.

"I'm not sure, ma'am. One of the things in the report was that when your daughter, Cherish, was found, she had with her a flash drive and a black feather."

"That's correct," Deputy Bynum affirms.

"And the Sheriff says the flash drive was lost."

Mr. Monroe snorts. Mrs. Monroe's eyes drop to her lap. And Deputy Bynum gives his friend a stern look.

I look between them. "So, it wasn't lost?"

Mr. Monroe gruffs. "More like the Sheriff put it in his pocket to keep for his personal use."

I frown. "Personal use? So you know what's on the drive?"

"Darnell, don't," Mrs. Monroe begins.

He slams a fist down on the table, making his wife jump and withdraw her hand. "Somebody's got to know." Rising from his seat, he goes to look out the window into the backyard.

I wait patiently while he decides what he wants to tell me. "Our girl was the third to be taken from this neighborhood, but we heard of others nearby. We went to the police, and they did exactly nothing. Said she probably ran off."

He barks out a sound that's half laugh, half huff. "An eleven-year-old...ran off."

"Our Cherish is a good girl. She would have never..." Mrs. Monroe starts and then trails off.

Mr. Monroe starts again. "When they didn't take us seriously, we asked for help."

"Help?" I echo.

"We got it, too. Got our girl back. When the police still did nothing and that drive went missing..."

"Darnell..." It's Bynum this time.

Mr. Monroe sighs and rubs his forehead as if he has a headache coming on. "We have our girl and those evil bastards are gone, hopefully burning in hell. That's all that matters. She was drugged, and they kept her in a dog cage. A dog cage. My baby girl might be in therapy for the rest of her life after what they did to her, but she's safe now."

"Who did you ask for help?" I query.

"It don't matter. Our girl is home and safe, and we'll do whatever it takes to keep her that way. We've said all we've got to say. I'd appreciate it if you'd go now."

"I'd like to..."

"No. I'm asking you to please go, but I'll make you if I have to," Mr. Monroe says, still looking out the window. "We just want to put this behind us and move on."

With a nod, I rise. "Thank you for your time."

"I'll walk him out," Deputy Bynum says as Mrs. Monroe goes to her husband and wraps her arms around this waist. He lifts his thick arm and puts it over her shoulders, pulling her close.

When we step onto the porch, Bynum says, "They've been through a lot."

"I understand. Do you know who they asked for help?"

"Not exactly. Someone told them they knew someone who knew someone who was good at getting information."

"Do you know who told them?"

He shakes his head, then holds out his hand to me. "Nope."

When I put my hand in his, something hard is against his palm. He leans in and whispers, "My son left his laptop at home that day and I was running it to school for him when I got the call from the Monroes. Knowing the Sheriff like I do, I copied the drive before calling the office. The stuff on there is...repugnant."

I nod, understanding he doesn't want anyone to notice he's given me the drive. Maybe he's afraid word will get back to the Sheriff. "Thank you for your time today, Deputy. Please let the Monroes know I won't be bothering them again."

"Have a safe trip home, Agent."

As soon as I get back to my hotel room, I plug in the flash drive. There are no words dark enough for the information I find on there. Repugnant doesn't even scratch the surface.

Files on the drive are full of documentation of transactions between the three siblings accused of taking the children and their customers. There are disgusting photos and descriptions of dozens of little girls. Obscene amounts of money changed hands.

Although the siblings have disappeared, there is enough information to go after their customers. However, I'm supposed to be learning more about the so-called help the Monroes mentioned.

This helper has gathered an incredible amount of detailed information. The transactional information contains bank account information and texts and emails. Dates and locations of transfers.

There are even photos of the location where Cherish was held. Photos of her and two other girls being held in dog cages, just as her parents said.

Raw, unadulterated rage surges through me and I find myself hoping Mr. Monroe is right and that they're burning in hell for what they've done. As the rage settles to a simmer, for the first time in my career, I find myself identifying with a potential vigilante.

It's obvious that if this so-called helper, this vigilante, hadn't stepped in, that little girls would still be taken and sold to perverted people because the Sheriff, for damn sure, wasn't going to do anything about it.

How do they do it? How does someone get this level of information without leaving a trail behind? And more importantly, how do they make people disappear without a trace?

CHAPTER ONE

Leopards and Spots

RAE

W hen we step inside the restaurant, Yona's hand tightens on mine. I'm not sure why at first, but when we sit down and he spends a lot of time perusing the menu, I get the feeling this place is pricier than he expected it would be.

He doesn't make a lot of money working for the Nation. Maybe he just picked the first restaurant he thought would be romantic. Or that could just be silly, wishful thinking on my part.

My heart, that used to be close to being, well, maybe not ice cold, but certainly morally ambiguous, has started trending toward tepid. I'd like to think it is because of Yona, that maybe we're creating something real here, an honest to goodness relationship.

As I peruse my menu, nonchalantly, I say, "I think you should let this be my treat as congratulations for such a big step forward on your career path."

"No. I invited you."

I look at him over the top of my menu. "Yona, you brought me all the way here. We have a great room, and I plan on eating those chocolate-covered peanuts in the gift basket they left you. I insist. Let me treat you to a nice dinner."

His eyes lower, but the corners of his mouth tilt up. "Okay. Thank you."

Wow. That was easy. For him, it would have been a struggle. For me, it's just pocket change. See, we can compromise.

So far, this weekend is starting off with a bang. Orgasms, an excellent meal, and Yona seems more relaxed than I've ever seen him. The conversation flows freely.

This conference thing must really be his element because he's been wound up and excited about it for days. I intend to sneak into the session where he's speaking so I can hear his presentation. Maybe he'll invite me, but he's so distracted he probably won't think of it. Either way, I'm eager to see how he's received by the audience.

When the server comes with the check and I send her off with one of my preloaded credit cards, Yona's hand covers mine where it rests on the table by my glass of whiskey. With a shy smile, he says, "Thank you, Rae. The meal was excellent."

"You're welcome, but you're the one who chose this place, so you deserve the credit. We'll have to come here again some..."

"Yona? That is you!"

Yona's hand jerks away from mine so quick it's as if he'd been touching a hot burner on a stove instead of my skin. I look up to see two young native women. Both are beautiful, with smooth brown skin, perfect makeup, and long, stick-straight black hair.

They're dressed to the nines in tight, colorful dresses and sky-high stilettos. If Barbie made an indigenous version of their doll, it would look like these women.

"Millie and Shauna, nice to see you," Yona says in greeting.

"Aren't you going to the reception?" Native Barbie number one asks, a slight pout on her pretty face.

"Yes. I arrived a little early and decided to have dinner with an old friend. We were just about to leave so I could make it to the reception on time."

His words are a knife to the heart. This is what tepid gets you. The server brings my card and receipt back. I sign it and slip a Benjamin into the folio for a tip. She really was an excellent server.

Barbie number two's eyes widen and she doesn't take them off the folio when I put it on the table, but she's apparently talking to Yona when she says, "Good. I was hoping I'd see you here. We need to have a drink and catch up."

Barbie number one looks me up and down and when I raise an eyebrow, she's smart enough to look away, her neck turning dark with embarrassment.

"We do," Yona answers. "I'll see you over there." They walk away, and Yona looks over at me. His expression is conflicted.

He knows he just fucked up, but it's the last time he'll have the chance. "Rae..."

I shake my head with a face made of stone, shutting down whatever empty words were about to roll off his forked tongue. Rising from my seat, I head to the restroom. As I pass him, I say, "I'll just be a minute."

Although I don't need to use the facilities, I do need a moment to collect myself. Stupid girl that I am, I had started to hope and believe that this man might actually want me beyond just getting laid. He said he did, but it was just another lie. I wash my hands and dry them, then head toward the front door.

As I pass our server, she smiles and mouths *Thank you* to me. I smile and nod in return. When I step out onto the sidewalk, donning my coat after collecting it, the area is empty.

That asshole wasn't even willing to wait for me on the sidewalk. I doubt that's how he'd treat me if we really were old friends. Or if I was one of those Barbies.

Instead of walking toward the hotel, I turn in the opposite direction and pull out my phone. "Allo?" my cousin Bridget answers. That makes my lips tilt, if even just a little, because Dad used to answer the phone the same way.

"Can you please come get me? I'm walking north on Robinson from Sheridan."

God love her. She doesn't ask any questions, just says, "We'll be right there."

I swear, the woman must be psychic. When I told them about coming here with Yona, my other cousin Bee was excited, but

Bridget was quiet for several moments, then said, "We should go, too. Not to stay in your hotel or anything, but you'll have downtime while he's doing whatever it is he's going to do. We can go site seeing and stuff."

Bee was all for that idea. As usual, Finn, Bee's bodyguard, was ambivalent.

A biting wind swirls down the street between buildings, so I pull up the collar on my coat and hunch my shoulders against the chill. I thought we were going to get some springtime weather, but a cold front moved in yesterday and the temps dropped.

"Fucking Oklahoma weather," I grumble to the empty street.

My feet pick up the pace, hoping that speed walking will generate some heat and beat back the cold, if even a little. With my stride eating up the bricks and still freezing my ass off, I'm concentrating so hard on moving that the phone buzzing in my pocket makes me jump.

Yona probably gave up waiting for me around the corner and realized I wasn't coming. Or, knowing him, he didn't wait at all and went straight to the hotel and just expected me to show up, trailing after him like some idiotic puppy.

Maybe he's a little panicked. That would serve him right. Most likely, though, he only just now figured out something was wrong.

How could I be so stupid about him? You'd think I'd have learned that leopards don't change their spots and Yona has shown me his deceitful fucking spots over and over.

That's what those spots are for, though, aren't they? They're camouflage so you don't see them coming until they're ready to chase you down and rip out your throat.

I see my family's rental car coming down the street and cross to the other side of the road. Finn stops the car and I slide into the back seat next to Bridget. No one says anything, and it makes a lump swell in my throat.

To avoid talking, I pull out my phone. Yep. There are several messages from Yona. As soon as I see his name, I minimize the screen.

I clear my throat. "He'll be going to his reception soon. When it starts, if you wouldn't mind taking me to the hotel, I'll run up and get my bag."

Knowing him, he won't miss any part of this conference, not even for me. He was too excited about this event. Too invested in what it might mean for his future.

Finn nods.

"Of course," Bee says.

Bridget scoots across the back seat and links her arm with mine, then rests her head on my shoulder. The damn knot swells in my throat again.

At a little past seven, I head into the hotel and go to the stairs instead of waiting in the crowd for an elevator. In the room, I gather up my things and shove them into my bag. It takes longer than I expected, because for some reason, Yona moved my things around.

Nothing is missing that I can tell, so I'm not too concerned. I didn't leave anything of value in the room, anyway. If he took something, I'll just replace it.

On my way out the door, I stop at the gift basket they left him for being a speaker and take the box of chocolate-covered peanuts. That's the least the asshole can do for me.

This time, I take the elevator down to the ground floor. As I'm heading toward the exit, people moving in a side hallway catch my attention. There are tabletops set up where small groups of two or three linger and talk, all dressed in fine clothes and looking very indigenous.

Wondering if this is Yona's reception thing, I head down the hall. I was so preoccupied with getting the peanuts that I forgot to leave the extra room key before I left. A profound desire to be petty fills me as I make my way closer to the open doors.

I stop in the doorway to the room where there are more tables and people scattered around and my eyes scan the crowd. The vast majority look just like Yona and the Barbies, their indigenousness undeniable. I definitely wouldn't have fit in with this crowd.

Standing at a high table about halfway down one side is Yona with one of the Barbies. They're standing close, heads together, and she has her hand on his chest. I stride up and put the card on the table, sliding it over to him.

He looks up at me and flinches, stepping away from Barbie. Shaking my head, I say, "Wow. It took you, what? Thirty minutes to move on?"

Weariness subsumes the hurt and pettiness and I bite back the comment on the tip of my tongue about hoping Barbie enjoys being fucked on dirty sheets. He's not worth any more of my time, attention, or words. Turning on my heel, I walk away.

A hand grabs my arm and swings me around. "Rae, I'm sorry, I just reacted..."

"Stop Yona. Just stop lying. You're embarrassed to be seen with me. That's clear and I'm worth more than being someone's secret fuck partner."

I take a deep breath and calm the anger that makes me want to punch him in the nose. "The meeting you had set up for Sunday afternoon still stands," I say. "I'll be there because we have business to discuss. Make sure your brother is there, too."

I jerk my arm out of his grip and resume walking away.

CHAPTER TWO

Moving on With Whiskey and Sweat

RAE

Back at the hotel where the Bs and Finn rented two adjoining rooms, it's clear which one the Bs have claimed, so I go to the other. I'm changing into comfortable clothes when Bee struts in and says, "Oh, hell no. Girl, we are going to go out and sweat our asses off on the dance floor. I talked to the concierge downstairs and found out there's a club just a few miles away."

"I didn't bring anything to wear to a place like that."

She grins. "Good thing I did."

I'm usually not much for dance clubs, but this one just might provide me with the distraction I need. The instant we step inside, the thump of the bass settles in my chest and makes my feet want to move, even though I am a lousy dancer. I mostly just stand there and wiggle my ass.

At the bar, I ask about the elevated area that looks over the dance floor. He checks his computer and says there's space available because of a cancellation and tells me the price. With a nod, I tell him we'll take it.

The upstairs area is slightly quieter than the floor below. We offload our coats and drinks and Bee grabs my hand to drag me back downstairs. Looking back, I stutter, "Wh…what about?"

She waves a hand. "Finn will watch our stuff."

On the dance floor, I mimic the actions of my cousins, who clearly know what they're doing when it comes to shaking their asses to the beat. After a few songs, I give up tugging down on the hem of the shiny, sparkly number that Bee made me wear.

It was probably a shirt on her, but reached to mid-thigh on me, barely covering my butt. She rolled her eyes when I insisted on wearing boy shorts underneath, but relented when she saw they were at least lacey. Thank God I brought them because the only other underwear I brought would have had me practically flashing my naughty bits with every move.

We're headed up the stairs for another break when I hear my name. Surely I must be hearing things, but no, there it is again, so I turn. Making her way through the crowd is Tori. Victoria, the gorgeous sugar baby I met on a plane ride from Boston to Oklahoma a few weeks ago.

"Tori! How are you?" I greet her as she draws near.

"Great! Did you get moved?"

"No. Long story. Come upstairs with me."

She follows me up the stairs and over to the sofas where the Bs and Finn are accepting fresh drinks from a server. "I'm glad I ran into you," she says. "A friend was supposed to meet me here, but she's thirty minutes late and just now canceled.

"Well, that settles it. You're with us from now on. Everyone, this is Tori. Tori, these are my cousins Siobhan, who I call Bee, Bridget, and our friend Finn."

Bridget scoots over to make room for Tori while I go to the other end of the sofa. Bee waves the server back over. "What are you drinking, Tori?"

"Oh! Thanks!" Tori says and gives the server her order, then turns back to the group. "I was so hoping you bought that house so I could finally see inside."

"House?" Bridget asks.

"What house?" Bee asks at the same time.

"Tori and I met on the flight from Boston the last time I was up there. She caught me looking at real estate and there was this house that I got stuck on."

The Bs do that silent stare thing again, then Bee asks, "Is it over by Tahlequah?"

I shake my head and answer, "No, it's here in the Oklahoma City metro."

A smile spreads on Bridget's face. "What?" I ask, scowling at her. "Did you have another of your psychic visions?"

She lowers her eyes, but still has that self-satisfied smile on her face, like a Cheshire cat. Bee giggles and claps her hands.

The first thing I'm doing when I get back to my computer is checking for an email from Emilie Sutton.

We head back down to the dance floor and shake our asses until we're sweaty, then head back upstairs for a drink. This cycle continues and after a few rounds of whiskey and shaking my ass, I'm feeling much better.

Getting out of that hotel room where I'd surely just sit and stew over being lied to again was the best idea ever. I'm moving on with whiskey and sweat.

I don't know how long it's been since we arrived, but I'm feeling buzzed all over. The air feels electric, and the tension has oozed out of me over the past few hours. So when some yahoo keeps sidling up to Bee even when she moves away from him, instead of beating his ass, I simply move closer to him, invading his personal space.

When I step between them as Bee moves away yet again, he looks at me with surprise before narrowing his eyes. I slide a hand up his chest and around the back of his neck, drawing his face down. He's so shocked that he doesn't resist.

With my lips close to his ear, words disguised as saccharine but full of venom pour out. "If you don't get the fuck away from my friend, I will gut you right here in the middle of the dance floor."

He jerks back in shock and looks from me to Bee. "You're fucking crazy."

I raise an eyebrow to top off my coy expression. "You don't know the half of it."

Stumbling as he turns, he hurries away, disappearing into the crowd. I throw my head back and laugh because I feel so good. Finally, I'm starting to feel like myself again and when I feel like this, I believe I could conquer the world.

Bee grabs my hands, laughing, too. "Thank you! He was getting creepy."

"Girl, we need to teach you how to get rid of creeps."

"I usually have Geno for that!" She spins away. I lock eyes with Bridget and she gives me a look. It's such a look that I can't define it, but remembering her words about how we need to talk, I suddenly agree wholeheartedly.

She and Tori are sticking close together, leaning in to talk occasionally. There's a lot of smiling and touching going on. I just smile and keep moving. The vibes I got from Tori on the flight were good, so if there's an attraction between them, I'm fine with it.

Bridget can be herself here and if what I'm seeing means that she's a lesbian or bi, I don't care. If that's the case, it might be the first time in her life that she's able to just be herself because the mafia in all forms frowns on anything but strict heterosexuality.

However, although I'm all for Bridget letting her hair down and just being, I make a mental note to do a full background on Tori. Her vibes may be good, but the data will tell me everything.

Later that night, after we've stumbled into our rooms and I've stripped off all my clothes, oblivious to Finn sharing a room with me, I fall into bed. I'm exhausted and fall asleep almost immediately. However, just as the Sandman is dragging me off to dreamland, I think I hear someone say, "He wasn't worthy of you."

Images of knights and dragons swirl through my mind, so I must already be dreaming, after all.

CHAPTER THREE

Guard Her Heart and Watch Her Back

BRIDGET

Sometimes I get feelings. Rae keeps accusing me of being psychic and maybe I am, if only just a little. It's not like I get full-blown visions or anything. Just feelings.

When she told us about coming with that jerk Yona to this conference, I had a feeling of unease in my gut. I knew something was going to happen that would hurt her.

However, I knew he was no good the moment I saw him in her bed that first morning we arrived. As soon as I laid eyes on him, I instantly disliked him and wanted to drag him out of her bed and throw him out onto the street.

It was her house, and he was her guest, though, so I refrained. Also, we didn't know each other well enough for me to speak frankly. We're getting closer to that point, but still aren't quite there yet.

The man is a taker, and he used Rae's vulnerability to worm his way into her life. She doesn't have many weak spots. Most of them arise from being alone for too long. Solitude, even when self-imposed, isn't good for anyone if it goes on too long and Rae's has definitely done that.

We've all grown up with the reality of being born into mafia families. It is brutal and unforgiving and Rae's was more brutal than most for a girl.

She had no buffer between her and her father once her mother died. Siobhan and I at least had our mothers and each other, but Rae was all alone. Then when she came to Boston to be around her extended family, they rejected her.

Oh, Uncle Keegan was civil to her face, but was full of venom and spite behind her back or when he was speaking in Gaelic and thought she couldn't understand. She did understand, though. When she walked away from the family and never looked back, I was proud of her.

Back then, part of me wished she would take me with her, but she couldn't do that anymore than I was strong enough to leave on my own. I wish I'd known then what I know now. But I didn't and there is no way to change the past.

As strong as she is, she was ripe for the picking for someone like Yona, for whom lying comes easily. So easily that I don't even think he realizes he is doing it. She needs someone watching out for her. Guarding her heart against men like Yona and watching her back.

"I'm glad we were here," Siobhan, or Bee, as Rae calls her, says. I wonder what nickname she would give me. Maybe I'll have to ask her for one. If everyone else has a code name, surely I need one, too.

"Me, too."

"Did you see the way she made that guy leave? The woman is fearless."

"She sure is something. I wish we'd gotten to know each other better when she was in Boston."

"Based on what she told us, it would seem Dah didn't want us getting to know her, which is pretty shite of him."

I don't answer. Uncle Keegan is Bee's dah, and she loves him. She loves me, too, at least I think she does, but he's her father and if he presses her, I can't trust that she won't tell him each and every word I might say against him. Considering how much I hate him, I have to watch what I say most of the time, which is why I tend to keep my lips together.

"You through in the loo?" I query.

"Yeah. I wish I could call Geno."

"Why can't you?"

"Dah said no distractions. If I call or text, Geno will be the one to pay the price."

"Well, that sucks. You don't even get to have phone sex."

She starts scrolling through photos on her phone. "I know. Maybe Dah won't make us stay here for too long."

In the bathroom, I close the door and stare at myself in the mirror. I hope we stay here for a very long time. In fact, I hope I never have to go back to Boston.

If Uncle Keegan insists and gets my mother's husband involved, he'll have to make me go back, even if it's by force. Even though I'm in my twenties, I'm under the rule of the men in my life.

My mother's husband has only met me on a few occasions because I've been Bee's companion at Uncle Keegan's home since coming back from Ireland. In our world, women have no say in what happens to them. They're given their fates and have to live with it regardless of what they want.

But I'd rather die than be forced to marry some man chosen for me because of the power or position he has. Just thinking about it makes me want to throw up.

Bee's looking forward to her and Geno finally getting married. By mob standards, they should have married years ago and have had a couple of wee ones by now. I wonder what Uncle Keegan will do if Geno isn't able to perform as he hopes over these weeks while we're gone.

That's borrowing trouble for another day, so I let it go and keep my thoughts in the now.

Besides seeing Rae relax and let go of everything that had her wound so tight, another bright spot tonight was Rae's friend,

Tori. She seems very nice. I think she'd be a great addition to our group.

We spent some time talking, and I found her to be smart and funny, just all around delightful. Maybe we can visit with her again. Hopefully soon.

With a sigh, I get on with my nighttime routine. Once my face is washed and teeth are cleaned, I go back into our hotel room. Bee is still on her phone. I glance into the other room and see Rae has collapsed on top of the covers with no clothes on. She really was quite drunk by the time we left.

I go into the room she's sharing with Finn. He's sitting with his back propped up on pillows at the head of the bed and scratching in his book. In all the time he's been our shadow, I've never been able to get a peek at that book, and I'm curious. He'd probably kill me and toss my body in the bay if I tried.

"Were you just going to let her sleep like this?"

He raises his eyes and stares at me. Sometimes I really wonder about him. I've never seen him show an interest in a woman sexually. Nor a man, for that matter.

Maybe he just hides it well, or maybe he doesn't have those kinds of feelings. Asexual, I think it's called. I'm no one to judge anyone's sexuality, and even though Rae's naked, I know Finn would never do anything to hurt her in that way.

I frown at him and go to Rae's bed to try and wrangle her under the covers. It takes some doing, but I get her covered up and actually get a shirt on her. After I fill one of the complimentary paper cups with water and leave it on her nightstand with some aspirin, I turn off her light and go to my own bed.

CHAPTER FOUR

Showing Them Who They're Dealing With

RAE

We arrive right on time to the meeting with Yona and his key people, that are composed of his father, brother, and Whiskey. If it hadn't been for Bridget insisting she and Bee and Finn follow me to the City, this meeting might have gone very differently. As it is, I'm feeling relaxed and happier than I have for a while. A very, very long while.

We spent yesterday roaming all over Oklahoma City, including doing a drive-by of the house Tori mentioned. Unsurprisingly, when we got home this morning and I fired up my computer, there was a message from Mrs. Sutton.

It seems the Universe is still orchestrating things and opening doors for me to stay here in Oklahoma. I just have to get today over with and tomorrow, everything is going to change.

That feeling of being empowered and in control has stuck with me, and I realized I don't need Yona, his crew, or his coat-tails. I'm the one with the connections and I'm the one who can make this happen.

For a moment, I feel like a rockstar walking into the warehouse where the Dick took me when he kidnapped me after breaking into my dad's cabin because my family, my temporary crew, follows me like my mother fucking entourage. It also pleases me to know that every single one of them is more legit than anyone Yona has on tap.

The Tribe that never was is waiting for me and when I step into the room, all four of the men stand up. Yona steps forward. "Rae, can we just talk for a few minutes?"

Ignoring him, because he doesn't deserve my attention, I step into the middle of the room and take off my jacket. Yona steps back when he sees my shoulder holster. It comes off next and I start offloading the knives I have stashed on my person and handing everything to Finn.

We didn't talk about it, but he makes a helluva second. When I'm down to my leggings and a tank top, I say, "First things first. Dan the Dick and I already had some unfinished business, but this latest infraction can't be ignored."

"What infraction?" his father asks.

Of course, he didn't tell his father, or anyone else for that matter, but they need to know just how much of a liability Dick is. He was mad at me, so recklessly acted out.

"It seems that Dick decided to inform his drug dealer buddies where I was staying in town. Not only did that endanger me, his actions endangered my family and innocents when the idiot Howk brothers came miming a drive by shooting at the coffee shop. If Billy Howk had used more than just his finger gun, people, possibly even the little girl and her mom, who were standing right next to me, could have died."

"How do you know this?" Yona asks, a scowl furrowing his brow.

I ignore him as Bridget hands him the papers she carried in which show transcripts of exactly what Dan told the Howk brothers. It's laughable the amount of information people banter back and forth on their phones because they believe it's unbreakable.

"I didn't do shit," Dan barks out.

"This says otherwise," Yona says, handing the papers to his father.

"So, Dick, I made you a promise after you hit me that first time and the only reason I didn't make good on it after you ambushed me with two other men outside the bar was because your brother thought he could keep you in line. Apparently, that was yet another lie he told me."

I tilt my head right, then left, my neck cracking, then I shake out my arms.

"What?" Dan blusters. "You think you can kick my ass?"

I give him a shark's smile, letting my inner predator shine through. "I know I can, big man."

He rubs a hand on his jaw, not hiding his cocky smile. "All right, bitch. I'm bout to show you just how wrong you are."

Although he thinks he's being sneaky, he telegraphs his wild swing and I duck it easily. It comes as no surprise that when he is close, I can see his pupils are blown. I put my hands on him, urging him on. "Your brother is high again, Yona."

This time, there's no playing because I want these people to see exactly who they're dealing with. Dan's punch carried him forward, and when I dodge and keep him going in the same direction, I step around him and jab him in the kidney. He stumbles, and I put my foot to his ass and help his momentum along some more.

When he sprawls face first on the concrete floor, I laugh. "Come on, Dick. Is that all you've got?"

Already breathing hard, he lumbers to his feet and puts his fists up. He's a little leerier this time. When he steps closer, I zoom in, punch him in the liver and sideswipe his knee.

He goes down like a howling oak tree and rolls on the floor, holding his knee. The entire fight probably didn't even last sixty seconds. I take one of my knives from Finn and saunter over to Dan.

Slowly, I kneel, putting one knee on Dan's chest and my knife to his throat. His father steps forward. "Please, don't kill him. I know you don't owe us anything, but I'm begging you."

Well, fuck.

Moving the knife around, I drag it over the concrete and slice off Dan's braid at the nape of his neck. Gripping it in my hand, I throw it down at him with disgust, the long black rope of hair landing in the middle of his chest. "Yet again, Dick, you owe me your life. If I ever see you again or if you ever speak my name or even think about me, I'll take it. Do you understand?"

He doesn't answer, so I kick him forcefully in the ribs, definitely bruising them, maybe even cracking or breaking one or two. I bend over him and growl, "I said, do you understand?"

"Yes," he finally gurgles.

I spin to Yona. "You're out. Not only can you not manage your men, but because you couldn't be straight with me for even one night, you're done. If you make any more attempts at entering the world of organized crime, I'll shut your shit down faster than you can blink and expose your secrets to the Nation and to the world. Stick to politics, where your forked tongue will best suit you."

"Rae..."

"No! Same goes for you that goes for Dan. I never want to see your face or hear from you again and you're never to talk about me to anyone. Are we clear?"

He gives me a terse nod.

"Good," I hiss. "Because I'll be watching, and you know exactly what that means."

Once I've put my boots, weapons and jacket back on, I hand a wrapped stack of bills to their father. "He's going to need knee surgery. This should cover most of it, if not the entire bill. The hospital will be good for him because he needs to detox, but they'll also be able to keep an eye on his kidney and make sure he eventually stops pissing blood."

He nods and whispers, "Thank you," as he takes the money. "I apologize for my sons."

I shrug and head for the door. Whiskey steps into my path, and I pat him on the chest. "I'm going to miss you, big guy."

He pulls me in for a hug and replies, "Same." Then he leans down and whispers in my ear. "Thanks. Always knew they weren't cut out for this. You just saved them both from gettin' killed."

Whispering back, I say, "There might be work for you soon, if you want it, but I'll let you make the choice when the time comes."

He pats me on the back to let me know he heard and lets go of me, then steps out of my path.

Back at the bunker below dad's cabin, we spend one last night before rising early the next morning to pack up everything we can fit into their rental car and on my bike. When both vehicles are loaded down and the cabin is shut up tight, we head across the state to Oklahoma City, where a new life awaits.

CHAPTER FIVE

Dream Houses and the Destruction of Evidence

RAE

Mr. Bradford Harland, III Esq. is not what I expected when Emilie Sutton told me I'd be meeting with her attorney. Instead of a stodgy, old money, geezer, the Third is only in his mid-thirties.

He has a jolly round face and thinning blond hair, but if you look into his vivid blue eyes, you can see the shark hiding underneath. I imagine his disarming appearance would cause people to underestimate him, and he probably likes it that way. Maybe I need to put him on retainer.

"Now, Miss Morrissey, it is my understanding that you and my client reached an agreement for some undisclosed service you provided for her. It must have been quite the service because the payment is quite substantial."

So, she didn't tell him exactly what I'd done. She'd be protected under attorney client privilege, but I would not, so I'm thankful she didn't enlighten him. I'm not about to clue him in, either, despite his probing statements.

The service I performed for her is erasing the data I found that linked her to the man she hired to kill her husband. She didn't plan for the nanny to be killed, too, but had told the man that she wouldn't be bothered if the young woman fucking her husband was collateral damage.

Harsh, but part of me understands. From what I could find out about the husband, he was quite the asshole. He hadn't gotten in trouble with his company at the time of his death, but they were investigating suspicious activity coming from his department. Dying probably saved him from going to prison for fraud.

Although it was over ten years ago and I doubted anyone would come looking for the information, she was still grateful to me for taking care of it for her. She was also more than ready to get rid of the house and is selling it to me for about one sixth of its value.

It's still a pretty penny at a cool mil, but enough of a deal that I am willing to part with the money. I'll make the purchase price back in a few months, anyway.

"Mrs. Sutton has given me Power of Attorney for some of her affairs here in the states, including the ability to act as signatory for her on real estate transactions. You've transferred the funds?"

"Yes, sir. We had accounts at a common banking institution, and I wired the funds yesterday evening. If you'll check your email, you should have something from Mrs. Sutton confirming they've been received."

He turns to his computer and logs in. "Yes, I see it here. Since that's taken care of, it's just a matter of signing the documents."

He presses a button on his phone and the woman sitting at the desk just outside his door answers. "Yes, Mr. Harland?"

"Will you please send Jessica in? I need her to notarize the signatures I discussed with her this morning."

"Yes, sir. Right away."

I wonder what it's like to have people at your beck and call like that. If things go the way I hope they do, I might just have a few people like that. Probably not anytime soon, but I can see it happening.

The Third pulls out a contract of sale and a warranty deed he has prepared for the property. Once I've reviewed the information to ensure it's being transitioned to the appropriate corporate entity, I sign everything where instructed, then the Third follows suit.

Once Jessica applies her stamp and signature, I'm the proud owner of a new home.

"Mrs. Sutton asked me to take care of filing the deed with the County Clerk's office and that will be done by end of business today. In here, you will find copies of all the codes for the gates and security system and instructions for resetting them. There is also a roster of the vendors that have been caring for the property. I've informed them the house would be changing ownership and that you would be in touch."

He folds up a copy of the contract and slides it and a photocopy of the deed into a manila envelope. When he hands it to me, it clinks, the sound a lot like keys moving around. I thank him and take the envelope, walking casually out of his office.

The Bs and Finn are waiting in the parking lot next to my bike and their rental car. Now that we have somewhere to store a vehicle, I think we just need to go buy something and return the rental.

"So?" Bee asks.

With a grin that is splitting my face in two, I shake the envelope, letting her hear the keys rattling around inside. I'd really like to jump up and down and hoot and holler, but I try to maintain my dignity while we're outside the attorney's office.

She claps her hands and laughs.

"Come on," I say. "Let's go look at our new digs."

Opening the envelope, I find the sheet that has the gate code. Once I get a look at it, I tell them the code and the address, then return the paper to the envelope and tuck it into my saddlebag.

I straddle my bike and put on my helmet, still grinning. "See y'all there."

Bridget smiles and shakes her head as I zoom out of the parking lot.

My heart is pounding as I plug in the gate code and wait for the enormous iron gates to swing open. This is, by far, my biggest investment to date and I'm beyond excited to make the place my home.

From the road, you can just see the upper level of the house because the drive inclines up one of the small, rolling hills that mark the property. Just inside the gate is a guardhouse, which I'm pleased about. I'm also pleased that the entire fifty acres are surrounded by iron fencing, but I wish it was a little higher than six feet.

As I cruise up the driveway, the house comes fully into view and up close, she's breathtaking. She's just over fourteen thousand square feet and styled like something you'd see in Spain or Italy. The exterior is butter colored stone with a red tile roof.

The house sits quite a way back from the road with a long drive. A branch off the drive goes toward the garages at the back of the house, and there's a roundabout at the top of the driveway with a tiered fountain in the middle. My cheeks are starting to ache from grinning so much.

I park my bike and stow my helmet before going up four steps to a wide patio? Veranda? Hell, I don't know what it's called, but it's a space tiled with large smooth stones which stretch out in front of the door with benches on each side and planters filled with pots.

Just as I'm sliding my key into the door, the others arrive and park. Bee races up to where I wait for them and she's practically as excited as I am. "Oh, my God! This place is gorgeous! I love all the wide open space around it."

With a turn of the key, I step inside. The furnishings were left with the house, so other than maybe replacing some beds - I have a thing about sleeping where other people have slept for extended periods of time - I can take my time making the place truly mine. Not that I'm any kind of decorator, but I'm sure I'll find some things I want to change out.

The interior is more stone accented with iron and dark wood. A curved staircase leads up to the second and third floors. All the furniture is covered with sheets, but what's not covered looks as if it has been well tended by the cleaning crew, which probably accounts for the lack of a musty smell. Based on the size of this place, I'll definitely have to keep the cleaning crew on because there's no way I'd be able to handle it alone.

We wander through room after room, oohing and ahing with every new space. There are living areas, one with what looks to be a grand piano under sheets. An enormous office, a dining room with its own fireplace. Some rooms have coffered ceilings, some have dark wood beams. Everything is high end and gorgeous.

The kitchen has an enormous island and a stove bigger than anything I've seen outside a commercial kitchen. We're still on the first floor, and it doesn't take long for me to get overwhelmed by it all.

This place is even bigger than my cousins' mansion in Boston. It will be nice while they are here, but when they leave, it's a lot of space for just me to putter around in. I step through the back door and take a deep breath of the cold, but damp air.

There's covered space with cozy seating arrangements that leads to another large patio. Lounge chairs are arranged around a swimming pool. Steps lead down from the patio to what looks like a garden area and a hot tub before the expanse of lawn rolls down a slight hill to a pond with a dock.

Bridget steps up and links her arm with mine. "You okay?"

"Yeah. I've just never had anything like this. While y'all are here, it will be wonderful, but I was just thinking that once you go back to Boston, it will be a big lonely place for just me."

"Well, you should know now that I'm not going back to Boston," she announces without ceremony.

"What?"

"If you're willing, I'd like to stay here. When you lived with us, I hated the way they treated you, but back then, I was too much under their influence to do anything about it. I see the way Uncle Keegan looks at me. Once he marries Siobhan and Geno, I know he has plans to marry me off next. Honestly, I'm surprised he hasn't already tried, but I don't want him choosing anything or anyone for me."

"Before you decide, we should talk so you know what you're getting yourself into by staying here with me. I mean, you don't have to stay here with me if you don't want…"

"You're setting up your own operation and I want to help you do it. We do still need to have that talk, but I have a feeling we're more kindred in spirit than you realize."

We stand there for a few minutes longer, taking in the expanse of property. I take the time to get a grip on having family that not only likes me, but wants to stick with me rather than going back to the blood relations they've known their entire life.

"You can stay here as long as you want," I tell her, a strange feeling of something all gooey uncoiling in my chest.

"Let's go back inside and finish exploring."

CHAPTER SIX

Celebrations and Connections

BRIDGET

B ack in the house, we move from the first floor to the basement. The vast, open, unfinished space helps bring Rae back to her equilibrium.

"I should've brought a notebook with me," she says. "We can put in a weapons room and gym down here."

"Bunk space, too, when you start bringing on guards," I say.

From the corner of my eye, I see how she stares at me. She thinks she's inscrutable, but I know where she's headed and as I told her, I'm all for it. For now, it's just the two of us. Bee is off exploring the rest of the house and Finn is probably sitting at a table with his book waiting for the giddy women to settle down.

"I see more than you think, cousin. It's clear to me that you're setting up to take over the city and probably the state, but I can also see that you're seeking to put something different in place. Something that balances the criminal with the beneficial. As I said, you and I aren't that different."

She makes a noise in her throat that's half-laugh, half-snort.

"Let's go take a look at the rest, then figure out what we're doing for supper. I'm starving."

I link my arm with hers again. "You're always starving. One of the first things you probably need to do is hire a cook."

"True."

We go to the third floor, which contains four smallish bedrooms, most likely for staff. On the second floor are several large bedrooms. Unsurprisingly, Bee is in the master suite, lounging on the bed.

"This is Rae's room," I say with a little bite to my voice.

Bee is my cousin and I love her dearly, but she's had everything handed to her on a silver platter. Sometimes her sense of entitlement gets the better of her and Rae's so pleased to have a family that she'd probably tell Bee she could have the room just to make her happy.

Although she was raised in this life, Siobhan was also raised by her father and was shielded from many things the rest of us weren't. She loves her dah and reveres him as only a beloved daughter can. Honestly, I wouldn't put it past her to act as a spy for him.

When Rae and I are alone to have our talk, I will have to warn her that as much as she might care for Bee, she shouldn't trust her wholeheartedly. Uncle Keegan would have zero qualms about using his daughter against Rae.

Bee rolls over and looks at us with a broad smile. "I know. It's just so pretty that I couldn't bear to leave. This house is amazing, Rae."

"Thank you, Bee. I think we need to go out to eat to celebrate. Bridget, if you have Tori's number, why don't you see if she has any suggestions for a place to get a good steak and if she's available to join us?"

The thought of seeing Tori again makes my pulse kick up. Perhaps I'm not the only one proving to be observant.

"I do," I say, doing my best to keep my voice even. "Let me go retrieve my phone and I'll give her a ring."

An hour and a half later, after Bee dressed herself and made Rae change clothes three times before just telling her what to wear, we park at the restaurant. Tori is waiting for us inside, and she looks absolutely beautiful.

Her long dark hair is pulled back into a ponytail. Her makeup is done so expertly, it looks like she's practically bare faced. Even in jeans and a sweater, she looks like a million bucks. But then, they are designer jeans and her stiletto heel boots are to die for.

She greets Rae and says hello to Bee, but when our eyes meet, my stomach does a flip-flop. I've never really dated anyone.

Dating isn't allowed in the world I grew up in. The only reason Bee has any experience with dating is because she and Geno were promised to each other pretty much at birth.

Usually, women in mafia families are told who they will marry, then they get married whether they like it or not. Whether they are attracted to the man or not. They're expected to smile and make the best of it, servicing their husband's sexual needs and pumping out babies.

There are no allowances for someone like me.

After a dinner of excellent food and a lot of laughter, we're walking out to the parking lot when Rae says, "So, Tori, when do you want to come take a look at the place?"

Tori stops in her tracks and grabs my arm. With wide eyes, she looks at me, then back at Rae. "Really?"

"Yep. You said you'd always wanted to get a look inside," Rae replies, still walking.

"If you're serious, how about now?"

"Fine by me." Rae turns as she's getting into the car and looks at me. "Bridge, do you mind riding with Tori and showing her the way?"

I'm thankful for the dim light in the parking lot because I can feel heat rising in my cheeks. "Um, no, I don't mind at all." Based on previous conversations, it would seem that Tori already knows the way, but I appreciate Rae giving us some time alone.

Tori still has her fingers wrapped around my arm. "Holy cow! I'm so excited. I've wanted to see inside that house for over ten years. Is it as beautiful on the inside as it is on the outside? No, don't tell me. Let it be a surprise."

Her excitement is infectious. She lets her hand slide down my arm and puts her hand in mine before she starts pulling me toward her car. "Come on, let's go!"

Her car is a Mercedes AMG and I'm surprised that someone her age can afford such a vehicle. I wonder what she does for a living. Or maybe her family has money. Rae said that the two of them met on a flight, but that's all.

There's so much more I want to know about Tori, so I use the car ride to ask some questions. "So you met Rae on a plane trip from Boston? Were you there on vacation?"

Unexpectedly, she chuckles. "No. I was traveling with a...friend who was there on business."

"A friend?"

She hesitates. "Rae didn't tell you?"

I frown. "Tell me what?"

"When we met, I was traveling with a man. A married man who paid me money to be with him."

She tells me about her work at a BDSM club called Cassandra's and how she got involved with Harold, the man Rae saw her with, and their subsequent break-up.

"Have you done that a lot? The sugar daddy thing, I mean."

"No. Harold was the only one. When he came along, I was in a tough place financially. I needed money for school and he was a means to an end. As soon as I didn't need him anymore, I broke it off. It just got to be disgusting to be with him."

"Disgusting?"

She sucks in a deep breath and doesn't respond right away.

"Tori?"

"I dated when I was younger...like...boys because that's what my strict Catholic family wanted. It didn't take me long to realize that I really didn't like boys. Or men. At all. But when you're economically disadvantaged and have big goals, you trade on what you have. I have this body and this face, so men were attracted to me."

Out of the corner of my eye, I see her looking at me, so I turn and meet her gaze. Barely more than a whisper, I say, "My family is Catholic, too."

Her lips tilt ever so slightly. "When a friend introduced me to Cassandra's club, I found it intriguing. The lifestyle stuff, but even more so that I could provide a service to men who were attracted to me without having sex with them. Then I discovered the internet and doing the same kinds of things. I could be friendly and flirty and connect with them, but not have sex with them."

My brow creases. I'd heard of people doing those kinds of things online. "Do you really make that much money doing that?"

She laughs. "You wouldn't believe how easy it is."

I smile, embarrassed at my naiveté. When she reaches over the console and takes my hand in hers, my embarrassment abates.

"I'll have to find a way to make money," I say.

"You don't have any?"

I shake my head. "No. My family has money, but I don't have anything. Rather than going back to Boston, I want to stay here with Rae."

She pulls up to the gate and plugs in the code I give her. We both watch as the enormous iron gate swings open.

"What happens if you go back to Boston?"

"My uncle will force me to get married."

It's her turn to frown as she looks over at me as she waits for the gate to open completely. "I didn't think the Irish Catholics did the arranged marriage thing."

"Some of them do."

She parks her car in the circle drive, and we get out. As we walk up the steps, she reaches over and takes my hand in hers again.

We step through the front door, and she looks over at me and grins. "I can't believe this is finally happening! Ooh...I was wondering if they left the contents behind with the house. This is so cool."

"Other than replacing all the mattresses, Rae said she'll probably live with it for a while to see what she wants to keep."

"Makes sense."

Throughout the house we go with Tori, taking everything in with oohs and aahs. She even wants to see the basement, although it's nothing but concrete walls at the moment.

The suspicious part of me, instilled by my family, wonders if she has some sort of ulterior motive. However, it's unlikely that a chance meeting on an airplane could have been orchestrated so effectively by Uncle Keegan. He thinks Rae is an insignificant woman, unworthy of his notice, except if he can use her as a tool to secure an alliance.

That thought makes me smile because I'd like to see him try.

After she's seen everything, we go to Rae's room and knock on the door. "Come in!"

She calls back. When we go inside, I don't see her.

"Rae?"

"Over here. Watch out for the cables."

I finally spot her on all fours under a desk and fiddling with several cables stretched out like black snakes across the floor.

"What are you doing?" I ask.

"Setting up my system," Rae replies, as if it should be obvious.

"You're not going to use the office downstairs?" Tori inquires.

Rae looks up at her and grins. "Not for this. So, what do you think of the house, Tori? Is it everything you thought it would be?"

"Even better," Tori says, taking a seat on Rae's bed.

Rae crawls out from under the table she's apparently going to use as a desk. "I've done all I can do until I do some shopping. How about we go downstairs and have a drink?"

Bee emerges from somewhere just as we reach the first floor and joins us in the kitchen where we perch on stools around the island and share the alcohol Rae must have stopped to buy on the way home.

A few hours later, Rae and I walk Tori out to her car. Tori wraps her in a hug and the look on Rae's face has me holding in a laugh. "Thank you so much for letting me come see the house."

"You're welcome," Rae replies as she extricates herself from Tori's embrace. "We'll have to have you out again. Good night, Tori."

She turns and heads toward the front door, leaving me alone with Tori. She steps closer to me. "Thanks for showing me around. I'd love to spend more time with you."

"Yeah, me, too."

It surprises me when her hand goes to my jaw and she runs the pad of her thumb over my cheekbone. "You really don't know how beautiful you are, do you?"

The comment is so unexpected that I'm gobsmacked and unsure how to respond. She leans in and gives me a quick peck on the cheek, then pulls away and opens her car door. "Call me," she says. "Let's get together soon."

Like the eloquent speaker I am, I reply, "Yeah. Okay."

As I watch her drive away, my fingers touch the place on my cheek where her lips brushed my skin. I would have thought there'd be a scorch mark there, but it's just my skin, chilly in the crisp spring air.

CHAPTER SEVEN

Sharing Our Secrets

RAE

I'm back up in my room fiddling with computer cables when Bridget returns. She takes a seat on the edge of the bed then flops backward, her arm going over her eyes.

Since hooking up my system is probably something I shouldn't be doing while feeling so pleasantly buzzed, I crawl out from under my desk and go join her. I sit next to her and lay back, putting my entwined fingers behind my head.

"So, you and Tori seem to be getting along," I say.

She doesn't answer for long moments and when she does, it's not what I expected. "I've killed three people," she says, her voice just above a whisper, as if she's afraid of someone lurking in the corners and listening in.

I roll onto my side, pull my stocking feet up onto the bed, and prop myself up on an elbow to look her in the eye. Only her eyes are closed. "Okay."

Then her eyes fly open, wide as saucers. "Okay? That's all you have to say? Okay?"

I shrug. "If you were expecting me to be shocked or judgmental, sorry, that's not me. As you know, I've killed people, too."

"How many?" she queries.

"With the Howk boys, my total is twelve."

She rolls onto her side to face me. "Were all of yours like them? People who were threatening you?"

I shake my head. "No. Most of them were like my first." I tell her the story of killing Pastor Brown, a man who had been kidnapping and raping girls in my hometown when I was only fifteen. Also about my subsequent attempts to feed information to law enforcement only to have it fail miserably. "So, for the truly evil ones, I sometimes take matters into my own hands."

She nods. "My first was the boyfriend of one of our housekeepers. She came to work with a face full of bruises several times. Uncle Keegan wouldn't lift a finger. One time it was particularly bad, and she let it slip that she went to the police and reported him. He was a firefighter, so talked his way out of it. He didn't see it coming, and no one suspected me."

"We apparently have similar motivations."

"Yeah," she says with a wan smile.

She reaches out and traces her fingertips over the ink on my upper arm.

"That's why I want to stay here. I want to help you."

"Hang on," I say and get up from the bed.

A glance over the railing to the first floor shows faint light spilling into the foyer from under Finn's closed door. I go down the hall and peek inside Bee's room to see her fast asleep. Quietly, I pull her door closed, then return to my room and close that door, too.

"You're smart to do that," Bridget says. "She is her dah's daughter. Part of her loves you, but she will always love him more, and she can be a vindictive cunt when she wants to be."

The frozen steel in her voice surprises me. Although I wonder what happened, I don't pry. I can't imagine spending time in the Morrissey household was easy on her.

I return to the bed. She's moved up to put her head on the pillows and I join her. We're facing each other again and for a moment, I hesitate.

But then I take her hand in mine and pour out all the information I have and all the things I've been thinking. I tell her about the leader of the Vietnamese mafia in the state, Tai Dang, taking out the Mexican cartel leaders and how it's opening doors.

"All I can think is that if someone like me doesn't step in, who else might? Dang seems a little too unstable to handle it on his own. He's an iron-fisted tyrant. A self-elected king who doesn't share his power with anyone. He has no seconds or anyone he trusts implicitly."

"So, if something happens to him, his underlings wouldn't know what to do."

"Exactly. And in the chaos, someone prepared could step in and seize power. However, I don't want to perpetuate his business model. He's mostly into drugs and trafficking people, and I loathe those avenues of making money."

"Drugs aren't going away."

"I know. But I've made contact with a client in Columbia, and we're negotiating. We're talking about me helping them come in as long as they follow my rules. The primary one is no selling to kids. Mostly, I want to make the state a pipeline. A place where product can come and then be distributed across the US. Guns, low-cost pharmaceuticals, and such."

"I like your plan. It will also help keep Uncle Keegan out of here and away from your Uncle Max."

"Precisely."

We talk more about the things I want and don't want. Bridget shares with me what she sees for herself and how she thinks she can help.

"I'm great at organizing things. Like how you said you felt like you needed a notebook to keep track of everything that needs to be handled. Just tell me what you want and let me handle it. I can be your right hand, so to speak. Your version of a consigliere."

"That sounds wonderful. I'm great with the data, but sometimes the practical stuff gets overwhelming, like there aren't enough hours in the day."

"Okay. Tomorrow we'll go through the house again and you tell me what you want and I'll handle it."

We talk a while longer, and eventually fall asleep there, lying on top of the covers, facing each other with clasped hands.

Starting in the basement the next morning, I take Bridget through the thoughts I have. One end will be enclosed as a weapons room. "We can tell them we're making it a safe room," she says, and I nod in approval.

"The contact I have for weapons distribution will get us anything we want, so if there's something specific you'd like, let me know."

On the other side, there needs to be a wall built to enclose the room for, as she mentioned, a bunk room for the eventual muscle we'll need to keep on site. "In the middle, I want a gym. Weights, mats, climbers, and treadmills. The works. Stop making that face! You can still run outside on the property."

Floor-by-floor, we continue with Bridget taking notes the entire time. New mattresses for every bed. We stop when she has a three-page list of things to take care of and I give her one of my pre-charged cards.

"This has a hundred grand on it. If you use it up, let me know and I'll give you another."

Bee shuffles into the kitchen, and Finn appears from the solitary downstairs bedroom as if on cue. "Good morning sleepy heads," I tease, because I know Finn has been up for a while. "I need to go to the electronics store. If y'all want to come, we can get some breakfast while we're out and stock up on groceries, too."

"Why are you all up so early?" Bee grouses.

"I hate to tell you, sweetheart, but it's not that early. It's almost ten. If you want to come with, you've got thirty to meet me by the front door."

CHAPTER EIGHT

Nicknames are Earned

BRIDGET

My latest interview with a potential cook has just left when Rae comes racing down the stairs and flies into the kitchen. She grabs a soda out of the fridge and paces while she drinks it down. "What's wrong?" I ask.

Her system is finally set up, and she's been glued to it for days, reviewing whatever her wee beasties, as she calls them, brought her.

She looks at me and then around. I know she's wondering if Bee is nearby. It's my fault that she doesn't tell Bee everything, but I can't be sorry. Bee can't tell her dah what she doesn't know.

Uncle Keegan is excellent at drawing information out of people without them realizing he's doing it and Bee is one of his favorite targets. When we first came back to the US, she didn't mean to tell her dah about the girl I'd been friendly with in Ireland.

After he beat me black and blue to drive home the point that that kind of nonsense wouldn't happen again, he swore to me that if I told Bee about the beating, I'd get another one. I know she didn't mean to tell. At least that's what I told myself at the time, but looking back, I'm not so sure.

Rae moves closer to me and lowers her voice. "I found something. Well, two somethings." She jerks her head toward the stairs. Taking my notebook with me, I follow her to her room.

When we're inside her room, she closes the door and locks it, then goes to her computer. I stand beside her and watch as she points at the screen. The stuff on the screen just looks like numbers and letters to me, so I give her an oblique look.

"I think Tai Dang is going to rob a bank."

"What?" I gasp.

"From what I've found, he's behind several bank robberies that have happened over the past two and a half years. I think he does it for the thrill because he sure doesn't need the money. However, he doesn't know the cops are onto him. If he finds out, he might not do it, so I have a crazy idea."

She chews on her thumbnail, her leg bouncing a million miles a minute.

"Tell me already!" I urge. "The suspense is killing me!"

After sucking in a deep breath, she says, "Because he's such a control freak, he has his liquid cash in very few accounts. So, I'm thinking about pulling out money to push him to go through with the robbery. Then the feds can snatch him up and he goes off to prison. Good riddance."

"Can you really draw out that money and redirect it so no one knows you did it?"

"Yeah. It takes time and finesse, but I can."

"I say do it. If the feds move him out of the way, you don't have to mess with him. Just step in when the way is clear before anyone else does. What's the other thing you found?"

"It's just something to keep in our back pocket for now, but there appears to be another group working against human trafficking in the state. I don't know who yet, but there's a lot of chatter about certain shipments being hijacked and the cargo being set free."

"Excellent. Perhaps we can tap them as a resource when we take over Dang's operations."

"My thoughts exactly. Okay, I'll get to work. I just wish there was a way to get someone close to Dang. Maybe I'll start looking into those closest to him more in depth. How was the cook?"

"She's morally opposed to pizza," I say as I shake my head, then a laugh bursts out of me at the look on Rae's face because pizza is one of her primary food groups. "Speaking of food, when is the last time you ate?"

She stares at me. "Um…"

I shake my head. How has this woman lived for so long without a keeper? She might be a bad ass in a lot of ways, but she still needs someone looking after her. It's not good to spend so much time alone.

"We have sandwich stuff and frozen pizza."

"Nah. I need a break. Let's go out. There may come a time when we can't move around as freely, so we might as well enjoy it while we can. Let's go find the others and see if they want to go."

Of course, Bee will want to go, and where Bee goes, Finn goes. She's been complaining about being cooped up all the time. I've told her she's free to go and do however she wants, but she's never been one to go do anything on her own.

She's also frustrated that I'm not following her around all the time here and have been spending more time with Rae than with her. Last night she asked me, "Why are you getting so involved? We'll be going back home soon."

I haven't told her yet that I won't be going back to Boston. It's better to wait and cross that bridge only when necessary. Like when she's boarding the plane to go back.

As soon as we return from dinner, Rae goes back to her computer and I return to the kitchen to weigh the options of hiring a cook versus using one of those meal kit services. Even those would be better food than the junk we constantly have around because none of us can cook, but perhaps one of us could manage following step-by-step instructions.

Before I even get started digging back into the information, I decide to let it rest for tonight. The house is quiet as I go upstairs to my room, but when I pass by Bee's room, I can hear her muffled voice.

She's probably talking to Geno on the phone. Somehow she either convinced her dah it wouldn't be too much of a distraction for them to talk from time to time or figured out a way to keep him from finding out.

There's still light spilling from the gap at the bottom of Rae's door, so I knock quietly enough that if she's sleeping, I won't wake her. "I'm up." Sounds from inside.

"You need to get some sleep."

"Backatcha."

I step farther into the room. "What are you still looking for?"

"Nothing now. Other than through his men, there's only one other potential in with Dang. His fiancé broke things off and is seeing someone new. Dang didn't take it very well. She's staying away from him, but her cousin isn't. I think there's something going on between Dang and the girl."

Rae shows me photos of a pretty Asian girl, a child, to my eyes. "How old is she?"

"Thirteen. From what I can tell, Dang is using her as a lure to get other young girls to follow her to one of his parties; then they disappear. Probably into one of his brothels. At thirteen, she's not going to be open to any of us. We've got ten years too many under our belts."

"Let me give it a try. I won't approach her. Just get close and see what happens."

She scrutinizes me for long moments before she nods and says, "Okay. It's worth a shot. Every day, she goes to the mall near her house after school. Usually, she's shadowed by one of Dang's men, so we'll have to be careful."

"Tomorrow then."

Rae's eyes go wide when she sees me coming down the stairs. "Ho-ly shit."

"What?" Bee asks, rushing into the foyer. A frown takes over her pretty face. "Why are you dressed like that? You look like a kid."

"Exactly," Rae interjects. "Arya Stark's got nothing on you."

"Who?" Bee asks. She never wanted to watch the program with the rest of us. Finn, who has emerged from his room, just smirks and nods.

"You're a regular chameleon. Come on Cam, let's go before we're late."

Bee stomps her foot and demands, "Where are you going?"

"To do recon," Rae tells her. "You can come, but if you blow our cover, I'll kick your ass."

Finn raises an eyebrow at her, but Rae just raises both of hers back at him. Honestly, I'd love to see the two of them spar. I'm not so sure that Finn would come out the winner and if he did, she would probably make him pay dearly for it.

Rae turns back to Bee. "It's at the mall."

"Oh," she replies, "we're going."

At the mall, Bee drags Finn off with her while she goes in search of retail therapy. Rae pulls around to a different entrance and parks. I get out and shuffle into the building.

Deciding to approach my search for Kimmy Pham methodically, I go upstairs. From there, I can roam from store to store while being able to look down at the lower level. Avoiding the higher-end stores, I focus on the ones targeted at tweens and teens.

I'm almost to the end where I planned to turn around and go down the other side when I spot her. She's leaning on the rail and watching the people moving around below.

Behind her is a store with shoes popular with skaters, so I stop in the doorway, staring at the display of shoes. I pick up a shoe and examine it, then with a sigh, put it back onto the display before I shuffle off.

Her eyes are practically boring holes in the back of my head. Inconspicuously as I can, I look for Rae. She is nowhere to be seen, but I know she's there. Watching. Keeping me safe.

Across from Kimmy's position is one of those stores with cheap costume jewelry that appeals to a lot of young girls. I go inside and even though the clerk is watching me like a hawk, a woman comes in and distracts her, so I let Kimmy see me slip a pair of earrings into the pocket of my jacket.

Then I shuffle out of the store and move on down the row of stores. Just as I step onto the escalator to go downstairs,

Kimmy steps on right behind me. "You were so smooth," she says, leaning close.

I slide my eyes and turn my head a fraction. "Don't know what you're talking about."

She shrugs. "Okay. I'm Kimmy, by the way. Where do you go to school?"

"Haven't started yet. Just moved here," I mumble and shuffle toward the coffee shop I spotted on my earlier rounds.

She keeps trying to start up a conversation while we stand in line, but I continue to keep my answers short. I place my order and she steps up close again, placing hers and saying she's paying.

When I slide my eyes to her again, I mumble a thank you.

"No problem. My boyfriend gives me money to get anything I want."

"Boyfriend? How does a guy our age have that kind of money?"

She jerks her head to a table away from the others. We sit and talk; her extolling the virtues of her older, wealthy boyfriend, while I mostly listen.

She hints at the party scene available through said boyfriend. Looking away, I drop my own hints about at a less than spotless past and parents who hover too much. Her commiseration seems so sincere.

How many girls have fallen for her act and been lured into Dang's clutches? Anger begins to simmer in my belly. As much as I want to shake some sense into her, I manage to keep my façade of cool indifference in place.

My phone buzzes. I pull it out and glance at the screen before I tell her I need to go and, as I expected, she asks for my number.

With a promise to keep in touch after I plug her number into the phone Rae set up for me, I make my way out of the mall and to the bus stop. At the station downtown, I change buses and take another to a neighborhood appropriate to my character.

Once I'm sure I'm not being followed, I slip into an empty house's backyard and transform my look before going over the back fence into the alley. When I call Rae, she's there quickly with the others, having followed my travel through town.

Sliding into the backseat next to her, I grin. "It couldn't have gone better."

"You definitely earned your nickname today," Rae says, her voice full of praise. "Cam the chameleon. The girl never had a clue."

Bee, of course, has a million questions, all of which Rae is very circumspect in answering. Although she's only getting half-answers and deflections, Bee is quickly mollified. She probably doesn't really care, she just doesn't want to miss out on something she might deem important.

We stop for food on the way home and Bee grumbles about eating out again. She's used to having a house full of staff at home ready to fulfill her every whim. I know she's being testy because she misses Geno, but Rae has bent over backwards to make us comfortable and has footed the bill for everything since we arrived.

Ungrateful isn't a good look for Bee.

CHAPTER NINE

Trading on My Pretty Face

VICTORIA

I hurry into Cassandra's Club and make a beeline to the dressing room. Cassandra's is a BDSM club where clients can play out sessions catering to their particular fetish. The sessions are about the fetish and there's really very little actual sex that goes on.

I've been working here for a while, but recently got onto a webcam site and have been doing very well there. My cam session at home today went a little long because the client was being particularly generous. Although I hated to cut him off, I have an early appointment at the club.

Juggling school, my online presence and working at the club can be exhausting sometimes, but it will be worth it. The light at the end of the tunnel is getting closer and it can't get here soon enough.

"Hey Tori!" Joelle says when I enter the room. She's putting on minimal makeup that goes with her schoolgirl outfit. She is a beautiful blend of her Asian and African American heritage and is blessed with a very youthful appearance.

Although she hates it now because when she's without makeup, she looks like she's about fourteen instead of her full nineteen years. I keep telling her that in a few years she'll be thankful for it, but so far, she doesn't believe me.

"Hi Jojo. Got the creeper again today, I see." One client always asks for Jo in the schoolgirl getup. He has her sit on his lap while he rubs her butt and spanks her occasionally.

His pushy requests for more and for an off-site get together have been denied, but he's not dropping it, and it makes me a little afraid for her. Some clients can get out of hand and Jo is too sweet to rebuff them effectively.

Thankfully, she says she's just doing this while she's in culinary school because I don't think she's cut out for it long term. One more year and she says she can leave this place in her rearview mirror.

Quickly, I stow my things and sit down to check my makeup. It's just my luck that my online client wanted the latex dominatrix outfit today, so I didn't need to change before coming in and just threw on a long coat to cover the outfit.

"Yeah," Jo replies. "He's my only appointment today, but he offered an excellent bonus if I'd come in for him."

The money at this place is hard to beat, so I totally get the lure, but sometimes it seems like Cassandra is a little lax in certain ways. Although I want to buy her out some day, I wonder if I'll be able to redirect the power from the clients to the workers.

If someone has enough money, they're allowed to get away with way more than I'd be okay with. More than once since I've been working here, girls have gotten hurt by a client who gets carried away and one was even stalked by a client and Cassandra only barred them for a short time before allowing them to return. I would not put up with that shit.

There is plenty of fun to be had within the limits of the rules and plenty of clients to go around, so there's no reason for them to be allowed to misbehave. Once a client gets away with something with just a slap on the wrist in response, they push the boundaries even further next time.

A lot of the girls are like I was when I first started, financially strapped with big dreams, and trading on my pretty face was a way to make money that couldn't be earned by flipping burgers. When you're in that position, you put up with a lot more than you would otherwise.

"Well, be careful. Don't let him do anything he's not supposed to," I admonish. "I only have two sessions tonight, but they're back-to-back so if you want to wait until I'm done, we can walk out together."

She smiles at me. "Thanks, Tor."

From what others have told me, there used to be a lot more security around here. Especially when one of the girls was kidnapped and killed by someone stalking one of the other workers in a case of mistaken identity.

Cassandra let that little tidbit slip one evening when she'd been indulging in a little too much merlot in her office. She begged me not to say anything and so far I've kept quiet, but if things keep going downhill, I might have to remind her of what can happen.

Now, there's security inside, right at the front door, but once you step through the exit, you're kind of on your own unless you get lucky with who's on duty. Some of the guys acting as bouncers are more attentive and protective. Some of them simply don't seem to give a shit and think that if you're working in a place like this, you deserve whatever you get.

I go to my session and paddle Mr. Bank President until his bottom is rosy pink. He gets off on humiliation, so I let all my pent-up frustrations from the last few days out on him and he loves it.

Frustration over one of my professors making a pass at me and over my cousin, who is essentially blackmailing me to allow her to live with me while she goes to school to prevent her from telling our parents what I do for a living.

It wouldn't be so bad, but she is too smart for her own good. That means she's a constant pain in the ass, so having her around all the time would not be fun. But mostly, I'm frustrated because I haven't had time to contact Bridget.

Her beautiful face has been on my mind since I left her the other night and I've wanted nothing more than to see her again. I'm hoping that tonight I can get out of here early enough to call her.

When my first session is over, I put an ear to the door of the room that's set up as a classroom and hear muffled noises from inside. Jo's voice is unmistakable even though I can't make out exactly what she's saying. She sounds fine, so I go change clothes and head to my next session with Mr. State Representative.

Jo's stuff is gone from the dressing room when I return, so maybe things went all right and she's already gone home. However, when I step outside, her car is still parked out front.

I turn on my heel and go back in and all my released frustrations come back when it takes forever to find one of the security team. He's sitting in the security room with all the monitors showing the Thunder game.

"Bruce!" He drops his feet to the floor from where they were propped on the desk.

"What the fuck do you want? Can't you see I'm busy?"

"I see you're not busy doing your fucking job. Jo's stuff is gone, but her car is still here. Please pull up the cameras for the past hour."

"Come on! The game's in the last minutes."

I pull out my phone and put one hand on my hip. "Do you want me to call the cops?"

Because of our high-profile clientele, one of the cardinal rules is that the police don't get called unless absolutely necessary. He glares at me, but turns his attention to the keyboard.

Leaving the game up on one screen, he puts the security view on the others. "Watch your fucking game, asshole. If anything has happened to her, I'm going to hold you personally responsible."

"Whatever," he says.

Although I needed him to log in and change the screens, I've been in here often enough to know how to run the system. I rewind quickly and when I see Jo walk out, I stop and start moving the video forward at a slower speed.

She walks out of the building, bundled up in a warm coat, and opens her car. Her bag is tossed inside, and she's just about to slide into the driver's seat when a car pulls up and blocks her car in. The window of the car rolls down, and she turns to go to it, closing her car door.

I don't miss the look on her face – part impatience and part fear. She doesn't want to talk to whoever it is, but she goes anyway. Her body is blocking the view of who is in the car, so I can't see what happens.

Her knees give way and she's pulled through the open window into the car before it pulls away and motors down the street. Although I didn't see the driver or passenger, in my gut I know it was most likely the client she saw tonight.

"I need to know the name of her client tonight," I tell Bruce.

"You know I can't."

"Fine," I say and dial 911.

While Bruce curses a blue streak as we wait for the police to arrive, I make another call. When Bridget answers with her lilting Irish cadence, I want to smile, but instead, I burst into tears.

CHAPTER TEN

Forces Our Agenda

BRIDGET

My stomach flip-flops when I see Tori's number light up my screen, but as soon as I hear her crying, my happiness dissolves. "What's going on?"

"I'm sorry, but I didn't know who else to call. Based on what you said, Rae is really good with the computer. You didn't say it, but I have the feeling that means she's able to do things a lot of people aren't."

"Hang on, if you're needing her, let me go find her so she can listen in." As usual, Rae is in her room, glued to her computer. I go inside without knocking and close the door behind me, then put my phone on speaker.

"Okay," I say. "Rae's listening in."

"Rae, this is Tori. I was working at the club tonight and one of the girls I work with was taken from the parking lot. If you can't do it, let me know, but I have a feeling you can. If I give you her number, can you trace her phone?"

"What's the number?" Rae queries, her fingers flying over the keyboard as she shifts the data display on her screens.

Tori rattles off the number and Rae goes to work. "I've got it. She's headed south."

"Can I come over?" Tori asks, sounding small. "That way, when she stops, I can go get her."

Rae nods.

"Yes," I relay. "Come on over."

"I have to wait until the police arrive, but will come as soon as I can."

We disconnect, and I hover as Rae works. It's amazing what she can do. Besides having a window open with the girl's phone's location moving on a map, she's already pulled up her name and address. Her driver's license, too.

Joelle Carter is pretty and looks very young but the birthdate on her license puts her at nineteen. While Rae works, I watch the red dot moving on the map. Suddenly, it blinks out.

Rae notices it, too, and utters a curse. Another window shows what looks to be a login and I notice the logo for Cassandra's Club. That window is minimized and her fingers are back to work.

Screen after screen is opened and closed, Rae absorbing the information before I can even grasp what I'm seeing.

Rae sits back in her seat. "Shit."

"What?" I ask, just as the doorbell rings. "That's probably Tori," I exclaim, racing out of the room and down the stairs.

Finn is opening the door just as I reach the ground floor. Tori starts to speak to Finn, but sees me and rushes past him. I open my arms and she steps into them, putting her face in my neck and crying.

Finn gives me a speculative look just before Bee comes into the foyer from somewhere. "What's wrong with her?"

"I'll tell you later," I reply, hoping my tone encourages her to keep her mouth shut and not comment further. "Come on," I say against Tori's ear. "Let's go upstairs to where Rae is and see what she's found."

Keeping her hand in mine, I lead her upstairs to Rae's bedroom. Rae looks up and gives Tori a sympathetic smile. "Well, I have bad news and good news."

"Just tell me what you can," Tori says, sounding weary.

"Okay. They took her to the south side of town, but either took the battery out of her phone or destroyed it here," she says, pointing to the spot on the map where the red dot had been before it disappeared.

"The good and bad news is that I know who took her."

"How?" Tori queries. "That's not even on Cassandra's records. She has code names for everyone and the code name is what she gave the police. She was so pissed at me for calling them that I may have lost that job. I don't give a fuck, though. I don't need her anymore and after this, I don't want to be associated with her."

"She has a customer bible, for lack of a better term, that gives the real identity for every code name. The last client that Joelle saw was Tai Dang, head of the Vietnamese gang in OKC."

"How?"

"Don't ask," I tell her. "It's better that you don't know the details."

Before she can respond, Rae says, "He's been killing off his competition and has had to step up staffing of his other business interests, mainly his brothels and it looks like that's where he's taken her, to his main brothel. A pretty girl like her that looks five years younger than she is..."

She doesn't finish the statement because it doesn't take much imagination to know exactly what is likely to happen to poor Joelle.

"Let's go get her!" Tori demands.

"We can't just go in there guns blazing and that's what it would be," Rae informs her in a tone laced with ice. "The place has armed gang members on duty at all hours and this time of night, probably most of the customers would be armed, too. Then there are the other victims to consider. Most of them have been trafficked and are there against their will. If I'm going in there, I'm not going to leave any of them behind."

Tori seethes for half a dozen heartbeats, but eventually succumbs to reason.

Softening her voice. "By now, Dang has probably already raped her. I know that's no comfort, but you need to understand that it's too late to rescue Joelle unscathed. However, for a while, he'll want to keep her to himself before sharing her with anyone else."

Tori kicks the solid wood armoire and slaps her hand against it before letting out a frustrated scream.

When she quiets, Rae goes on. "I'd already been working on a plan to clear out that brothel and have cultivated a contact that will be able to offer transition support to the trafficked individuals. It will mean going sooner than I'd hoped, but I might be able to manage a quick change-up of the plan. I'll also get in touch with my contact to see if they can step up the timeline."

"Let's leave her to work," I tell Tori and lead her by the hand toward the door. "We have coffee, tea, or just about anything alcoholic you could want."

We go downstairs, where we retrieve the tequila bottle and take it back upstairs to my room. Tori blames herself for what happened to Joelle, saying that if she'd just made her wait so they could go out together, Joelle wouldn't have been taken.

My logical argument that she likely would have been taken right along with Joelle doesn't even make a dent in her what ifs. Between the stress, crying, arguing with herself, and drinking, she eventually exhausts herself and falls into a fitful sleep.

Once I pull the covers over Tori, I return to Rae. She's putting on her jacket. "Where are you going?" I ask.

"Like I said, there was a loose plan in place, but this forces our agenda. It's more loosey goosey than I'd like, but I can't just leave that girl there to have God knows what done to her."

"You still didn't answer my question."

"I don't have a vehicle large enough to transport a dozen women, but my contact does. However, before they put their asses on the line, they want to meet. So, I'm going to go meet them in Okemah because if they don't show up, the plan is fucked and I'll have to regroup before attempting it without them, which means leaving Joelle where she is, possibly for a few days."

"I'm going with you."

"All right, but the bike will be fastest, so dress warm."

CHAPTER ELEVEN

Interesting Allies

BRIDGET

Rae and I hurry out to the garage even though Bee is in a huff that we aren't telling her where we're going. There's just not time to explain. Once Rae gets a spare helmet for me and shows me how to put it on, she gets on the bike.

"Get on behind me and wrap your arms around me. We'll be moving fast, so however I move, you move."

"Got it," I reply. "There was a boy in our village growing up that had a motorbike and I rode with him a few times. I think he mostly did it to get the girls to put their arms around him."

Rae grins and pulls up the bottom of her balaclava to cover her mouth and nose. I do the same and climb on the back of the bike. We're off like a shot and headed down the drive where the gate is opening for us.

After a terrifying but exhilarating ride, we pull up to a twenty-four-hour gas station in the town of Okemah. Rae parks the bike and I go inside to use the restroom. As I walk back out to the mostly empty parking lot, two men step out of a truck that has seen better days.

One is smallish, about the same height as Rae, but he's all rawboned, hard muscle, and scrap. He'd do in a row, I'd bet, but he's quite the contradiction because his eyes are full of care and laughter.

The other man is tall, stoic, and radiates power and authority. If I was alone with him, I'd tread with care, but Rae steps right up and holds out her hand. "You must be Kieran. I'm Rae."

I'm not sure if it's because he's not used to people approaching him without fear or hesitation, but the look on his face transforms from stony hard to slightly bemused. "Aye, that would be me."

"So, do you think you can help us?"

Kieran looks at the other man and asks him, "John, what are your impressions?" However, he does it in Gaelic.

For some reason, that gets my back up. "It's rude to talk about people in a language you don't think they'll understand," I say, also in Gaelic, letting every bit of Ireland within me shine through.

"Sorry, lass," the smaller man says with a grin. He's still speaking in Gaelic. "No offense was meant."

"Actually," Rae says, also continuing the language trend. "Since we can converse like this, it's probably a good idea. Gentlemen, this is my cousin Cam. She was born here, but grew up on the other side of the pond. I learned from my father, who was born in Belfast."

"Please tell us more about the situation you're facing," Kieran requests.

Rae fills them in on what happened tonight to push up the timeline. Then she repeats a lot of information that I hadn't known when we left the house. She's apparently been watching the brothel long enough to know how many victims are kept there and their approximate age ranges and possible ethnicities.

"They've probably been fed a steady diet of drugs and alcohol to keep them compliant and easy to control," Rae adds.

"We can handle that," John says. "We've had a lot of experience with detoxing victims."

"The owner of the brothel is the head of the Vietnamese gang, the Viet Cong Boyz, and seems intent on taking over the state," Rae tells them. "So...it could be dangerous."

"Your concern is appreciated, but unnecessary," Scary Kieran replies. "Our people will be fine."

Rae shows them a copy of Joelle's driver's license. "This is our gal. We'll take her with us, but the others will need transition help. The target address is written at the bottom of the page."

Kieran hands the paper to John. "Time?"

"Oh six hundred?"

Kieran checks his watch and raises an eyebrow.

Rae shrugs. "They usually close around two, so that gives them four hours to get relaxed and ready to sleep the day away.

The two to three guards on duty usually stay for twenty-four hours at a time, changing out with a new crew before they open for the day around noon."

"Got it." John says. "See you in a few hours."

We race back to the house to try to get a few hours of sleep before we have to meet our allies to raid the brothel. I'm so wired that I don't know if I'll be able to rest at all, much less sleep. In my room, Tori is still out, so I move cautiously so as not to wake her.

After a quick trip to the bathroom to wash my face and teeth, I change into comfortable clothes and climb onto the bed. Although I was careful, not wanting to wake her, when my head hits the pillow, I look over to see her looking back.

"Where'd you go?" she queries as she reaches out to take my hand in hers. Her touch is electric and I'm no longer tired.

"We went to meet with some people who are going to help us get everyone out and they'll help them transition into a regular life."

"Do you think we can trust them?"

"Yeah. Rae's checked them out. This is something they do all the time, rescue people being trafficked and help them start over. They even said they're experienced with rehabbing addicts."

"That's amazing," she replies around a yawn. "When are we going to get Jo?"

"In a few hours, so I'm going to see if I can get a few hours of sleep."

She scoots closer and frowns, tugging at the comforter. "Why are you on top of the covers?"

"I didn't want to wake you."

Pulling at the comforter again, she says, "Get in here. We've got a big day in a few hours."

I settle under the comforter, and she moves closer, taking my hand in hers again. Without warning, she leans in and kisses me lightly. "Thank you, Bridget. I can't tell you how much your help means to me."

"You're welcome."

I try not to read too much into that kiss, but as I drift away into sleep, it consumes my mind. Her lips are so soft. And mine are tingling in the aftermath. My entire body is tingling.

We are ready early to go to the location where we think Jo is being held. Rae skimmed through the camera feeds, but says she can't be positive the young woman wasn't taken somewhere else. She wants to scope the place out in advance of our allies' arrival.

Bee was still asleep, but Finn was up. He wanted to go with us, but Rae convinced him he should stick to his charge and stay at the house with her.

It shocks me when he actually argues with her. With words. "You shouldn't go alone."

"I'm not."

"Bridget is not trained and doesn't have experience in these types of situations."

He has no idea of the things I've done, so I bristle at his comment. However, interjecting myself into the conversation wouldn't help anyone.

Partly, he's right. I've never gone into a building with guns blazing against an unknown number of opponents. When we get back, I want to start training so that when we inevitably go into another dangerous situation, she can be confident in my ability to be an asset.

"She's not the only backup I'll have," Rae informs him.

Finn closes his mouth. Smart man.

Tori and I take her car and park two blocks away from the building that houses the brothel. I view the back of the place through binoculars while Rae stops next to us on her motorcycle.

There's very little ambient light because several of the streetlights are dark, either broken or just burned out. The darkness benefits us, but from this vantage point, the outside of the building looks like a small, rundown warehouse with a few cars parked in the alley behind it.

"Cam, my tablet, please," she says through Tori's open window.

I hand it to her and she does some kind of electronic wizardry as her fingers move over the screen. She pauses for several heartbeats, then hands the tablet back, and says, "All right, their cameras are blind, so I'm going to do a drive by and be back in a few."

Tori and I watch as she zooms away down the street and disappears around the corner. "Why does she call you Cam?"

I smile to myself, remembering how it felt to be christened by Rae with my new secret identity. Like I was accepted. Like I belong. "It's a nickname, short for chameleon, because I am good with disguises."

"What exactly does Rae do? I mean, she's not that much older than me, but seems to have a lot of money. Even if she got a phenomenal deal on that house, it had to cost over a million dollars."

Rather than answer directly, I hedge, "What do you think she does?"

"I don't know. She's super nice, but also kind of scary. The way she was able to track Jojo and how she shut down those cameras just now, she has to be some kind of computer genius, but also a bad ass because of the way she's going to go into that building to rescue people she doesn't even know."

"She's definitely a computer genius and our family kind of necessitates being familiar with dangerous situations."

"You've said something like that before. Who is your family?"

I hesitate even though I want to tell her everything. However, as much as I would like to explore this attraction I feel toward her before she runs away screaming at the idea of mob ties, she deserves to know what she's getting into so she can decide if she wants to explore it, too.

"I'm going to tell you because I believe I can trust you, but I'm going to ask that you not tell anyone because it wouldn't be safe, especially for my other cousin."

"You don't have to worry about me. After today, I owe you. No one else would have stepped up to do this for me, much less people who don't know me any more than you all do."

My nerves jangle despite her assurances. This isn't something we talk about. People in Boston hear the name Morrissey and just assume, but here, no one is familiar with who Bee's father is.

Sucking in a deep breath, I dive in. "My other cousin that's at Rae's house, her father is Keegan Morrissey, and he is the head of the Irish mob in Boston. His wife's cousin is my mother, and my father was one of his high-ranking captains before he was killed. Rae's father was his half-brother. So we all have ties to organized crime."

"I thought Rae was from here."

"She is. Rae didn't grow up in Boston because her father was sent down here by his father, who was in charge at the time to look into setting up a distribution hub. Because her father was born out of wedlock, he was treated badly in Boston. When he fell in love with a woman here and wanted to stay, no one balked. However, knowing that someday she'd be exposed to his family, he prepared her for that life."

"Wow."

Rae stops next to Tori's window again. When it's down, she says, "That black car on the far side of the three parked out back is Tai Dang's, so it's a pretty good indicator that Joelle was brought here. It's also an opportunity and a problem."

"With him here, that means two more combatants than you'd be facing," I reply.

"Exactly...but..."

She doesn't finish her sentence because a wash of light appears in the alley as the back door is opened. Through the binoculars, I can make out three figures. As I watch, Rae puts down her kickstand and gets off her bike.

She pulls off her helmet but leaves her balaclava on and unzips her jacket. Her hands move. One to the inside of her jacket to pull out a weapon and the other to a pocket, where she takes out a cylinder and screws it to the end of the gun. It's a silencer, I realize.

Then she's gone, a dark smudge on the night moving silently closer to the target building.

Chapter Twelve

Rescue Operation

Rae

As much as I want to run right up and shoot whoever it is at the back of the building in the head, it would be stupid because they'd just pull out their weapons and shoot me first. So, I approach it a little more circumspectly.

By the time I'm close enough to hear the murmur of their voices, too much time has gone by because I hear someone, probably Dang, barking out...something...just before a car door closes. Shoes crunch on the rough pavement as a second someone moves, probably Dang's driver, since a second car door opens then closes.

The car starts and pulls away. Holding my breath, I listen to see if the other man is moving. He's not, but he does mutter under his breath, apparently a little irritated by his boss's orders. A flick and hiss of a lighter is followed by the stench of weed.

Tsk. Tsk, big boy. But you do your thing and smoke up because that will make your impaired ass easier to kill.

When I left Cam and Tori, it was about twenty minutes until our cohorts were due to arrive. Quickly, I debate whether I should wait for them, or go ahead and take this guy out. The decision to move wins out because if he goes back inside and locks that door behind him, it will be a bitch to get inside.

Stepping out of the shadow I'd been using to conceal my presence, I see his back is turned. He knocks the cherry off his blunt and instead of shooting him, in quick, fluid moves, I flip the safety on, slide the gun in my jacket, pull out a knife and jab it into the side of his throat.

He spins, his hand going to his neck, and lurches toward me as he reaches for his weapon. The idiot must have left it inside, because he comes up empty as blood spurts through his fingers, down his arm, and onto the dirty, broken pavement and trash of the alley.

When he takes another step, he falls to one knee. After a feeble attempt to regain his footing, he falls face-first into a puddle of his own blood.

Stepping around his prone form, I'm careful not to leave any footprints in the growing red stain. I crouch and open the back door to peek in.

The lights are dim inside, but I don't see any movement, so I take a deep breath and step inside. I pull my gun back out and start moving through the space.

I'm in a hallway with doors on both sides. When I try the knobs, they're locked. On the other side of one of them, a feminine whimper sounds from inside. There are seven doors on each side, so that means fourteen potential victims, which is more than I'd counted during my surveillance.

"Fuck," I breathe.

From previously studying the camera system, I have an idea of the layout of the place, but there are no cameras back here. I'm almost to the end of the hall of doors when the exit behind me creaks open slowly. Swinging around with my gun in the lead, I lower it when I see John's face.

Relieved, I move back to meet him. In a whisper, I relay my suspicions about the rooms containing the trafficking victims. "I have one last door to check, but so far, I haven't seen any other security."

Just as I move back down the hall again, the last door I hadn't had a chance to check opens. A giant, heavy-set Asian man steps into the hallway. He's wearing a white t-shirt with stains that look suspiciously like blood under an unbuttoned white dress shirt. The man is pulling up his pants and zipping them when he sees us.

"Whotha fuck are you?" he shouts and whoever is in the room behind him begins to shriek with fear.

"The Morrigan," I reply as rage surges through me.

When I step forward, John puts a hand on my arm. "Please, allow me, Lady Badb. You work on getting these doors open."

"But there might be other security..."

"I'll handle it," he replies casually, as if he takes on men three times his size every day.

The back door opens and Kieran comes in with the dead man draped over his shoulder. In quick, efficient statements, I catch him up as I take out a lock pick gun to start opening doors.

It would be faster just to kick them in, but that would only serve to terrorize whoever was inside even more. Inside the first two rooms, the occupants are sleeping. One is a girl who looks to be about fourteen. I recognize her from the camera feeds.

The other room is a boy, also in his early teens. On and on it goes until all the doors are open. Almost all of them are asleep, or most likely drugged out of their minds.

Behind the door where I heard the whimper is Joelle. She's naked, sitting on a bed, wrapped into a tight ball in the far corner with her eyes shut tight as tremors of fear course through her slight frame.

"Joelle," I say, keeping my voice even. "I'm a friend and I'm going to get you out of here."

"Here," someone behind me says and I turn to see a woman.

She must have come with the others because she hands me a folded stack of sweats with a pair of slippers on top. Of course, they'd be prepared. Kieran's group has done this before and I'm thankful to have them as allies in this sort of thing.

I take the clothes from her and nod my thanks. "Jojo," I say, "that's what Tori calls you, right?"

That finally gets a reaction other than fear from her. At the mention of her friend's name, Joelle's eyes pop open. "Tori?"

I nod, holding the bundle of clothes out to her. "She's here with me, but she's outside, so we need to get you dressed."

Joelle, finding her strength, darts off the bed and takes the clothes from me. Hurriedly, she pulls them on and slides her feet into the slippers. I take her by the hand and lead the way to the door.

Ducking my head around the corner, I see the others carrying the sleeping victims dressed in their own sweats out the back door. "Come on," I tell Joelle and pull her into the hall behind me.

She's got a death grip on my hand and sticks close to my side. When she sees one of the men, she ducks behind me. "Who are they?"

"Friends," I tell her. "They're going to take the others to safety and help them with whatever they need."

Kieran rounds the corner carrying the boy I saw earlier. He hikes his chin. "Go. We're almost done and will handle things here."

"Okay. Just so you know, I shut the cameras down before you arrived, so you don't need to worry about that."

He nods and we take our leave, hurrying out the back door. I guide Joelle around the puddle of blood and two passenger vans as I lead her toward the street. As soon as Tori sees her, she's out of the car racing toward her friend.

Joelle is limping, but hurries to meet Tori. They embrace. "We need to get gone," I tell her. "The others are almost done and said they'd handle cleanup or whatever they intend to do. Take her to the house; we can keep her safe there."

I race toward the car where Cam waits. Her face is full of worry, so I tell her, "I'm fine."

She nods and slides into the back seat to make way for the others to get in. I hop on my bike, quickly put my helmet on, and we all take off, moving fast, but not so much as to draw police attention.

As we slide through the dark like specters in the depths of the ocean, my mind replays John calling me Badb after one of the sisters that make up the Morrigan goddess. A thrill ran through me when he said it and it felt so very right.

What happened tonight, seeing all those victims of Dang's ilk, just solidifies what I want to do here. Considering all the chance meetings, like with Kieran and crew, and how things keep falling into place, I think the Universe wants me here, too.

CHAPTER THIRTEEN

Adrenaline Burn Off

RAE

Back at the house, we get Joelle settled in one of the rooms on the third floor. When she saw Cam's room had a terrace with doors that opened to the backyard, she had a panic attack, started screaming and hid under a table. Although it took a while to coax her out, I can't say that I blame her.

It was either one of the plain rooms on the third floor that must have been used by staff, or the basement. Considering the basement is nothing but concrete walls and very prison-like, the third floor was the best option.

Only one of the doors on the third floor had a lock on it, which is weird to me. Were the staff not allowed to have their privacy? If not, why was one person allowed to?

We put her in the room with the lock because it makes her feel better. Almost immediately, we hear the shower start. I just hope there are things like shampoo, conditioner, and soap in there.

After the adrenaline burn-off, I'm a jangled mess of wired and exhausted. I go to the kitchen and fix myself some cheesy eggs and grab a beer, taking everything to my room, where I turn on the television.

A breaking news bulletin flashes on the screen, reporting a fire in a rundown part of town. Three dead bodies were found in the ruins after the fire department extinguished the flames. Being an old property, it was mostly gone by the time authorities arrived.

For a moment, I think about going in and doctoring the ownership records to ensure they can tie it to Dang, but I think better of it. I'd have to be quick about it and I'm too tired to be as meticulous as I'd need to be.

Sitting back in my chair, I zone out on the television, letting my body settle so I can get some sleep. My phone buzzes on the desk. When I pick it up and see who it is, warm fuzzies roll through me, pushing everything else out.

Davis: *Miss you.*

I really should ignore it, but after seeing some of the worst in humanity this morning, I need some good. And Davis is definitely good.

He's an FBI agent, so I should stay far, far away from him. But for some reason, after what should have been a one-night stand a few months ago, our paths cross over and over.

Every time they do, I feel more and more connected with him. It seems obvious that the Universe has some purpose for us to be in each other's lives, but at the same time, doors keep opening for me to dive deeper into criminal activity.

It makes no sense, but I gave up trying to figure it out and am just enjoying the way he makes me feel all mushy inside.

Me: *You've taken up entirely too much of my brain space, too.*

Davis: *Was wondering if I'd hear back from you. Very glad I did. What have you been up to?*

Me: *Working. Dealing with company. Working some more.*

Davis: *Company? Does that mean you've settled in one location for a change?*

As soon as I hit send, I knew it was a mistake and that he'd pick up on the one thing I didn't want him to. I won't lie to him, though. Whatever this thing is between us, I meant it when I said I always try to tell the truth. Especially to him.

Me: *Yeah. Running the roads all the time wore me out. Decided it was time for a home base. How's Boston?*

I breathe a sigh of relief when he lets it go and doesn't push for a location.

Davis: *It's okay. Spent a week in North Carolina and it was gorgeous there. Much more conducive to getting outdoors.*

If I had spidey senses, they'd be tingling right now. As it is, the hairs on the back of my neck stand on end.

Me: *What took you to NC?*

Davis: *Work. Tracking a possible serial killer.*

Fuck.

Calm down. Just because he was in North Carolina doesn't mean he's looking into my activities there, right? I mean, no one even knows those three assholes are dead, right?

For a moment, I panic, but get myself under control. I can't let on that anything is wrong. He's too smart, and I don't need to give him any reason to get suspicious.

Me: *Serial killer? That sounds dangerous.*

Davis: *Are you worried about me? That's awful sweet of you.*

Me: *That's me...I ooze sweetness and sugar.*

Davis: *I remember. Sux that this is just getting good and I've gotta go inside the office now. Thanks for texting me back. Maybe next time you'll let me hear your voice.*

I'd meant it sarcastically, but his words make me squirm in my chair as heat blooms in my belly. He remembers. Remembers how he told me how sweet I tasted when his mouth was on me between my legs.

Me: *Have a nice life, Davis. Be safe.*

He sends me back a winking emoji.

Asshole.

I take my dishes downstairs to the kitchen, where I find Bee eating breakfast while Finn looks on. "Why are you grinning like that?" Bee asks.

Am I grinning? I wasn't even aware, but I stop doing it immediately. Inside, I still feel very smiley, though. Warm from my hair follicles to the tips of my toes.

"No reason."

"Where did you all go this morning?" she queries.

"Rescue mission."

"To rescue that girl upstairs? Her screaming is what woke me up."

My first inclination is to scold her for being so bitchy about Joelle screaming after what she's been through, but she doesn't know, does she? So, I push my protective mama bear back down and turn to face Bee.

"She was kidnapped from work and has spent the night being raped, so yeah, she's probably going to have some nightmares and panic attacks."

"Oh, my God. Really?"

"Yeah. We brought her here so she could be safe. She lives with a lazy bum of a boyfriend, so if she went there, the man who took her would likely just take her again."

Then she shocks the shit out of me when she says, "Of course you had to bring her here. Did you kill the guy who took her?"

I shake my head. "No. He wasn't there."

"Shame," Bee says. "I think all rapists and child molesters should be drawn and quartered like they used to do to people in the middle ages."

Wow; I'm impressed. I didn't think she had that in her. Once I put my dishes in the dishwasher, I turn to go back to my room.

"Anyway, I'm going to go get some sleep, but I should be up in a few hours. Cam and Tori will look after Joelle, so if you and Finn want to go do something..."

I leave it open-ended, letting them think they lost the end when I turned the corner to go upstairs. Back in my room, thoughts of Davis return. He said he misses me. If I'm honest, I miss him, too.

With memories of the nights we spent together rolling around in my brain, I take out my vibrator and use a little self-service to release the last bit of tension in my muscles. Several minutes later, I'm as sated as I can be without him here in the flesh, so I roll over and give in to the exhaustion.

CHAPTER FOURTEEN

Firsts and Possible Lasts

CAM

O nce we hear Joelle enter the shower, Tori and I go downstairs to raid my closet for some clothes for her. She and
I are of a size and I can't imagine she'll want to keep running
around in sweats and slippers for however long she's here.

Thankfully, I used the credit card Rae gave me to purchase a
few things I needed since I didn't really pack to be here for as
long as we have been. I didn't go crazy with it or anything, but I
did buy some plain underwear and comfortable, casual clothes.

While we gather clothes, Tori looks as if she's on the verge of
tears. "Are you okay?" I ask.

Her eyes meet mine. "Yes... No... Um, maybe." She lets out a breath. "The past twenty-four hours have been so overwhelming. You and Rae, you're both so calm. How do you do that?"

My response is a mirthless chuckle. "We were trained by our families and have been through trying times before. Nothing quite like this, though."

"So, is this the kind of thing your family does?"

I shake my head. "No. My family would have been on the side of the men who took Joelle. They traffic in drugs and guns and people without regard for anything or anyone but power and money."

"But... Then why?" She doesn't finish the question, but I understand what she's asking, so I answer as best I can.

"That's Rae."

"I don't understand."

"I know, but it's not my place to tell you her story and what her goals are. It's hers. However, I can assure you that she will never abide by those who seek to prey on those too weak to defend themselves."

She nods and takes the bundle of clothes. "I'll just take these up to Jojo." Putting a hand on my arm, she whispers, "Thank you, Bridget."

I watch as she leaves the room, and I'm unsure of where we stand. If she can't handle something like today, then she won't be able to handle what's coming. Better to find out now than later.

Later would hurt a lot more.

She's gone a while, so I go to take a shower to wash away the gritty feeling in my eyes and on my skin. I am beyond exhausted from the adrenaline rush and emotional roller coaster I've been riding all morning.

Once I'm clean and rested, maybe everything will look different.

I'm facing the wall, letting the water run over my head and warm the muscles of my shoulders, hoping to release some of the tension there. The shower door opens and hands slide onto my shoulders.

"You're tight," Tori says as she kneads my muscles.

"Mmm."

"I don't..."

Cutting her off, I say, "Let's not talk anymore until we're rested and clear-headed, okay?"

She moves my hair to the side and her lips press against the nape of my neck. "Okay." Fingers tickle down my back and over my hips. Her lips continue kissing my neck.

"You're so beautiful," she breathes between kisses.

Those tantalizing fingers move around my hips and up my ribcage, making me flinch and giggle. "Shh..." she soothes.

When her fingers brush the curve of my breasts, I suck in a breath. "If you want me to stop, just say so."

"No," I gasp. "Don't stop."

Her hands move again and cup my breasts. The sensations of her hands and lips on my skin are short circuiting my brain.

When I was in Ireland, there was a girl. We kissed and petted, but I've never been naked with another person to whom I'm sexually attracted. Never felt their touch on my bare skin. I've never had an orgasm except by my own hand.

Maybe I should be nervous, but I'm not. I want this.

A lot.

So when she smooths her palm down my stomach and slips it between my legs, I spread my feet wider to give her access. With my hands pressed to the wall to keep me from melting to the floor, I close my eyes and get lost in the delicious sensations she's creating at my core.

The orgasm slams into me faster than I've ever been able to bring one on myself and the intensity is off the charts. Tori's arms around me are the only reason I don't slide to the floor when my legs turn to jelly and give up supporting me.

Embarrassed that my inexperience is showing, heat crawls over my skin. Tori doesn't comment. She just kisses my shoulder again and moves around under the spray.

I want to touch her like she touched me, but I feel awkward and unsure so I simply squirt some body wash into the palm of my hand and begin to stroke it over her skin. When she's washed and we're rinsed and dried, she leads me to the bed.

Both of us are still naked when we pull the comforter over us. I meet her eyes for the first time since she left the room earlier. "That was the first time I..."

My face flames, so I stop speaking and look away. She tilts my chin up. When my eyes return to hers, she kisses me.

This time, it's no quick brushing of lips. It's deep, sensuous, and lovely.

Pulling back, she says, "Go to sleep, Cam."

I turn onto my side, and she tucks herself behind me, putting an arm over my waist. Finally, I've had my first sexual experience with another woman, but it may be my last. If nothing else, it has confirmed that I could never be intimate with a man.

Coming to Oklahoma has been a godsend. Knowing Rae will let me stay here has been another. If I'd been forced to return to Boston and marry a man, I don't know that I could have done it for long before I ended my husband or myself.

When I wake up, Tori's arm is still around me and I love the weight of it. I turn over to see her eyes flutter open. "Hi," I say shyly.

A tender smile spreads across her face as she reaches out to smooth a strand of hair out of my face and tuck it behind my ear. "Hi."

I lean forward to kiss her and she meets me halfway. She lets me take the lead and I'm grateful for that because I'm eager to explore.

We taste each other with lips and tongues dancing as my hands caress her skin. Her face, her neck, and her shoulders. She feels as if she's wrapped in silk.

Feeling much braver than I did last night, my fingers trace over her skin, and my lips are drawn to follow. When I cup her breasts in both hands and stroke my thumb over the stiff peaks, she sighs as if she is absolutely and utterly contented.

She doesn't balk, just keeps stroking my hair as I explore and tease her nipples. My kisses trail down her chest and I'm filled with excitement as they draw closer to her breasts. I've dreamed and fantasized of this sort of thing, but with it about to become reality, my heart is racing like a thousand wild ponies.

The moment my lips draw that bit of hard flesh into my mouth, I swear I think I have a mini orgasm. At first I'm tentative, but when I pull hard on her nipple, she gasps.

Breathlessly, she says, "Yes. Like that."

To know I'm the one who made her breathless is exhilarating and makes me eager to see if I can do it again. I do when I slip my hand between her legs and dip a finger through her folds, stroking over her clit.

Mimicking the motions she used on me in the shower, I push two fingers into her and the walls of her sex clench around them. They slide in easily because she is so wet and I'm amazed that I'm the one who aroused her like that. She moves her hips in time with the scissoring of my fingers.

Accidentally, my thumb brushes over her clit and she gasps out, "Yes!" So I put my thumb on the bundle of nerves and apply some pressure to my stroke. "Perfect."

Eager to taste a woman for the first time, especially this woman, I kiss my way down her torso and pause to flick her navel piercing with my tongue. When I reach my destination, there's no hesitation. I pull my fingers out of the way and stroke the flat of my tongue over her sex all the way from bottom to top.

Another mini-orgasm grips me, and my cunt is throbbing with arousal. Thinking of the things I've imagined someone doing to me, I use them as inspiration for the movement of my tongue over her pussy before sliding my fingers back inside her.

The taste is better than I imagined, creamy and salty and I can't get enough. Although I am not the most skilled, I hope I at least make up for it with enthusiasm.

Her fingers fork into my hair as the music of her moans and whimpers fills the room and her hips dance to the tune against my mouth. Without warning, her vagina grips my fingers like a vise and she cries out in Spanish.

She was already wet, but a flood of her juices coats my mouth and chin and it is glorious. I did that. I actually made her cum.

Feeling on top of the world, I move up her body and she pulls me into her arms, kissing me fervently. I'm so worked up from pleasing her that the moment she touches my clit, I explode, the orgasm more intense than it was in the shower.

Never, ever did I think it could be like that.

CHAPTER FIFTEEN

Surprises and Settling In

RAE

I go downstairs after my nap and it's immediately clear that Cam and Tori had some intimate time together. Once people have sex, they act differently around each other.

Good for them.

Bee and Finn are gone somewhere. Since she hasn't had Cam glued to her side, she's been dragging Finn all over the place. Mostly shopping, which I'm sure he adores. Not.

One thing occurred to me when I was vegetating in front of the television before going to sleep; we need another car. Also, Cam needs to be compensated. She's taken on a lot of responsibility by handling logistical things for me, and she has excelled.

In their family, money given to women is tightly monitored mostly by giving them credit cards so every charge can be reviewed by their father or husband. I wonder what Bee's dad is going to think of the money she's spending while here.

Now that I've drained the first of Dang's accounts and bounced the money all over the world, I diverted some into an account for Cam. I have no idea of how much people get paid for what she's doing, so I basically picked a number out of a hat.

On a piece of paper, I write down the account balance and put it into an envelope with a card tied to the account which she can use for purchases.

"How's Joelle doing?" I ask them.

"She's dealing," Tori replies. "Still refuses to go to the hospital, though, which worries me."

"Give her a day or two," I reply.

Since it's just the three of us in the kitchen, I hand the envelope to Cam.

"What's this?" she asks, looking at it as if it's a snake that might bite her.

"Well, you've been working hard and I appreciate everything you're doing, so I figured you should be getting paid. I set some money aside into an account for you and it's yours. No one will know how you use it but you. There's a log in so you can check the balance, but I'll transition funds into it."

Uncomfortable, I wave a hand. "We can talk about it if you think it's not enough and how often to do transfers. Once things get rolling, you'll get a share of...whatever."

She tilts her head, and for a moment, I am relieved when it seems as if she's just going to set it aside to look at later. But I guess curiosity gets the best of her because she opens the envelope and peeks inside.

When she sucks in a deep breath, I'm concerned. "Like I said, if it's not enough..."

She practically leaps off the stool where she's sitting and hurries to wrap me up in a hug. "It's way more than enough. Probably too much, but thank you! I've never had my own money."

"You're suffocating me," I wheeze. "And you're welcome."

When she releases me and steps away, she's wiping tears from her eyes.

"Also," I say, "we need to get another car. Since you'll be the one driving it most of the time, I want you to pick out what you want."

Her cheeks turn pink. "That sounds wonderful, but I've always had a driver and I don't know how to drive."

Shit...I know that. Not allowing their women to drive is another point of control in their world. Their fathers and husbands say it's for their safety, and in part, I'm sure it is, but they're more afraid that a woman who can drive will just get in the car and leave to never come back.

"I'm sorry. I knew that and totally spaced. It wasn't my intention to embarrass you."

Her smile is ornery. "No, I get it. That just means you get to teach me."

"Deal," I assure her. "We can get something for the interim and trade it in when you're ready to pick something out if you want something different."

"I like Tori's car. Can we get one of those?"

"Yep. You'll just need to pick the color."

Tori's mouth literally drops open. She catches herself quickly and turns her back, but I can tell she has questions. When she faces me again, I ask, "What?"

She sucks in a breath and lets it out slowly. "What exactly do you do? I mean, when we met, you said you were moving because of a job, but from what I can see, you don't have a job."

For a moment, I think about misdirecting her because that's what I usually do. However, her being involved with Cam changes things. If they're going to be together, she needs to know what she's getting into.

I level a look at Cam. "Do you want me to tell her?"

She shrugs and I know she's conflicted because this is the first relationship she's had a chance at and if I tell Tori what's going on, she might decide it's too much.

"She has questions, and I told her you would need to answer them because so much of it is tied to who you are and your plans."

It's my turn to suck in a breath. "I'm going to say something and it's going to come off pretty harsh, but I need you to know who I am. Okay?"

Tori nods.

"As you saw this morning, I'm no stranger to dangerous situations. I killed a man this morning and two others were killed to rescue your friend and the others who were being trafficked. I'm going to tell you some things and if you talk about them to anyone but our inner circle, you'll be a threat and I will eliminate any threat to me and mine. So, you need to decide if you really want to hear this."

Without hesitation, she nods, reaches out to hold Cam's hand, and says, "Yes. I want to hear it."

"I've told her about our family ties," Cam tells me.

"That cuts out a lot, then," I reply and tell her a little about how Dad prepared me for their world. "A talent I discovered I had early on was hacking and I've been doing it since I was eleven or so. Up until now, I have mostly been a hacker for hire and used my skills to gather information for my clients and got paid very well for it."

I pause to see how she's handling that much. She seems fine, so I go on. "Occasionally, I get requests for help to gather information on people like the ones we dealt with this morning. Sometimes the police can't find the evidence or their hands are tied for one reason or another. If I come across people like them, people that need to be unalived to stop their evil, I take matters into my own hands."

Again, I watch for her reaction, but she still seems fine. She's not squeezing the shit out of Cam's hand or anything, and her eyes aren't round as saucers.

Now I go into what I want to set in place for the future. How I want to make Oklahoma a distribution hub, but also keep a tight rein on what actually happens here.

I'm fine with prostitution as long as the women are there voluntarily. Some women like sex and, like Tori, can make a ton of money doing it on their terms.

There are myriad reasons why people use drugs, but if someone is an adult and chooses to abuse themselves in that way, that's up to them. Stopping dealers from hooking kids will help prevent some of that.

However, I want to put money into programs to help people kick drugs if they want and after-school programs for kids to help them see a life off the streets is possible. In my mind, there can be a balance and money made from criminal activity can be used to do a lot of good.

The activity is still going to happen, so why not by me? People like Dang are just looking for more power and money, hoarding their coins like a dragon just for the sake of having it.

Yeah, I have a nice chunk of change in the bank, but that's mostly because I was traveling all the time and didn't have anywhere I felt was home. Now that I've decided to settle here and make it my home, it's time to be a benefit to my community.

"So, you're like a morally gray vigilante do-gooder," Tori observes, and I have to laugh.

"Something like that."

"Tori?" a voice calls from somewhere. I don't recognize it, so it must be Joelle.

All three of us go toward the stairs to find the young woman standing on the bottom step looking a bit dazed, but better than she was the last time I saw her. Tori goes to her and takes her hand.

"Jojo, how are you feeling?"

"Okay."

"Are you thirsty? Hungry? In pain?"

"I could use some aspirin and yeah, some food might be good."

"Come on," Tori says, pulling her toward the kitchen. Then, as if she forgot we were here, she sees us and stops. "Oh. I'm not sure if you remember, but this is Cam and Rae. They are the ones who got you out of there this morning."

"I remember," she replies and drops her eyes. "Thank you isn't enough, but it's all I have to give at the moment."

"No thanks needed," Cam says, and takes Joelle's other hand and they lead the way to the kitchen.

Joelle stops in the kitchen's doorway. "Wow. I love your kitchen." She moves confidently into the room, her fingers brushing over every surface she passes. When Joelle reaches the refrigerator, she opens it and begins rummaging around inside.

The door closes, and she's standing there with her arms full of ingredients. Just as she sets them on the counter, Bee comes buzzing in. Startled, Joelle leaves the ingredients in a haphazard mess and races over to duck behind me.

Not Tori. Although she knows Tori better, she apparently feels safest with me. I attribute it to me being the one who escorted her out of the hell she'd been dragged into.

Her cold, clammy hand wraps around mine. When Finn walks through the door, she whimpers and presses her face to my back between my shoulder blades. He raises one ruddy eyebrow.

"It's okay," I tell Joelle patiently. "This is my cousin Bee and our friend Finn. You don't need to be afraid of them."

She moves behind me and although I can't see her, I get the impression that she's peeking around me like a shy toddler faced with strangers. When Finn's eyes settle to a point about the height of my left shoulder, I figure I'm right.

"Lass," he says. "You need not be afraid. No one will harm you while you're here. I swear it."

Well, damn. He might not speak very often, but when he does, he makes his words matter.

Ever so slowly, she moves from behind me. Not looking at anyone, she says quietly, "Is anyone else hungry? I was going to make a frittata."

"You can cook?" I ask.

"She's in culinary school," Tori supplies. "Jojo is a fabulous chef."

CHAPTER SIXTEEN

Adding to the Flock

RAE

That night, Joelle asks if she can stay awhile in exchange for cooking our meals while she, as she put it, tries to get her head on straight. Of course, I tell her she can stay as long as she needs to. And while Joelle stays, Tori will probably stay.

You're welcome, Cam.

The two of them are so cute together, but sometimes I worry about Cam. Tori is much more experienced and when we met, she was immersed in playing a role for a lover when her heart wasn't even remotely in it.

I like Tori, but as far as I know, this is Cam's very first experience with investing her heart in another person. Who am I to judge, though? I've never risked my heart with anyone.

At least someone is having sex. I've been so fucking horny that I think I'm going to wear out my vibrator.

That's what I blame it on. My horny hormones that simply aren't being satisfied by my buzzing boyfriend. They're responsible for me doing the last thing I should do.

"Jeffries," he answers, his voice sounding gruff with sleep, and it sends my hormones into overdrive.

Shit. I didn't think it was that late.

"Sorry. It sounds like I woke you."

"Rae?"

"Yeah. Go back to bed. I'll call again some other time."

"No! Don't hang up. I'm fine."

Snuggling deeper into my bed, I pull the covers up as if they might hide my idiocy in calling Davis.

"I couldn't sleep and was just thinking about you." Thinking about how good it would feel to have you inside me. "And wanted to hear your voice." Because your voice, when it's all husky like this, is incredibly sexy.

And I miss you.

"I'm glad you called," he replies. "What's got your mind so tied up that you can't sleep?"

"Nothing really." Just everything. "How's the hunt going?"

He tells me about his case while not really telling me anything at all. I completely understand that he can't give details about an active investigation, but I'm honestly curious whether mine is the trail he's on.

Listening to his voice is so relaxing that without warning, a yawn cracks my jaw.

"See, my work is boring," he says with a chuckle. "What have you been up to?"

"Not much. Playing hostess to my cousins. Mostly hanging out, going shopping, painting our toenails. You know, girlie stuff like that," I tease.

"Mmm...that, I'd like to see. Send me a pic of your toenails."

"Pervert," I reply with a voice full of laughter. Playing with fire, I push down the covers to snap a pic of my polished toenails and send it to him.

"I think purple is my new favorite color. Whoa. Nice room. Are you in a hotel?"

"Nope. Anyway, I've kept you from your beauty sleep long enough. Get some sleep Agent Jeffries."

He chuckles again, probably knowing I've given him enough of a peek into my life and it's unsettled me, so now I have to run away.

"You, too, Rae. Call me again; anytime."

"Good night."

"Night, beautiful."

Beautiful. I wonder if he really thinks I'm beautiful or if he says it because he knows it's something women like to hear.

Although I'm still sexually frustrated, talking to him has taken the edge off. I wonder if he's sleeping with anyone. That thought surprises me.

Why should I care if he's sleeping with anyone? It's not like we're in a relationship or anything. Plus, I know what it's like to need to blow off some steam. You know, to take the pressure off.

Night, beautiful.

I smile to myself as I turn off the light and roll over to go to sleep.

When I wake, I feel rested like I haven't in a while, so I put on running clothes and head downstairs to see if Finn's up. I find him sitting at the island in the kitchen reading a paper he got from who knows where.

Bumps and clatters sound from somewhere. When I go investigate, I find Joelle in a closet. Well, I call it a closet, but it's more like an extra room lined with cabinets and a long countertop.

There are appliances, serving dishes, additional dinnerware sets, and dried and canned goods of all sorts. I didn't even realize it was here. Jo looks up at me and beams.

"You have everything here. It's dated, but there's a lot of good stuff," she says as if she's just found the best treasure ever.

My lips quirk. "I didn't even realize this was here. The kitchen isn't my forte, so I didn't explore beyond the refrigerator."

"This is what's known as a butler's pantry or scullery. It's mostly an extra storage space."

"Oh."

I lean a hip against the counter and toss out something that popped into my head when she said she wanted to stay for a while. She's only been here a day, but seems to be dealing all right at the moment.

"I know you said you'd like to stay for a while and we've been looking to hire a cook since all of us are useless in here. So I have a proposal for you. While you're here, I'd like to pay you to cook for us. There's no pressure. If you don't want to, or if it's too much, you can say no and I won't..."

She holds up a hand, so I shut up.

"Yes," she says. "Absolutely yes. There's no way I can go back to Cassandra's, and I was trying to figure out how..." she pauses and sucks in a deep breath. "Anyway. Being able to be here takes the pressure off."

"Hold that thought, because I have one condition."

She takes a step back and fear flickers behind her eyes.

"Hey, it's okay. It's only a little scary. I simply want you to see a doctor to get checked out and make sure you're all right."

She thinks about it for long moments and nods her head. "I'll call my doctor and make an appointment. Also, I'd like to collect my car and some clothes from my apartment, if that's okay."

"Fine by me," I reply. "Also, whenever you're ready, I'll give you money to go grocery shopping."

She nods.

Thinking I've probably given her enough to deal with, I go back into the kitchen where Finn still sits. "How about we take a jog around the property to check it out? I'd like to upgrade and extend the security system and would appreciate your input."

We identify several locations to post cameras to eliminate blind spots. Then we debate the merits of putting gun turrets in two spires that seem to be only for decorative purposes. Well, I talk and mostly Finn listens and occasionally nods, shakes his head, or shrugs.

Back in the house, we interrupt, not an argument, really, but a tense discussion. Tori needs to go to her place and get her computer and other equipment so she can work while she's here, as well as more clothing.

A trip also needs to be made to Joelle's place to get her things and her doctor had an appointment cancel and can get her in right away, but Bee says no one can drive the rental car but Finn. Also, Joelle understandably doesn't want to go anywhere alone.

"Okay! Everybody calm the fuck down!" I interject. "Christ, we need another fucking car. Anyway, Tori, take us to pick up Jo's car. Then you can go to your house to get whatever you want. Jo and I can go to her appointment and then to her apartment. As soon as we get another vehicle, we start driving lessons!"

"Driving lessons?" Bee asks.

"Yeah. You can have them, too, if you want."

"Really?"

"I know your dad would shit bricks if he knew I taught you how to drive, but he's not here, is he? All right people, let's get moving. We can sort out cars and lessons when we get back."

CHAPTER SEVENTEEN

For Once in My Life

JOELLE

The closer we get to the club, the more my hands start to shake. It gets so bad that I finally sit on them. I guess I didn't do it soon enough because Rae puts a hand on my leg, which, much to my embarrassment, makes me flinch.

When I look over at her, she has a fierce look on her face. In a low voice, she says, "No one will hurt you."

I nod and take a deep breath. For some reason, I believe her. She's not big or scary, but I still believe her.

Tori pulls up in front of the club right next to my car and puts the car in park. Rae opens her door and gets out. When I don't follow, she ducks and looks inside.

With a kind look, she holds out her hand to me. "I promise."

I called ahead to ensure Cassandra would be here, and she informed me they'd retrieved my belongings from my car and would have them inside. Although it's the last place I want to go, I need to get this over with.

Taking Rae's hand, I slide across the seat and step out onto the parking lot. She leads me right up to the front door and we go inside like there's nothing to be afraid of, because there isn't. I've got Rae on my side.

"Where's the office?"

I point, and she gently pulls me down the hall. Seth, one of the guards, steps out. "Took you long enough, Bubba," Rae bites. "We're here to get her things."

Seth steps toward me. "Jojo, I'm so..." He stops speaking when I whimper and duck behind Rae.

He moves aside when Rae continues toward Cassandra's office. After a quick knock on the door, Rae turns the knob and we go inside. Cassandra looks up with a frown on her face until she sees me.

She stands and rounds her desk, coming toward me. The look on her face is all pity and fake concern. At least that's what it looks like to me.

"I'd like my things," I say. Belatedly, I add, "And I quit."

"I understand you need to take some time off..."

"She didn't say she wanted time off. She said she's done," Rae remarks.

"And just who are you?"

Rae doesn't answer. She levels a look at Cassandra, and the older woman is the first to look away. She goes back around her desk and sits in her chair. Once her hands are folded together and resting on top, she looks at me.

"It's clear you've gone through something traumatic. If we could just talk about it, I'm sure we can come up with some resolution. You don't have to resign."

Rae snorts. "Let me get this straight. Thanks to your shitty security team, a woman was kidnapped and brutalized. It took one of her fellow employees to alert the police that something had happened because you've instructed that laughable security team to not call the authorities."

She stops talking, but Cassandra just stares back at her with a pinched look on her face.

"You would think you'd have learned your lesson when...what was it? Ten or so years ago, when Samara Stephens was taken from the same parking lot. Thankfully, your victimized employee didn't end up dead this time."

My eyes snap to Rae's face. Someone else was taken like me and killed? Why didn't I know that?

"But because of her childish looks, Jo here is quite popular with your clients and probably a real moneymaker for you, so you'd really like to convince her to come back to work in a few weeks. She said she's done, so hand over her belongings now so I can get her out of this place instead of compounding her trauma by keeping her here a moment longer. You're lucky she doesn't sue the shit out of you."

Cassandra has the wisdom to not respond. She opens a drawer and hands over my purse. After a quick look through the contents, I nod at Rae.

My keys and wallet are still there and when I open the wallet, everything seems to still be intact. The man who took me, I don't know his real name, busted my phone, so I'll need to get a new one, but my license, cash, and the one credit card I have are still in place.

"All right then," she says. "Do you have anything else to say to your former boss?"

I shake my head and wrap my fingers around my keys, clenching them in my fist. Rae leads me back through the building and out the front door. With a sigh, I tilt my face up to the sun and draw in a deep breath of the fresh air.

"Are you okay to drive, or would you like me to?"

I hold out my keys to her and go around to the passenger door. She lets me be quiet for a while after we drive away. Finally, I speak up and start giving directions to my apartment.

I let out a groan when I see Jamal's car parked out front. "What's wrong?" Rae asks.

"My ex-boyfriend is home. When we broke up, he'd just been laid off, so he begged me to stay and help with the rent until he found a job."

"How long ago was that?"

"Almost a year. For the first few weeks after he lost his job, he said he needed a break. Seems as if he enjoyed sitting at home on his ass all day playing video games while I worked. I was so busy between work and school that I never had time to find a new place, so I stayed."

"Asshole," she breathes. "How much of what's inside is yours?"

I shake my head. "Mostly just my clothes and a few personal things. I moved in with him and he already had everything. That's another reason I stayed. If I moved out on my own, I'd have to buy everything new."

"So, can we fit everything in your car?"

I look up at the front door of the apartment and nod. "Yeah."

She opens the door. "Well, let's go get everything."

When I open the front door, Jamal snaps, "Where the fuck have you been?"

From behind me, Rae says, "Well, aren't you a little ray of sunshine?"

It's all I can do to not laugh. This woman is like a sledgehammer, unafraid of busting down doors and saying exactly what she thinks.

"Who the fuck is that? Where have you been? You disappeared, and the fridge is almost empty, so I haven't had a decent meal in over a day. I had to go buy stuff for sandwiches."

I don't answer and scurry past him to my room. Again, Rae takes the lead. "Wow. You haven't seen your roommate in over twenty-four hours and your first move is to curse at her and whine about having to fix yourself a fucking sandwich?"

"Who the hell are you, and why are you with my girlfriend?"

"Hmm...that's interesting because Jo says you're her lazy, out of work asshole ex. Actually, she said you were her ex. I embellished a bit. Jo is moving as of right now, so your free ride is over. Time to get a job, Scooter."

His game controller clatters on the coffee table. Then I hear Rae speak. Her voice is filled with menace. "Sit your goddamn ass back down. She's been through enough and doesn't need you making it any worse."

I open the suitcase I bought when I went on a trip to Padre Island with some friends after high school graduation. It's funny that we were so wrapped up in each other's lives then, because we don't even talk anymore and it was less than two years ago.

Working quickly, I start tossing clothes and shoes into it. Another thing about working so much and going to school is that I didn't have time to shop, either, so I don't have a lot of stuff. When the suitcase is full, I roll it out to the living room, then go to the kitchen for a trash bag.

"Jojo," Jamal coaxes. "I'm sorry I yelled at you. Can't we just have a minute to talk about this?" His eyes slide to Rae. "Alone? What happened?"

I sigh and stop in the doorway and without looking at him, I say, "I'm done financing your lack of motivation. You've been promising for a year to get a new job, but you haven't. The only reason I stayed is because it was easier."

Before he can reply, I hurry back down the hall and throw the little that's left in the bedroom into the bag. Next, I go to the bathroom and take the last bit of my things from there, including my quality hair products that Jamal likes to use.

He thought buying sandwich stuff was bad. Just wait until he gets a load of what that shampoo costs.

My last stop is in the kitchen, where I gather up my specialized cooking tools and the expensive pans I purchased. With one final look around, I believe I have everything that's mine, so I go back to the living room where Jamal is glaring at Rae. She's giving him a look that's a dare if ever I saw one.

"Is this everything?" she asks.

I nod.

She takes the heavy bag from me and I put a hand on the suitcase to roll it to the door. Jamal pops up. "Jo! Talk to me!"

"I've tried talking to you for a year. I'm done talking to you."

At the top of the stairs, Rae jerks her head for me to go in front of her. She drapes the bag over her shoulder and grabs the handle of the suitcase.

At the bottom of the stairs, I turn and watch, hoping she doesn't overbalance from all that weight and go tumbling down the stairs, but she doesn't. She must be hella strong. I hurry to the car and open the back door so she can put everything inside.

Feeling a bit stronger now, I move to the driver's seat and, without a word, she goes to the passenger door. As we're driving away, she asks, "How are we doing on time for your doctor's appointment?"

"Perfect," I tell her.

The appointment isn't as bad as I expected. My doc gives me some shots and a morning-after pill. I'm able to avoid losing my shit when she performs a cursory exam to make sure I'm not torn bad enough to need stitches. I'm not, thankfully.

After a stop at my wireless carrier to get a new phone, we go to the grocery store where I spend an obscene amount of money stocking up on spices and staples as well as enough food to feed all the people at Rae's house, but she doesn't even blink. I'm looking forward to cooking for everyone.

As we're driving back to the house, Rae asks, "Do you have family or anyone else we should contact?"

"No... I mean, I have family, but we were never close and they pretty much disowned me when I told them I wanted to cook for people instead of cutting them open."

"Doctors?"

"Yeah," I say, and it almost sounds like a curse word.

I never really wanted to go to culinary school, but if you love feeding people, that usually means working at a restaurant or as a private chef and getting hired is easier if you have training. My style isn't super fancy, so school has mostly been not so fun.

I've been focused on the end result instead of the day-to-day thinking that once I have enough experience, I can find a way to do my own thing. Despite all that's happened in the last day or so, I'm excited to have a safe place where I can just be and cook good food.

For once in my life, someone has my back. It should be interesting to see where this change leads, but for now, I'm just going to cook.

CHAPTER EIGHTEEN

Fraid I'll Kick Your Arse?

RAE

A clap of thunder so loud that it sounds like Thor is right outside my window wakes me. When I check my phone for the time, it's close to when I usually get up, so I roll out of bed and go downstairs.

I was going to take Cam car shopping, but that's on hold. It's no fun buying a car in a downpour. It's also no fun running in a rainstorm, so I head down to the basement to test out our new workout equipment.

Finn is in the kitchen reading the paper. Sheesh. Does the man ever sleep?

"Where do you get those newspapers?"

"Gate."

"Hmm. I wonder if ten years of papers have been delivered and someone is pissed that you've started picking them up."

"Gardener did. Bridget told him to leave them."

As if called by her name, Cam comes into the kitchen. "Is there coffee?"

"Not yet. Seems the storm is waking everyone up early. I was going to go downstairs and use the new equipment, but I'm thinking maybe Finn and I could spar. Seems like that would be a better workout."

Finn looks at me and raises an eyebrow.

"Ooo," Cam says, drawing it out. "That I want to see."

"What do you want to see?" Tori asks as she shuffles over to Cam and kisses her cheek. "Is there coffee, baby?"

"Not yet," Cam answers, her neck flushing. "Rae and Finn are going to spar downstairs."

Tori's eyes go wide mid-yawn. Joelle comes into the room, freshly showered and fully dressed for the day.

"Gee," she says. "I guess the storm woke everyone else up early, too. Coffee will be ready in a few minutes."

"Whadda ya say Finn? Feel like a spar?"

He just looks at me.

I plaster my best smarmy smirk on my face and add an Irish lilt to my voice. "Dat a no? Wha's the matter, boy-o? Fraid I'll kick your arse?"

That gets him. His lips tilt up on one side, a micro expression of amusement. He rises from his seat and goes toward his room.

"Put on something you don't mind getting bloody," I call after him, my voice full of laughter.

Downstairs, I stretch a little to warm up my muscles. Cam has done a great job getting things set up down here. We have a full set of weights, a couple of treadmills, one of those climber things, and an elliptical. There's even a weighted punching bag and a speed bag.

Finn arrives a few minutes later. We face each other on the mat. There's no ring, no protective gear, no gloves, just us, on the padded surface. We're both barefoot and wearing close-fitting, stretchy clothes.

I reach out a fist, like I used to do in MMA fights to signal the obligatory handshake. Finn frowns. "Fist bump, dude," I supply.

He nods and puts up a fist to bump mine. I dance away and the fight is on. Finn is fast and strong, so I have to stay moving to avoid the worst of his punches, even though I know both of us are pulling them so we don't do any real damage. I'm still going to have some bruises. Hopefully, he does, too.

Everything else fades away as we dance. The cheers and hoots of the spectators become white noise. Finn jabs and I dodge. I kick and he blocks.

He feints, then does a combination and catches me on the shoulder as I'm a hair too slow getting out of the way. But I manage to land a roundhouse to his hip and he stutter steps sideways to regain his balance.

On and on it goes with punches and kicks. Neither of us tries to take it to the ground, though, and I think he's doing that for my sake. If he got me down, he'd be more likely to force me into submission because he outweighs me and, while I'm strong, he's stronger. On our feet, we're evenly matched.

I'm not sure how long we have been fighting, but we're both sweating and have lost the sharpest edge of speed and reaction. When the lights flicker and go dark, eliciting squeaks from the other women, we pause and everything goes quiet. Half a dozen heartbeats later, they flicker back on.

"I'm starving," I say into the silence with a grin. "What's for breakfast, Jojo?"

Finn's lips tilt slightly, and he holds out a fist to me. I bump it as the others laugh and the match is officially done. Finn was an excellent opponent and I'm glad he's the one looking out for Bee.

I know I'm no match for a well-trained man who's expecting me to be who I am, but most men see tits and think I'll be a pushover. That's my advantage most of the time.

As we make our way to the stairs, I link my arm with Finn's. A look of surprise flickers across his face before he wipes it away. "Thanks," I tell him. "That was a good fight. Been a long time since anyone has challenged me."

"You'll do," he replies quietly. I bump into his side, but he doesn't miss a step.

I race upstairs to my room to shower and Finn fades away to his room. While I let the water run over my head and wash the sweat away, my stomach gurgles its displeasure, so I keep it short, towel off, and put on fresh clothes, leaving my hair to air dry to its corkscrew delight.

Back in the kitchen, everyone but Finn and me chatters about the fight while we drink coffee and watch Joelle make breakfast.

"Dah told us we were getting trained to defend ourselves, but we're in no way prepared for anything like that," Bee says.

"That's why you have Finn to watch over you," I tell her, then belatedly add, "and Geno."

She gives me a sour look, but doesn't speak more. Maybe she's thinking what I'm thinking; that Geno isn't prepared to be in that kind of fight, either. Geno isn't prepared for much of anything. Not for the first time, I wonder how much longer Bee and Finn will be here.

When the time comes and they leave, but Cam stays, what will be Bee's dad's response? I can't even think of him as my uncle anymore. Now, he's just Bee's dad.

He's always treated Cam like an afterthought, but I know without a doubt he has plans for her. Plans that would make her life a living hell.

However, she wants to stay, so she'll stay. Defying him like that is likely to bring a shit storm down on me, but I have the advantage in that he really has no idea what I'm capable of.

Over the past five years, I've uncovered many of his dirty little secrets that he probably thinks are buried deep enough they'll never see the light of day. But knowing him like I do, I knew it would be smart to have leverage against him should I ever get crossways with him.

If he does anything to prevent Cam from doing as she pleases, I'll make it costly enough for him to wonder if it's worth the life of one young woman.

CHAPTER NINETEEN

Car Kismet

CAM

I stand near the window that looks out on the back of the property, watching the sun rise bright orange in a clear blue sky the next day. As the lingering moisture from the day before heats up, a dense fog hovers over the rolling hills of home.

Rae's home. My home, too.

Tori rolls over in the bed with a sigh, and it makes me smile. She was up late working last night while I dozed in bed. When she joined me, we made love for what felt like moments, but was much, much longer.

I simply can't get enough of touching and tasting her and she seems to feel the same way about me. At least I hope she does. My naïve heart is falling hard and I hope it doesn't get broken.

We haven't talked about much beyond the here and now, but once Jo feels settled in or decides to move on, I wonder if Tori will move on, too. Not wanting to think about such things, I leave the room so I'll let Tori sleep instead of waking her with kisses like my libido wants me to.

My first thought was to put on some running clothes and take a few spins around the property, but the grass is wet and running in wet footwear does not sound ideal. So, instead I go to the kitchen. If the wet burns off, I'll run this afternoon.

Finn is sitting at the kitchen island reading the newspaper and drinking coffee while Jo is mixing items in a large bowl. "Good morning," I say, as I enter the room.

"Good morning!" Jo chirps, seeming happy as a clam whenever she's here in the kitchen.

I go to the coffeepot and fix myself a mug. Leaning a hip against the countertop, I inhale the magnificent aroma of whatever quality coffee Jo has started making instead of the generic crappy stuff we started having after no longer going to the coffeeshop in Tahlequah.

Jo pours the contents of her bowl into a casserole dish and puts it into the oven just as Rae shuffles into the kitchen, looking like she's been up all night. She zombie walks to the coffeepot. "Dia dhuit," I say to her.

"Mornin," she mumbles.

"Did you get any sleep?"

She sucks in a breath. "Not really. Had client requests and started on phase two of my coup."

"Your coup?" I ask, confused. Then I realize what she's talking about.

She said she was going to drain Tai Dang's financial resources to drive him toward robbing the bank in the hope that the authorities would arrest him and remove him from the board. Better them than Rae having to kill him. Although she's willing when needed, I understand it's not something she enjoys.

Without waiting for it to cool much, she drinks down half her mug of coffee. "What's for breakfast, Jojo?"

Jo looks around with a smile. "I love that you like to eat. It's a breakfast casserole with sausage, eggs, hash browns, peppers and onions. Some cheddar will go over the top of it to melt just before it's done."

"Sounds wonderful," Rae replies. "Cam, the dealership opens at eight-thirty, so be ready to go. We'll just need to find someone to drive us into town."

"I can take you," Jo says. "As long as we can stop by the grocery store either before we go or on the way home."

"Deal," Rae says and shuffles off with her mug of coffee.

She returns an hour later looking bright eyed if not bushy tailed and dressed for the day. Before she's even settled on her seat, Jo sets a plate in front of her along with a fork and napkin. Rae lets out a groan of pleasure as soon as she takes a bite and then she proceeds to vacuum up the rest as if she hasn't eaten in a year.

Rubbing her belly, she sits back in her seat. "Dang, that's good. Keep that on your roster of greatest breakfast hits, Jojo. Ladies, are you about ready to head into town?"

"Yeah," Jo replies. "I'll just cover this with a cloth. It should stay warm for a while."

"Finn, Tori is still asleep. She was working late last night, so I don't want to wake her. Would you mind letting her know where we've gone if she gets up before we get back?" I request.

He nods, and we're on our way.

We swing by the grocery, following a power walking Joelle around as she zips up and down the aisles, pushing a cart with a list in her hand. She pauses occasionally to grab something off a shelf and put it into the basket. I'm glad she knows where she's going because the products on the aisles pass in a blur.

She takes minutes to do what would have taken me hours and before I know it, she's heading to the checkout. On the way, Rae grabs a container of dried mango and eats it as we wait. Pointing a finger at a magazine, Rae asks, "So, what do you think? Is Bigfoot real, or some elaborate hoax?"

I laugh. "There's no way it's real!"

"I don't know," Jo replies. "A cousin of mine went camping down in southeast Oklahoma and swears he saw one."

We discuss the possibility of the existence of cryptids, that's what Jo says they're called, while we take the groceries out to the car and put them in the back next to where Rae's sitting. Apparently, her cousin was deeply affected by the encounter and has become one of those people who roam around the woods and supposedly haunted places with video cameras and post their adventures online.

"He's got like a hundred thousand followers now and actually makes a living from all the views he gets," Joelle assures us.

"Seriously?" Rae asks.

Jo nods. "Yep. It's not much of a living, but considering he lives in his parents' basement and doesn't pay rent, it doesn't take much money to live."

That makes me laugh as we get back into the car to go to the dealership. When we pull into the lot, my nerves begin to jangle. All the cars look so expensive. Maybe I've asked for too much.

Rae pulls me out of my thoughts when she hands me a pistol over the console. "Here, put this under your seat." I'm not sure where she had it, but I take the weapon and put it under my seat as she asked.

Without batting an eye, as soon as Jo parks, Rae gets out. When I just sit there, she looks through the passenger window at me. "Come on, Cam. This is your car we're picking out, so you need to do the picking."

I look over at Jo and she gives me an encouraging look as she opens her door and steps out. A smarmy looking man approaches Rae, a broad grin on his face. Rae looks him up and down and says, "No."

He stops in his tracks and his smile fades. "You don't need to schmooze us," she says. "We know what we want and just need to peruse colors."

He cocks his head at her and asks, "What is it you're looking for, little lady?"

She cocks her head right back and says, "How is it you think calling a grown woman little lady is a good idea in this day and age?"

His neck pinks, but before he can apologize, she tells him, "We're looking for an AMG GLC, but my friend here wants to pick out the color. Do you have one of those handy dandy color chart thingies she can look at?"

"Yes, ma'am. Let me just go get one."

"Let's go peruse what they've got, ladies. I have a feeling we're going to need more than one additional vehicle, and soon," Rae says as she walks into the middle of the lot and turns in a circle, her eyes scanning their inventory.

With a raised eyebrow, she heads straight for a large SUV and circles it. When she looks at the price sticker on the window, she frowns and turns back toward the building just in time to see Mr. Salesman puffing his way across the lot.

He holds out the brochure he has in his hand to her. She takes it and hands it to me before asking, "Why is the price on this almost double what it should be?"

"Well," he says, taking a moment to catch his breath. "There was a visiting, let's call them a dignitary, in town, some bigwig in oil. His team bought the vehicle, and we sent it down to be armored before his arrival. They drove it for the two weeks he was here, then sold it back to us."

While they talk, I flip through the brochure and narrow the options. "I know you'd probably like it best if I get..."

I was going to say black, but Rae holds up her hand. "This is going to be your car. Pick whatever you want."

With a nod, I hold out the brochure. "These three are nice, but I'd like to see them in person."

"All right. We'd like to see cars in these three colors."

Two of them are similar, dark gray colors and the third is silver. White cars are everywhere, it seems, and I don't like going all the way to black. I've also never been a fan of brightly colored cars.

They have the car on the lot in the silver color, but not in either of the grays, and one of those colors is my favorite. I start to settle for the silver, but remember what Rae said and tell the man the one I like best.

"We don't have one of those in stock, so we'll have to locate one at another dealer. I can probably have one here in a few days, but it shouldn't take more than a week unless we can't find one and have to order it."

"Okay," Rae says. "Let's go see if you can find one. I'll also take the armored SUV."

His jaw drops open. "All right, let's go see what we can find and we can talk financing..."

"No financing," Rae replies. "I'll be paying cash." Then to Jo and me, she says, "I know Jo's got ice cream in the car. You're welcome to hang out here with me, but if you two want to go back to the house, feel free. It gets really boring from here on out and I can drive the SUV home."

I can read what she's not saying. We can stay, but when Jo leaves, she doesn't want her going home alone and I don't blame her. Even though it's not that far and there's probably no one looking, it's better not to leave her without some protection.

Because I'm excited and want to know how long I have to wait for my new car, I reply, "Jo, are you okay staying for a few minutes? I'd like to find out if they're going to be able to transfer it or will need to order it."

She grins at me. "Excited, huh?"

I look down, but can't help the smile that's splitting my face in two. "Aye, just a little." Lowering my voice as we walk toward the building, I ask Rae, "Do you really think we'll need an armored SUV?"

"Yeah. You know that's what you ride around in all the time, don't you? I've been thinking about it and was really surprised to find one here when we were looking for a totally different vehicle. It's like car kismet or something."

They have one of the cars I picked at their sister dealership in Tulsa and will have it brought down from there. Mr. Salesman says it should only take a day or two. When Rae sits down with the man to handle the sales contracts and stuff, Jo and I take our leave.

I'm fairly bouncing as we go back out to her car and head toward home. As soon as that car arrives and I learn how to drive it, I'll have one more layer of freedom, bringing me to a level I never imagined possible.

CHAPTER TWENTY

Driver's Education

CAM

The instant I see her, my jaw goes slack and I'm not able to close it. There, in front of me, is my car. My car. Those are two words I never thought I'd utter.

But I can and she is the most beautiful thing I've ever seen. Well, next to Tori, anyway. She needed to go to her apartment for some more things, so she dropped Rae and me off at the dealership. Her parting kiss was sweet and her smile was wide as she drove away with a small wave.

That's another thing I never thought I'd be able to have – the ability to show affection publicly to another woman. Every time Bee sees us touch, or hold hands, or hears one of us call the other by a term of endearment, she looks at me with narrowed eyes.

She's probably thinking of how much to tell her father when we go back to Boston. However, I've never known her to take my side in anything, so she might be memorizing every moment so she can tell him everything.

"Damn, she's purty," Rae says with a grin.

A thrill runs through me. "I know."

Mr. Salesman saunters out to meet us. His chest is puffed up like he was personally responsible for making this car. Or maybe he's just thrilled with the commission he's probably getting from the two vehicles Rae bought.

"She's all yours," he says, holding out two small, plastic, rectangular objects to me.

When I frown, Rae steps up and takes them. "Thank you."

Without ceremony, she goes to the car, so I follow her lead and move to the passenger door. I slide onto the soft leather seat and groan with pleasure.

We glide through town back toward the house. I've never really paid attention to anyone driving, but I watch everything Rae does as she operates the car.

When we're waiting in front of the gate, instead of punching in the code, she puts the car in park and gets out. When she opens my door, I'm confused.

"Go on, go sit in the driver's seat," she urges.

I don't hesitate. Racing around the car, I get behind the wheel. She tells me how to adjust the seat. When I get it in a position to where I can reach everything, she instructs me what to do.

"Punch in the code to open the gate. Put your foot on the brake, then move the shifter down to the D for drive. Now, wait for the gate to be fully open, then take your foot off the brake and gently press down on the accelerator."

The car crawls forward through the gate and I feel like I'm going to pee my pants because of the emotional overwhelm. Instead of driving straight to the house, she directs me to a small side track just inside the gate that leads to some storage buildings on the far side of the property.

I press the pedal a little harder and the car jumps forward. With a half-gasp, half-giggle, I take my foot off and the car slows. We're almost to the storage area, so I put my foot on the brake, but I mash down a little too forcefully.

"Sorry," I tell Rae.

"No worries. You're just getting the feel of her."

I turn around and go back down the side road, then turn up the driveway and go around the circle drive and go back out to the sheds. Over and over, I make the trip between buildings and Rae just rides along patiently, all the while telling me how to pay attention to the information in the readouts on the dash.

"How is texting going with Kimmy?" Rae asks and it makes me relax a little, not being so focused on...everything.

"Okay. When everything happened with Jojo, I didn't check the phone you gave me because I forgot about it, but I told Kimmy that I'd been caught smoking weed and making out with a boy and my parents had taken my phone away."

"I'll bet she jumped on that."

"Yeah," I laugh. "She was back to trying to get me to come party with her boyfriend. But then she stopped, saying there wouldn't be any parties for a while because her boyfriend was mad about something."

"Probably about losing some of the people he was abusing."

"Probably."

I stop talking and make another turn to go back the other way. At first, it was a little overwhelming, but after about the dozenth trip, I'm feeling much more comfortable and confident. "Do you want to try it on the road?"

My eyes snap to hers. "What? No. I don't think I'm ready for that."

She shrugs. "Okay."

"Maybe tomorrow."

"Okay."

It must have been because it seemed she was confident in me by even making the offer, so when we are about to pass the gate again, I turn toward the street.

"You've got this."

With a death grip on the steering wheel, I look both ways before pulling out onto the street. I know I'm going too slow, but my heart is already racing. If I go any faster, it just might explode.

We drive a little less than a mile to a stop sign and Rae tells me how to turn on the blinker for a left turn. "We're just going to go in a big square and we'll end up right back home and you can go again, or turn in."

With a nod, I turn and continue down the road. My speed increases, but when I go too fast, she tells me about the speed limit signs and how to monitor the speedometer. By the third time around, I feel like I'm starting to get the hang of things, but when Rae's stomach starts growling, I turn into the gate and go up the drive to the garages.

She gets out and goes inside to open one of the doors, then gets back in, patiently coaching me until I'm parked. The car is a little crooked, but it's in the garage. I didn't run into the back wall and the door closes without taking off a bumper.

It's a win all the way around.

When we go inside, Bee is there waiting. "Why were you all driving back and forth only to leave, then come back again? And what's with all the cars?"

"That was me! I was driving!"

"What?"

I nod emphatically. "Aye! Rae showed me how and let me drive back and forth until I got comfortable. Then we drove around the mile section a few times, too."

"So, when will it be my turn? Did you go buy a car just to teach us how to drive?" Of course, she has to turn it to herself. Although it's uncharitable, part of me wishes she'd hurry up and go back to Boston.

"No, that's..." When I give Rae a look, she must glean the fact that I don't want Bee to know the car is mine, so she covers quickly. "just another car. I figure if we get any more people in here, we're going to need one. Driving lessons are done for today, but we can continue tomorrow. I need some food and a nap, and then I need to get some work done."

The order of her to-do list is curious, but when I narrow my eyes at her, she ignores me and goes off to the kitchen. Bee moves up next to me. "Why do I get the feeling there's something you're not telling me?"

I don't answer, just shrug and watch Rae move down the hallway until she disappears around a corner.

CHAPTER TWENTY-ONE

Gone Hunting

RAE

After a generous helping of lasagna and garlic bread, I go upstairs to my room. A quick data review for an update leaves me satisfied with where things stand. I'm pulling the blackout curtains closed when there's a knock at my door.

"Come on in."

Cam sticks her head in. "Good, you're still up."

"Not for long." I'm hoping to get several hours of sleep before I need to go out. Taking care of all this domestic stuff cuts into my work time. What I can't get done during the day, I have to do at night, which means I'm just catching naps here and there when I can.

"Where are you going tonight?"

Before I answer, I hesitate. Should I tell her? I mean, she's here and knows what I do. Plus, she's been an excellent right hand. "Hunting, but mostly in the form of surveillance of another bad person."

She sits on the bed and watches as I continue pulling curtains closed. "We should have shades installed that you can close with the push of a button."

"That is an excellent idea."

"What has this person done?"

"He started out contacting young girls in chatrooms, acting like he was close to their age, just a year or two older. After several grooming conversations with him saying all the things a teenage girl wants to hear from a super cute boy, he would get them to take compromising pictures."

The last curtain is stubborn, so I give it a powerful yank and am greeted with the sound of fabric ripping. She's not grinning, but I can hear the smile in Cam's voice, anyway. "I'll order the shades and let you know when they'll be installed."

"Perfect. Thank you. Anyway, the guy, who is in his thirties, not the teenager he claims to be, was satisfied getting pics for a while. Of course, once he had one, he'd use it as leverage to get more. Then he started using it as leverage to make the girls meet face to face."

The curtain finally closes, casting the room into darkness, only lit by a small bedside lamp and it's silent except for Cam's sudden, sharp intake of breath.

"Yeah. He'd rape them and threaten to release their photos online if they told. It didn't take long for him to escalate again and kill his first girl."

"Oh, no." Cam's smile has been replaced by a tone of horror, summed up in those two words.

"Because they've been in different jurisdictions, the police haven't tied them together. He's also a little tech savvy because he was able to erase all communication with the girls from their phones and enough data online that it will be difficult to tie anything to him. After the first, it took him a while, but there was a second about a week ago."

"Who contacted you?"

"No one. I saw the information about the murder of the first girl and decided to look into it when the investigation stalled. It's not something I usually do because no one contacted me for help, but I just felt I needed to."

Cam nods in understanding. If anyone is going to relate to doing something just because you have a feeling about it, she would. "Okay. What time are we leaving?"

I'm not surprised that she wants to go. "A little before sunset. It's not far, but I'd like to get a look at the place before the sun goes down and see if there's a place we can easily do surveillance."

With a nod, she turns to go. "I'll be ready."

Sure enough, when I come downstairs several hours later, she's in the kitchen talking with Tori and Jo. She's dressed in black and has her hair pulled back into a braid, pretty much identical to me.

"Here," Jo says, handing me a zippered cooler. "Some sandwiches and stuff. I know you'll get hungry if you're out long."

"You are the best."

Cam stands and kisses Tori. "I'll be back later."

"Y'all be safe."

"Absolutely," I reply, taking the bag and heading out to the garage, where I open the SUV and put the bag in the back. Once Cam's settled in next to me, we're on our way.

Isaac Sparks lives on the outskirts of a small suburb on the southeast side of the Oklahoma City metro. We drive by his house and around the block. There's an empty house a few doors down from his that we can use as a hidey hole if needed.

While we wait for darkness to fall and people to turn in for the night, we park down the street in a church's parking lot where we can see the front of Sparks' house, but can't tell what's going on.

We eat the food Jo sent with us. God bless her, she even sent a couple of brownies.

With a mouth full of chocolate, I observe, "Tori seems to be making you happy."

The flush of her skin is practically lighting up the inside of the car with a faint red glow. "She is."

"But? I sense a but in there."

"How do you know if it's real?"

I draw in a deep breath and sigh it out. "Fuck if I know. Romantic relationships aren't something I've done. I'm mostly good for a few nights before I get bored and wander away. Just tell her if she breaks your heart, I'll kill her."

She laughs, as I intended her to.

I'm used to this sort of thing, but she's not, so after a few hours in, I'm not surprised when Cam falls asleep. While she dozes, I take out my tablet. Doing what I do, I monitor Sparks' online activity. He has another girl on the hook, a fourteen-year-old.

She was a little more circumspect than others and only sent him a couple of photos. He's pressing her hard, possibly because she is proving more difficult to get. She's more of a challenge that will give him more of a high if he gets her.

Working fast, I log in with the user I set up several weeks ago and send her a message. Because we're not friends on the chat site, she's going to have to notice and accept the message request. I hold my breath while I wait, but she responds.

In quick succession, I tell her to agree to meet him and tell me where he says. If she's led to believe I'm a cop because of certain things I allude to, that's all the better. She won't be meeting him, Cam and I will.

Cam will play the bait, and I will be there to turn the tables so the predator becomes prey.

The girl plays along perfectly and sends me the meeting information. They're supposed to hook up in two days and she sends me the meeting information, which I verify on the screen monitoring his activity.

I tell her in no uncertain terms that she is to come home after school that day and stay inside. No exceptions. She agrees and I hope she sticks to it, because Sparks might get an inkling that he's going to be set up and snatch her early.

As soon as she logs off, he changes profiles and starts up a conversation with another girl. This one is only twelve. Thankfully, he'll be gone before he has a chance to do her any harm.

CHAPTER TWENTY-TWO

Interesting Encounters

RAE

For the next two days, I monitor Sparks, glad he stays inside his house chatting up unsuspecting girls. As long as he stays put, I can watch him from afar without having to follow him around.

On the day of the meet, Cam dresses in an outfit similar to one we saw on the girl's social media and styles her hair similarly. With her makeup done just right, the resemblance is astonishing.

"That girl from the dragon show doesn't have anything on you," I tell her.

She flushes with pride.

I give Cam a burner phone cloned to reflect a lot of the intended victim's information in case he looks at it. If he tosses it, turns it off, or destroys it, Cam has a tracker in her shoe.

We drive to the meet with Sparks and I drop her off a few blocks away so she can walk to the set location. Completely in character, she waves at me with a grin and says, "Bye mom!"

I pretend to drive away while she pretends to walk ever so slowly up the sidewalk of the house I dropped her at. As soon as I round the corner, she bounces back toward the sidewalk and moves toward her actual destination.

Her cover story is that she's being dropped at a friend's house to study and that her mom is going to be back to pick her up. As soon as she reaches the corner, Sparks is there to pick her up instead of letting her walk the additional block to where they were supposed to meet.

I follow at a discreet distance and can't believe it when he seems to be taking her to his house. Is he really that stupid? Taking her home increases the chances of DNA transfer from his victims.

The sun has set, so I park down the block and watch as he lets Cam into his house. Hopping out of the car, I hurry toward his house, keeping to the shadows and enter his back yard. Not wasting a moment, I pull out my lock pick gun and am preparing to shove it into the lock, but the knob turns in my hand.

Moving carefully to not make a sound, I step through the back door and find myself in the kitchen. The sink is piled with dishes and the trash can is overflowing. It seems that bad guys are either slobs or anal retentive clean freaks.

I'm almost to the door leading to the living room, when I hear Cam say, "Who are you?"

Then Sparks blusters, "Yeah, who the fuck are you?"

A man's voice I don't recognize speaks, but I can't make out what he says. If this thing has gone tits up, I need to get Cam out of there, so I step through the door, drawing her attention. Sparks notices and spins around. "Who the fuck are you, and why are you in my house?"

His face is so red, it looks as if he's on the verge of a stroke. Ignoring him, my eyes move to the tall, thin man across the living room from me. Like me, he's dressed all in black with a black beanie covering his head. It appears he has emerged from the hallway, which leads to the bedrooms.

The back door being opened was probably his doing and he must have been laying in wait until Sparks returned. He looks at me, his plain face stoic. "You can go. He's mine."

"Why is he yours?" I query.

"I ain't nobody's!"

We both ignore Sparks' outburst. Still devoid of emotion, the man replies, "He killed Amaris' sister Alina. She was alone at the funeral, the last of her family gone thanks to him, and her mourning was great."

His words are odd, but it seems we're here for the same reason. I need to be sure, though. "My intentions were to be final."

"As are mine."

"Okay. I don't have a personal stake, so you can have him. My intention was to prevent more girls like Amaris' sister from being harmed."

He nods and shocks the shit out of me when he hands me a white card. I tuck it in my pocket and jerk my head at the back door, signaling to Cam that it's time to go.

Having stood there watching our byplay, Sparks blusters again. "I don't know who…" The man steps forward and injects a syringe into Sparks' neck. Within the span of a heartbeat, Sparks crumples to the floor.

"Are you sure you don't need help?"

"I'm sure," he assures me.

"Thank you." On impulse, I pull one of my cards that only has a contact number printed on one side out of a pocket and hand it to him. "If you ever need help with something technical, I'm good with computers."

Solemn eyes study me, then suddenly go wide. "Are you her?"

My brows furrow in response. "Her who?"

"The computer wizard who destroys the truly evil?"

Holy shit. Are there rumors floating around about me? I've worked hard to keep eyes pointed westward. "I've heard that's a guy in California."

The look he gives me is oblique and he just stares at me again for long moments before responding.

"No man would care so much about women and children like the Raven does. A man would be more concerned with higher-profile targets because they would feed a man's ego. You are not simply a predator; you are a protector of those who cannot protect themselves. While my opinion is in the minority, I know the Raven is a woman, a Dark Queen of Justice."

The hair on the back of my neck stands on end.

Fuck.

His opinion.

That would seem to indicate that people are discussing the Raven far more than I'm comfortable with. I need to do some damage control and start scrubbing those opinions from existence.

As if he can read my distress, he soothes. "You have nothing to fear from me because I believe you are doing the work of the angels. Feel free to call on me should you need to."

When I put Sparks on my target list, I had no idea where it would lead. Never in a million years would I have been able to predict something like this. Following my gut is leading me into the most interesting encounters.

Again, I jerk my head at Cam. Before we pass into the kitchen, our new...friend?...tells us, "There are boards missing in the back fence that will allow you to enter the yard behind. The house is empty, so you can emerge on the next block. It is better shielded with trees."

"Thanks."

Neither of us speaks until we're back in the car. Before she buckles in, Cam turns to me. "What the hell?"

"I have no fucking idea."

I take the card he gave me out and hand it to Cam, then start the car. Slowly, I pull away from the curb and drive down the block. She reads the card by the light of the street lamps.

"It's for a funeral home and crematoria."

Great for getting rid of bodies. It would appear that I'm not the only one doling out vigilante justice in the metro area. Or in the state when I take Kieran's group into consideration.

"The Raven?"

I suck in a breath. The number of people knowing who I am and being able to assign a name to my alter ego is growing at a frightening pace, even if that number is now going to be three that are still breathing.

"Raven was my nickname when I was fighting, but it has been my hacker name for much longer. Most people in the hacker community think it belongs to a guy that lives in northern California."

"And you're fine letting them believe that."

"Of course. It deflects the attention from me. Mostly it's because he took credit for some things I did when I was a kid and mostly just playing around and testing my limits. That phase didn't last long, though. So far, no one has connected my more recent activities to the name. Or so I thought."

"So Rae is for Raven."

It's a statement, not a question, so I only respond with a hum.

"He called you the Dark Queen of Justice. That was kind of cool."

"Also kind of weird," I reply with a laugh.

She shakes her head as we pull through the gate at home.

"No. It's not. I'm not as blind as you must think I am if you believe I haven't noticed your tattoo or the grips of the pistols Max gave you. The Morrigan is your totem and influences your actions. She is the Raven Goddess, the decider of who lives and dies in battle. One of her other names is the Dark Queen, so it is more à propos than weird."

Having dropped her bomb of perceptive insights, when I park in the garage, she gets out without another word and goes into the house. Stunned, it takes me a moment to get myself collected enough to follow her.

CHAPTER TWENTY-THREE

Safe and Sound

VICTORIA

While Cam is gone, I try to work, but my heart just isn't in it. I know she's safer with Rae than with anyone, but I still worry. She didn't tell me exactly where they were going, but with her dressed the way she was and Rae in her dark angel all black getup, it was probably dangerous.

I know they're not likely to tell me because, in most ways, I'm still an outsider. Cam...I'm still getting used to that nickname...has been amazing. A breath of fresh air, considering the other people I've been with who seem to always be wanting something or have ulterior motives for a relationship.

It's my own fault, really. When you put yourself out there to be someone's dream girl, you're setting yourself up for disappointment. Most of my relationships haven't been anything more than transactions.

But Cam, she's so easy to be with. Beautiful, smart, and so tender hearted it makes me want to protect her. Which is funny, because she's had a lot more training in how to kick someone's ass than I have. I have exactly zero.

Making love with her is just that. It's not the fucking that I've done pretty much ever since I lost my virginity and it's on a level I'd never thought possible. With Cam, it's like every time we're together is a journey of discovery, not only for her, but for me as well.

She says she's staying in Oklahoma, but I'm taking it with a grain of salt. Especially because I have heard what her cousin Bee says about it. Bee has said many times that there's no way her father will allow Cam to stay in Oklahoma.

So, I keep my heart guarded, waiting to see what happens.

All evening, I've been keeping one eye on the front window and one on my screen. I'm yanked out of my thoughts by my client. "Baby, are you with me?"

Beaming at him, I cover, "Si, mi corazon, I was just thinking of what I'd like to do to you and it had me distracted in the best way."

"Mmm...why don't you tell me?"

With a purr, I tell him all the things he wants to hear me say I want to do to him. He's a fifty-something, bald, overweight computer programmer and I want to do absolutely nothing to him, but he's paying me a lot of money for me to create the illusion of desire.

As a generous regular, he also pays a lot of my bills, so I make it convincing. Just as I'm wrapping up my session with him, headlights wash over the windows when a vehicle comes around the house and turns into the garage area. Assuring him of my undying love one last time, I log off and leap to my feet.

As I pass the bed, I grab a robe and throw it on as I hurry out of the room and down the stairs. Rae is holding the door for Cam to come in and I zoom right past her, wrapping Cam in my arms.

Once I kiss her thoroughly, I am inspecting her to be sure she hasn't been harmed. She cups my face in her hands, putting a halt to my frantic searching. "I'm fine. Come on, let's go upstairs and I'll tell you all about it."

Her touch calms me, and I follow as she leads me by the hand out of the room. With the click of our bedroom door as it closes, she starts telling me about their outing, including more details about what the guy had done.

"Other than him putting his slimy paw on my leg while he was driving, he didn't touch me. Inside his house, he didn't have a chance to do anything before that guy stepped out of the hall and then Rae came in."

"Did Rae kill him?" I'm surprised when the hope that she did bubbles up. Killing someone is illegal, but when there's no other way to stop someone...let's just say I understand. I couldn't do it, but I understand.

She shakes her head and starts unbuttoning her shirt. "No. The other guy wanted to because of what had been done to one of the victims. It left someone he knew alone. He insisted, so Rae and I left him with Sparks."

I move behind her and unzip her skirt. You know, just being helpful. "That's creepy."

When it falls to the floor, I help pull the unbuttoned shirt off her shoulders and let it fall to the floor, too. I place kisses along her shoulder as I unfasten her bra.

"The creepiest thing is that he knew who Rae is. He knew her hacker name and that she's a woman even though everyone else seems to think it's a man. Of course, she didn't confirm or deny anything, but he was insistent."

Slipping my fingers under the straps of her bra, I push it off, too, and as it falls, I cup her firm breasts in my hands, moving my kisses up the side of her neck. I love it when she sighs and leans back into me.

"Do you think he'll cause trouble for her?" I murmur.

"No. When he thought he knew who she was, he was almost reverent."

"That's good. I'm just glad you're back safe and sound."

When she turns her head, she's smiling sweetly, but doesn't speak.

"I know I'm being silly. You're safe as can be when you're with Rae, but I still worry."

She opens her mouth, but I kiss her before she can say anything. The kiss deepens, and she turns in my arms to face me, her hands moving up to tangle in my hair.

Hours, or maybe minutes later, I pull away, feeling dizzy and breathless. "On the bed. Now."

"Yes, mo chroi," she replies, looking at me coyly as she backs onto the bed, then lays back, posing for me.

"Dios mio, you're so hermosa," I tell her as I remove my robe and move onto the bed with her.

She opens her arms and legs to me, so I settle on top of her and she closes me in, cradling me in arms and thighs as our lips find each other again. Her hips move, grinding her center against my pelvis.

Even though she has assured me she's fine, I need to check for myself. I pull back and smooth her dark hair away from her face, inspecting her eyes and face. As if she senses my need, she remains still, letting me look my fill.

I kiss her along her jaw and neck and shoulder, tasting, touching, checking for even the slightest of bruises. Her skin is flawless, so I continue my journey of reassurance.

When my kisses lead me to her breasts, her small pink nipples are stiff and in need of attention, so I draw one peak between my lips and suckle it. Her mewl of pleasure sends a thrill through me.

I move to her other breast, nipping the tip before soothing it with my tongue. Sucking and teasing until she's bucking beneath me. Before I pull away, I nip the side of her breast, then put my mouth there, sucking and wanting to leave my mark on her.

Settling my shoulders between her thighs, her need is glistening all over her beautiful pink pussy. Tasting her is a visceral experience. She is sweet and briny, like the best salted caramel, and I can't get enough.

As soon as my lips begin to lap up her juices, her back bows and hips begin to move. My fingers dig into her hips, trying to keep her in place, and her fists grip my hair, trying to pull me closer. Any closer and I'll be climbing inside her.

She's so sensitive that it doesn't take long before she cries out my name and her hips jerk in my grip. I kiss her inner thighs, then move up her body to press my lips to hers, then wrap my arms around her. When she reaches a hand down to my breast, I know she wants to please me in return, but I nuzzle her neck and whisper in her ear.

"Please. Just let me hold you for a bit."

We must fall asleep because the next thing I know, Cam sits bolt upright in bed and says, "I need to tell Rae."

CHAPTER TWENTY-FOUR

Have To Go To Boston

RAE

As if the night isn't already weird enough, after I respond to client requests, I'm about to dredge up everything I can about the solemn stranger in Sparks' house when my phone buzzes, making me jump.

Davis.

Of course, he'd send me a text when I'm fresh on the heels of murdering someone.

But then I didn't murder anyone, did I? The murdering was done by...I flip the card and read the name. Donovan Newberry was the one doing the murdering.

Davis: *WYD?*

Because I'm too tired to be able to text coherently, I hit dial.

"Hey," he answers and his rich, rough voice sends warmth through me all the way to my toes.

"I was just sitting down to get some work done. Nothing important, tho."

"My lucky day. How have you been?"

"Good. Settling in. I never realized how much work it is staying in one place."

"Maybe someday you'll let me visit."

That makes me smile. But it's never going to happen. He'd get one look at this place and know I didn't buy it with clean money. Your average data jockey can't afford a six million dollar home, even if I did get a fabulous deal and didn't pay nearly that much.

I'm about to reply when Cam bursts through the door.

"Hang on a sec. I have a cousin who seems to have forgotten how to knock."

"Good," she says. "You're awake."

Tori comes into the room right behind her and closes the door. Both of them appear to be wearing robes and nothing else, so I'm not sure what's happened to cause the frantic look on Cam's face.

"What's up?"

"You have to go to Boston."

Of everything I might have guessed she'd say, that would not have been in the top one hundred. I tuck the phone against my chest, hoping Davis didn't hear Cam's words.

"What?"

"You have to go to Boston. Right away. Finish your call and I'll tell you everything."

I stare at her so long she puts her hands on her hips and tilts her head. With a sigh, I return to the phone call with Davis.

"Sorry about that."

"So, you have to come to Boston..." I can tell he's trying not to laugh.

"Apparently so. My cousin is a little bit psychic. She insists she has more to tell me, so I'd better go."

"Let me know when you're arriving. No sneaking in and out this time."

"Fine."

"Later, babe."

"Good night, Davis."

I put the phone down, take a deep breath to clear my head, and turn to face Cam. She's still standing there with hands on hips, her pretty face pinched with anxiety.

"Lay it on me."

"I had a dream and you need to go to Boston right away."

"You already said that. Do you know why?"

Her posture deflates. "No. Nothing certain, but I think there's something you're supposed to see. You were having dinner with a crow, which was weird enough. But then the crow cawed, and you turned your head and saw...something."

I take a moment to absorb what she's said. "It can't wait until this weekend?"

"No!" she exclaims, as if the very thought is going to give her a stroke. "Oh, and you can't fly commercial. Uncle Keegan has contacts that let him know if anyone on his list is arriving on a flight."

That makes me frown. "He has me on a list?"

"Yes."

"And a crow, huh?"

As if she has too much energy coursing through her body, she starts pacing. "Aye. It makes no sense to me, but the crow was important. If I figure out what it means, I'll let you know."

"You don't need to. I know what the crow means, or rather, who the crow is."

Halting abruptly, she turns to me. "How?"

I tilt my head to my phone. "It's the person I was on the phone with."

Her mouth drops open. Knowing I'm not going to be able to stay awake long enough to do a deep dive on Donovan New-berry, I move to my bed, ready to lie down. "Have a seat. You probably need to be sitting down for this."

I settle back against my pillows as Cam and Tori sit on the other side of the bed. When Cam's robe rides up, I hold up a hand and tease. "Cover up that coochie, girl. I do not need to be flashed."

Heat crawls up her neck as she pulls a throw blanket from the foot of the bed to cover her lower body. Then I launch into the story of Davis, who has the nickname of Crow from his time in the military.

From him seeing me take on four frat boys at my Uncle Max's bar. He saw me, but I didn't see him. To what I thought was a one-night stand at a casino the next night. Being on the same flight to Boston the day after that when he again saw me, but I didn't see him.

And finally, to how our apartments in Boston are directly across the street from each other. Not only on the same street, but literally, window-to-window, directly across the street. He can see into mine and vice versa.

When I finish, both of them are staring at me, openmouthed. "That is an amazing love story," Tori says.

I shake my head. "Can't be."

"Why not?" Cam asks with a frown.

"Because. Davis is employed by the Federal Bureau of Investigation, and I'm pretty sure he's investigating some of my previous activities, although he hasn't figured that out yet."

They both gasp.

"Yeah, how's that for a kick in the pants? I've never felt as connected to anyone as I do to him, and he's a cop."

Cam reaches out and touches Tori's arm, giving her a tender look. "He has some purpose in your life that is still unfolding. We're going back to bed, but you can't; you need to book your flight for tomorrow. Oh, and take something nice to wear."

I grumble. Since they've been here, we've gone shopping a few times, and they have forced me to expand my wardrobe options to include things like dresses and heels. Those are two things I never thought I'd own.

However, they also introduced me to cashmere sweaters and other finery that I don't know how I ever lived without. Well, crap. Packing stuff like a dress and heels means I can't just cram my things into my backpack. That means I'll have to be driven to the airport instead of taking my bike.

Speaking of which, I need to figure out how I'm getting to Boston on short notice without flying commercially.

CHAPTER TWENTY-FIVE

Wow – You're Good

RAE

Once I flew first class, I was spoiled for flying coach or even business class ever again. Now that I'm flying on a private jet, I don't know that I'll ever be able to return to flying commercial, even if it is first class.

When I arrived at the small terminal at Wiley Post airport, there was no waiting for service. No long lines. No fussing about my luggage weight. Just a greeting from a pleasant desk attendant and getting ushered to my plane.

The attendant gave me a brochure for their membership program. I read through it on the flight and see they have counters at both the smaller airport and at the primary commercial airport.

As I'm reading the brochure, I realize both airports are named after men who died in plane crashes. So someone has a morbid sense of humor.

In Boston, when I descend the steps of the plane, Davis is there waiting. He's leaning against a black BMW sedan. I never saw his vehicle, but I would have pegged him for something more rugged, like a Jeep or knobby tired SUV.

"Hi," he says.

I can't help but smile because, damn, he looks good. His ebon hair is slightly disheveled and looks as if he's been running his hands through it. The once perfect necktie has been loosened and the top button is undone on his shirt.

He's lost the jacket to his suit and the sleeves of his crisp, white shirt are rolled up. There's dark scruff on his jaw, but it looks like more than just a day's growth, so maybe he's working on a beard. When I draw near, I see his blue eyes are clouded with weariness.

"Hi," I reply, feeling shy, which is so unlike me.

Shyness isn't something I'm accustomed to, so why the hell am I feeling that way now? Fuck if I know. Davis throws me off kilter because he's like no man I've ever known.

He rises and moves toward me and I'm drawn to him like he's gravity. I'm helpless to resist. As soon as I'm within reach, he pulls me into his arms and kisses me.

His hands splay open on my back as my fingers curl into the front of his shirt. I lean against him, kissing him right back and damn, it feels good. Feels right.

The scent of musk and man washes over me and makes me a little lightheaded with an overwhelming sense of...relief? Affection? Because I'm emotionally stunted, I can't name it, but it's like nothing I've ever felt before.

It feels comforting and like coming home. I should probably be a little worried about that, but I can't muster the wherewithal to manage it. He might be putting me in cuffs someday if I let him get too close, but I can't seem to be bothered by that at the moment, either.

I'm not sure how long we stand there while our lips get reacquainted, but Davis breaks the kiss when someone clears their throat behind me. Davis looks up at whoever it is and tucks my head against his chest, all protective like. It's so cute.

"Sorry to interrupt, ma'am, but I have your luggage."

"Thank you," Davis replies, his voice gruff. He tightens his arms around me in a gentle squeeze, then lets me go. "I'll take those."

After making quick work of putting my luggage in his trunk, he comes around and opens the passenger door for me. I think he kept it locked on purpose just so he could do that. Yeah, I tried to open it myself, but he's forcing me to allow him to be gentlemanly, the rat bastard.

His look is smug when he opens the door and holds it until I'm settled in the passenger seat. The driver's door opens, and he slides in to sit behind the wheel. "Did you eat on the plane, or are you hungry?"

I can't help but grin because he's starting to know me so well. "Starving."

He reaches over the console and takes my hand in his. "In the mood for anything in particular?"

"Nope. Just good food, and if you're up for it, good booze. I know it's a work night for you."

"But it's not for you. I know just the place. When do you fly back?"

"Not until whatever is supposed to happen happens."

"Isn't that just like a psychic to not give you any details?"

I almost laugh because it's so spot on. However, Cam is my cousin and I've learned not to discount her feelings, dreams, and visions. After the fact, it's always kind of spooky how, even though it seemed vague on the front side, from the backside, it's spot on.

"Yeah, but she has proven herself to me. Her dream was that I was having dinner with a crow and until last night, she knew nothing about you." There's no way she could have known that Davis's military nickname was Crow.

"Seriously?"

When I don't answer with anything more than a "Hmm," he stares out the windshield as he navigates traffic. Several miles later, he pulls my hand to his mouth and kisses the back of it.

"That's creepy."

Now I do laugh. "I'll be sure to let her know."

He squishes my hand. Not hard enough to hurt, but with just enough pressure to get my attention as he growls. "You'd better not. In fact, I'm going to send her a thank-you card and some roses. Maybe some chocolates, too."

Whenever I'm with him, my defenses turn to mush. Hell, he doesn't even have to be in the room. Just talking to him on the phone sends butterflies flapping their feathery wings in my stomach, sending tsunamis through my blood.

"She's already a fan. Told me you have some purpose in my life that's still unfolding."

"I can't wait to see what it is."

We continue to chat as he moves us closer to wherever he has in mind for dinner. He parks on the street and, after he puts his jacket back on, we walk down the block toward a restaurant. We're about halfway down the sidewalk when a door opens on the next block and two men walk out.

One of them is Keegan Morrissey. I step in front of Davis, stopping him, and turning my back to the men. As I slide my palms up his chest, I say, "See those two men on the next block?"

His look of confusion fades when he glances up surreptitiously and smiles down at me as if I've said something interesting. "Yeah. I recognize your uncle."

"Do you know who the other man is?"

He leans down and brushes his lips across my jaw. "No, but I can probably find out if I can get a photo. Just go with me, okay?"

I nod and he puts his arms around me, backing me up until we're three quarters of the way down the block when he stops next to a streetlight. "Lean on the pole like you're posing for a photo."

He backs up a few steps and starts taking photos, telling me to smile and change up my poses. Laughter bubbles out of me as he tells me to bend over and show my cleavage, as if I have any. Then he says to smile bigger, so I stick my tongue out and cross my eyes.

Suddenly, he steps to me, takes me in his arms and kisses me with one hand cupping my face and the other around my back. For a moment, I forget what we're doing and get lost in him. Footsteps are coming up the sidewalk and my uncle's voice passes behind me, pulling me out of my lip lock stupor.

Although I can't make out what he's saying, it's definitely him talking. The other man responds. He has an accent and cadence I don't recognize, but I can tell it's for sure not Irish or Italian.

From the corner of my eye, I watch until they disappear around the corner, then pull my mouth away from Davis's even though I don't want to. "Please send me those pictures."

"Do you want the recording, too?"

"Recording?"

"Yeah. As soon as they started heading our way and I moved to you, I put my camera on record, hoping to catch them as they went by."

Well, isn't he quick on the draw? I can't say I would have thought of that so quickly.

I grin up at him. "Wow. You're good."

He nods. "Yep, and don't you forget it."

I laugh and link my arm with his as we continue to the restaurant. When we're seated and left to peruse the menu, without looking at me, he asks, "Seems like that was probably what you were supposed to see. Does that mean you're going to fly out tomorrow?"

His tone is casual, as if it doesn't matter to him, but I can hear the disappointment lurking in the dark corners of his voice. I reach out and cover his hand with mine.

When he looks up, I hold his gaze and say, "To be honest, a few days of peace and quiet sound wonderful. It's difficult to get my work done at home because I'm pulled in a million different directions. I can work at the apartment across the street for a few days while you're at the office."

The smile he gives me is positively beautiful.

Yeah, I know, I'm being stupid, but I'm going to quit fighting so hard against this attraction. It may end with him putting me behind bars or me having to do something violent to him to get away, but according to Cam, he has some role to play in my life.

Besides, I haven't even been able to think about hooking up with someone since Yona. I tried to force things with him and look where that got me. With Davis, things just work.

So for the next few days, I'm going to be present without thinking about what a terrible idea it is because of what might happen in some unknown future.

CHAPTER TWENTY-SIX

Let Everything Else Go

DAVIS

She's going to stay for a few days. Although it's only a few days, it's an enormous victory. This woman has more walls than a funhouse maze, but my chipping away at them seems to be yielding results, so I'll keep at it.

I've never worked this hard for sex before. However, this odd connection is also a completely new experience for me and definitely about more than just great sex. Now her cousin saying there's some purpose for me being in her life. I want to see where it goes.

When I park in my building's garage, she doesn't get out until I come around and open the door for her. She apparently got the hint when I purposely made her wait for me at the airport.

I get her luggage from the trunk and we cross the garage to the elevator, then I push the button and wait. She's quiet the entire time, so I wonder if she's nervous. The woman can take on a group of drunks at her uncle's bar without batting an eye, but my apartment makes her apprehensive?

Wanting to ease her doubts, I stroke the back of my hand over her cheekbone. She looks up at me and smiles, but it seems as if I've pulled her out of some deep thought. "You okay?"

Leaning into me, she answers, "Yeah. I'm good."

I gently pull her head toward me and lean down to kiss her temple. The elevator dings and the door slides open. As we ride up to my floor, she leans into my side again, so I lift my arm around her shoulders and draw her close. Yeah, I'm thinking she's nervous.

It's strange to see her this way. Although I don't know her as well as I'd like, I've never seen her be anything but self-assured, so this skittish side is another glimpse into who she is.

Once I unlock the door, she steps inside and stops a few paces in. I follow and close the door behind us, then drop my keys in a bowl on a table by the door. "Well, it's not much, but it works."

"It looks a lot like the place I use across the street."

"Florian Moreau."

I can't see her face, but hear the humor in her voice when she replies. "Figured you'd check it out once you knew which apartment I was in."

Damn right I did. It was a surprise when her name wasn't on the ownership records and another surprise to discover it was owned by a company owned by Florian Moreau. Moreau is a French national with significant holdings in real estate, tech, and aerospace.

I take her suitcase to the bedroom and move it beside the bed. "I cleared out a drawer and some space in the closet for your things." Trying to sound blasé, I ask what I've wondered since I found the records. "So, is he a former boyfriend or something?"

A laugh barks out of her, and she finally moves into the apartment. "Florian? No. He's a client who hired me to see if his wife was cheating on him. She was, but had also hired someone to kill him. When I told him, he said I'd saved his life and could have use of any property he owned. Since I figured it would be good to have access to a property here that didn't have a paper trail to me, I chose Boston."

I don't want to push, but there are so many unanswered questions about her that I'd like to remedy. "How exactly do you find the information?"

She steps close and does that thing where she puts her palms on my chest and slides them up to circle her arms around my neck. My skin tingles in the wake.

Looking me in the eye, she says, "Davis, I don't want to lie to you, but with you being who you are, there are some things I'm not going to be able to tell you. If you ask me something I'm not comfortable answering, I'm just going to say, no comment."

Taking her in my arms, I sigh. "Who I am...as in a cop."

She nods.

"Because you're a criminal."

She doesn't respond. Probably because saying no comment or anything else beside a flat-out no would just confirm it as fact. "Let me tell you what I think. You don't have to respond, but I don't think I'm as oblivious as you might believe me to be."

With a sigh, she tries to move away from me, but I just hold her tighter and put my mouth against her ear. "You don't have to be afraid of me being a cop, Rae. Mostly from guesswork based on the little bit you've told me, I think you're probably a hacker and use your skills to gather information for your clients."

She's tense and stiff as a board in my arms. "Also, you moved around a lot to make yourself difficult to track, but now that you have some time and experience under your belt, you probably know how to mask your activities using other means, so moving isn't as important."

I kiss her on that sensitive spot just behind her ear, hoping it will soothe her nervousness, and I whisper. "Even if I'm completely off the mark, we can pretend I'm not and just let everything else go. Okay?"

A shiver shudders through her body. It might make me a lousy cop, but in the military, I was ordered to do a lot of messed up shit in the name of duty and country that would probably make anything she's done pale in comparison.

So I'm not going to get all worked up about her gathering information and selling it. Especially when the information is stuff like a man wanting to know if his wife is cheating on him. It sounds like she's kind of a private investigator type.

She nods, her cheek rubbing against my chest. "Okay."

"Good. Since we have that settled, we can relax for the rest of the time you're here. So, what do you want to do? Take me to bed and have your way with me, or snuggle on the couch and watch basketball on TV?"

Her laugh is muffled against my chest. "Well, for starters, I'd like to change out of these clothes into something more comfortable. Who knows what might happen between taking off one set of clothes and putting another on?"

Rae pulls away and shrugs out of her jacket. I pull at my tie until I can take it off. Picking her up on time meant going straight from the office out to the airport, but there was no way I was going to miss her arrival.

As I watch her, she watches me. Mimicking her actions, I shrug out of my suit coat and go to the closet to hang it up, then hold out a hand for hers. She gives me her jacket and I hang it next to mine.

Turning back to her, I toe off my shoes as I unbutton my cuffs and start unbuttoning my shirt. She steps out of her heels and pulls off her sweater to reveal a lacy tank top like shirt underneath.

My dress shirt comes off, and she sucks in a breath. "I know it's weird, but I've always thought it incredibly sexy when a man wears a t-shirt under a dress shirt."

With a smirk, I shake my head. Of all the things a woman has said about me, being turned on by a t-shirt isn't one of them.

Simultaneously, I pull off my tee, and she pulls off her tank. Our unbuttoned pants fall to the floor next and we're standing there in our underwear, her hard nipples straining against the satiny fabric of her bra as my cock creates a tent in my boxer briefs.

Moving out of the closet, I take her by the hand and lead her to the bathroom. I, for one, need a shower before being intimate with her. She stands there for me as I unfasten her bra and remove it, then pull down her panties.

Her passivity is something new and I can't say that I hate it. The willingness to let me do something as simple as undressing her signifies a heightened level of trust, and I'll take every bit she gives me.

Once I'm naked, I move her into the shower, remembering she doesn't like her hair to get wet, so I put my back to the spray to shield her. Finally, I lean down and kiss her.

At first, it's slow and easy. We have days together, so there's no reason to rush. But then she puts her arms around my neck and presses her body against mine, the hard peaks of her nipples dragging through my chest hair.

The sensation makes me want to turn her around, bend her over and drive my cock into her tight, wet heat and fuck her like a neanderthal. Just as I'm trying to force the caveman back into my amygdala, one of her hands drops and circles my cock at the base.

She pulls her mouth away from mine and, with a husky voice, says, "Pick me up. I can't wait any longer to have you inside of me. It's been too long."

Well, hell. Who am I to deny her? Caveman, it is.

"Yes, it has."

Bending, I hook my hands under her thighs and lift as she puts one arm around my neck and wraps her legs around my hips to keep her balance. I hold her in place as she reaches between us and guides the head of my cock into her entrance, then I slowly let her slide down as her body takes me in.

She groans as her lids fall shut. "I've missed you."

"I was about to say the same thing."

A grin splits her face, but she doesn't open her eyes. "Great minds."

I withdraw until only the head of my dick remains inside her, then plunge back in deep, impaling her on my shaft. "Yes," she hisses, and we stop talking. She feels so goddamn good as our bodies move together, me driving into her while her hips undulate in time with my thrusts.

Since Rae saw me with Linda, there's been no one else. Another woman hasn't even caught my eye or made my dick stiff. The last time I went this long without having sex was when I was deployed on a mission.

It sucked then, but I had a purpose driving me, so delayed gratification on returning to base was manageable. Now, it's even worse because she is the only one I want and knowing she's out there, but unreachable, is too much to bear sometimes.

Before her, if you'd asked me, I would have told you that one pussy was pretty much like any other. But now I know better. She fits me like we were made for each other.

Because it's been a while since I've been with anyone, it doesn't take long before I sense the telltale pressure at the base of my spine and heavy tightness in my balls. Her forehead falls to my shoulder, and she clutches me like she's holding on for dear life.

"Davis," she breathes into my neck.

"Me, too, baby. Just let it go."

"Davis," comes out of her again, half whine, half growl, just before she sinks her teeth into my shoulder and her inner walls grip me like a vise, dragging me into orgasm with her.

CHAPTER TWENTY-SEVEN

Return To How Things Were

CAM

Without Rae in the house, Bee seems to think she's in charge. As soon as I came downstairs this morning, she told me her plans for us for the day.

Apparently, she has grand plans for the rest of our time here in Oklahoma, however long it may be. I know I'll have to tell her I'm not going back with her, but not yet.

After breakfast, she has instructed Finn to give her driving lessons like Rae gave me and to supervise when and if we go out on the roads. Tori looks over the rim of her coffee mug and raises an eyebrow at me.

In response, I roll my eyes and give her a secret smile.

Finn seems to have an endless supply of patience as I tell Bee how to operate the car, then settle into the back seat to grip the door handle. It takes her a few tries to get the hang of the accelerator and brake. She stomps on them so often I'm thinking we might end up with whiplash.

Eventually, she settles down, and the ride smooths out. Of course, her time behind the wheel takes priority, but she finally concedes and I get some practice under my belt before we go in for lunch.

That afternoon, poor Finn is yet again put to work because Bee thinks we need to be better fighters, more on par with Rae and Finn. I don't tell her that being able to fight like they can takes years of actually being in fights.

But again, I want to learn more, so I will go with it. She seems so pleased to see me falling in line with her wants again, like we've returned to how things were when we first arrived.

After dinner, she wants to watch a movie, so Jo, Tori, and I join her. Finn disappears to his room. Toward the end of the movie, Tori is keeping an eye on her phone. I know she has an appointment with one of her regular clients tonight.

While everyone else watches the movie, I text with Kimmy. Although I don't think we need an in with Tai Dang anymore, I have kept up the communication. She seems so lonely that I can't bring myself to just cut her off.

Since she told me her boyfriend, who must be Dang, and not one of his minions, was upset, she's been mostly quiet. That's why her text tonight surprises me.

Kimmy: *U ever done sumthin u wish u cud take back?*

Me: *Sure. WYD?*

Kimmy: *Hurt my cuzin.*

She lives with her cousin, a doctor. What could Kimmy have done to hurt her? I don't want to think the worst of her, but that's the first thing that pops into my mind. Could she have killed her?

Me: *WYD*

Kimmy: *Few wks ago set her up so my bf could grab her. He took her @ work n hurt her. Thot it wuz funny @ the time but wuz flyin but felt rl bad after.*

Me: *Y u do it?*

Kimmy: *She's prfect. Evry1 lvs her. I'm always the fuckup.*

Me: *Don't u live w ur cuzin?*

Kimmy: *Yeah. She won't tlk to me nemore. Wish my bf wud let me live w him.*

Me: *Y won't he?*

She doesn't answer right away, so I turn my attention to the movie and snuggle closer to Tori. She's been reading the text exchange. I'm not sure what she thinks of this whole thing.

The stuff we've avoided talking about is stacking up like a pile of books. I think it's high time we start talking about it because I want to know where I stand.

If she's just staying here until Joelle is settled in, I want to know, so I don't let my heart get any more invested than it already is. My phone buzzes.

Kimmy: *I asked, but he won't let me. Think he just wnts me 2 get 2 my cuzin. Dsnt rly wnt me. No1 duz.*

I don't know what to say. Could her cousin be that terrible? I can't see her taking the girl in and agreeing to be her guardian if she didn't care for her at least a little. But then, Uncle Keegan took me in and was my guardian until I turned eighteen, and he didn't hesitate to beat the shit out of me when he found out about the girl in Ireland.

Me: *Thts not tru.*

She doesn't respond. I try a few more times to reach her, but she stays quiet.

As soon as the credits roll on the movie, Tori pops up to go upstairs and I follow her. "Where are you going?" Bee snipes.

"Upstairs," I reply. "Tori has a client."

"That doesn't mean you have to go."

"I know; but I want to."

She huffs as she rolls her eyes and flops back to sink into the cushy sofa, mumbling something too low for me to hear. Ignoring her, I continue up to my room.

Tori is a flurry of motion as she changes clothes, trading her comfortable yoga pants and tee for sexy lingerie covered by a silky robe. She fluffs her hair up and is about to go live when I race over with her lipstick.

"Oh, my gosh, thank you!"

I've known what she does for a living practically from day one. It doesn't bother me, but I haven't ever watched her work other than being here in the beginning or coming in at the end to watch her wrap up.

However, I've had enough of Bee being a demanding grump today, so I'm going to watch my girlfriend...if she even is my girlfriend...have chat sex with some rando on the internet who is paying her for the privilege.

I'd probably pay her, too, because she is just that beautiful. And sexy. And smart, and funny, and amazing. But even with all that, she has a heart so beautiful, her exterior pales in comparison.

Every time I look at her, I'm overwhelmed. Never in my life did I think I'd ever be in a relationship with another woman no matter how much I craved it, and I never dreamed she'd be so incredible.

Tori blows me a kiss, then plasters a broad grin on her face as she clicks on the button to go live with her client. I quietly move a chair into position so I can watch her and see everything.

"Hey baby," she says to the screen, but I know she's talking to me. "I've been thinking about you all day. Have you been thinking about me?"

It's fascinating to watch how she handles her client so adeptly. She leads him where she wants him to go. All the while, he thinks he's the one steering the conversation.

Her fingers drag along the edge of her bra and he comments that he wants to see her beautiful tits.

"Sure, baby," she says huskily. "You know I want to show them to you, but you know what I need from you to do that."

She told me most of her clients start out with a basic chat for the cheapest price, which means no nudity. However, they inevitably ask for more, thinking they can ply her with flattery to give them what they want without the extra expense. She teases and flirts, but never crosses the line until they cough up the cash.

As soon as she gets confirmation that he's paid, she makes a show of taking off her bra. When my hands slip underneath my shirt, her eyes slide in my direction and if I'm not mistaken, they're filled with desire.

For her audience, she fondles her breasts, shaping, molding, and jiggling them for the man on the screen who thinks he's the only one watching. His comments are lewd, telling her all the things he'd like to do to her.

I pull off my shirt and bra and fondle my own breasts in tandem with her, tweaking my hard nipples as I imagine doing the same things to her that he's saying. Her breasts are full and round, with brownish pink areolas and large nipples. In comparison, my breasts are small, with blush pink peaks.

The man wants her to take off her panties, and again, that requires another level of payment. He quibbles and grouses, but pays the money and she rises to her knees to turn her back to him.

Looking over her shoulder at him, she pushes her sheer panties down slowly to uncover her gorgeous ass. Falling forward onto her hands, she gives him a closeup of her ass and the lips of her pussy through the gap in her thighs.

My pulse kicks up and my core throbs. I want to crawl up behind her and taste her sweet cunt. At first, I was inept in my efforts of tasting her and acted more out of curiosity and enthusiasm than any actual skill.

However, in the time we've been together, I'm learning about her body and what pleases her. When I do something that makes her gasp or grind her hips, I catalogue it away so I can remember to repeat it.

Now I want to slide in beneath her and taste her when she's in this position. And if she decides she's inclined to bend a little deeper and reciprocate at the same time, all the better.

Her client asks her to fuck herself on the dildo she has at the ready. I watch as she slides the silicone cock in and out of her pussy, moaning and cooing the entire time.

Part of me wonders if she misses having an actual flesh and blood dick inside her. Maybe we should get one of those strap on things and I could fuck her with it.

I'm so lost in watching her that I don't realize my hand has slipped into my shorts and I'm stroking my own pussy as she fucks herself. "Show me," she says a little louder than her other conversation with the client.

"Oh, I'm showing you baby," the man replies, but when I look up, she is looking at me.

With a flush of pleasure crawling over my chest when I understand she means me, I stand and shuck off my shorts. I spread my legs wide and drape them over the arms of the chair, then resume rubbing my clit.

Breathing heavily, we stare at each other as we pleasure ourselves. The man on the screen is so caught up in the show, he
doesn't even realize she's not looking at him any longer.

"I'm close," he says.

"Come for me, baby," Tori demands, but again, I know that's
for me.

"Close," I breathe.

She and I moan in tandem. "That's it, baby," the man growls.
"You know you love this cock."

"Yes, you're so perfect," Tori replies, looking at me.

He groans.

She moans.

I gasp.

Then we're all silent as we ride the waves of endorphins.

CHAPTER TWENTY-EIGHT

Modern Way of Counting Coup

RAE

Sitting back in my chair, I relish the quiet room. There are no voices carrying through the halls. No one knocking on the door or just plain barging in.

My time here is limited, so I'm going to buckle down and get as much done as I can. Things in Oklahoma are coming together and I can't afford to drop the ball or the whole fucking thing will fall apart.

I log into my system, and while I wait, my mind drifts back to last night. After the shower, we moved to his bed for round two. It was like our bodies needed to make up for lost time because round two quickly turned to round three.

We fell asleep with tangled arms and legs. When I woke up this morning, I felt more rested than I have for a while. Maybe it was just being able to sleep for more than a couple of hours, but I have a feeling it had a lot to do with the man I woke up with.

I don't know what it is about him, but I feel more relaxed with him than I've ever felt with anyone since my mom died. The knowledge that he has an inkling of who I am and was fine with it helped, too. It's a start, but I doubt he'd be so nonchalant if he knew everything.

We went for a run and had breakfast together, then had a quickie in the shower because that's all we had time for before he had to hurry into work. "I hope you're still here when I get back," he teased as he slipped behind the wheel of his car after kissing me.

I just grinned at him and, carrying my laptop, walked out of his parking garage across the street to my apartment. When I realize I'm lost in reminiscing about the night before, just sitting there grinning at my computer screen like a loon, I shake myself.

"Quit swooning over a boy and get to work, you dork," I chide into the silence.

"Easier said than done," I reply, because Davis Jeffries is no boy and he's definitely swoon worthy.

When the first bit of information I see is an email from my weapons contact, I push everything and everyone else out of my mind. Once I have arrangements confirmed, I upload the pictures Davis sent me and set my spiders searching the web for the unknown man's face.

I listen to the recording several times, but it's too muffled to make much sense of. Audio isn't something I've ever had an affinity for, so I send the file off to a contact to see if he can clean it up for me.

Hours later, my growling stomach forces me to find food. Instead of going out, I order something to be delivered and get enough to take care of a few days.

In the past few hours, I've accomplished more than I did in the past few weeks at home. That's something I need to deal with. When the cousins first came to stay with me, I thought they'd be there for a week or two, but we've blown by that timeframe.

Once I'm back home, I'm going to have to set up office hours or something so I can get my work done because my hacking work is still the primary source of income. Well, outside of draining Tai Dang's bank accounts, that is.

The man was so oblivious that I had drained one and was halfway through another before he noticed. Even then, he probably wouldn't have clued in at all, but he lost out on some real estate deal because he didn't have the cash on hand. That was worth a belly laugh, at least for me.

The bank is investigating, but they haven't found anything because it looks like he did it himself. I love it when a target has no tech game because it makes things so easy. Like taking candy from a baby.

Based on the tone of his texts to his men, he's beyond angry about it, but I can't really blame him. If someone were stealing my money, freeing my prisoners, disrupting my ability to do business, and I didn't have a clue who it was, I'd be pissed, too.

Because of my skill, I'm able to strike my enemy without being harmed, stealing his valuables and getting away unscathed, like a modern way of counting coup. He's losing face and is powerless to stop it.

Hopefully, soon he'll be behind bars and unable to do anything because his loyal soldiers will have disbanded without him to keep them in line. Soldiers need a leader and Dang doesn't have any seconds to run the show for him if he's taken off the playing field. I doubt they'd be willing to follow his orders if he's giving them from prison.

I'm crawling through his system when I make a discovery. We cleared out the brothel in the City, but from his text messages, I discovered he had another and closed it down, moving the victims to another location.

Although I'd been searching for the location, I hadn't had any luck. Until now.

I take out my phone and send a message to Kieran. Rescuing trafficking victims is his wheelhouse, so I'll give the information to him and let him handle it.

Me: *Found the new target.*

I'm surprised when he texts me right back.

Kieran: *Excellent.*

Me: *Encrypted address coming right away. Be careful. BG on edge.*

Kieran: *You, too.*

We worked out some code for our communications early on. BG stands for bad guy, which is kind of comical because we're all bad to some degree. In this case, Dang is the badder bad guy and a common enemy for Kieran's group and mine...or me. I guess I'm still mostly a group of one. Or two if we count Cam, which I do.

In an effort to equip my allies, I also got Kieran's crew hooked up on my encryption software. Go me, because I didn't even include a backdoor to make it easy for me to hack into his phone and other systems.

Like it was with this relationship or whatever it is with Davis, the collaboration and alliance with Kieran and his crew was just easy. There's no physical attraction between us, but in my gut, I immediately knew Kieran was trustworthy.

The brothel where Dang moved everyone to is in Tulsa and that's why I couldn't find them in the City. That actually works out well because they're closer for Kieran's group to deal with.

With that taken care of, I check in on my spiders and am pleased they've found some juicy tidbits for me. The man who was talking to Bee's dad, Keegan, is named Ilia Starova. Unsurprisingly, he's mob. The surprising part is that he's Albanian mob.

What the hell is Keegan doing cozying up to the Albanians? The Italians with whom Keegan has alliances, namely Geno's family, hate the Albanians. It's a feud that goes back many generations.

Also, until recently, Starova was in Albania, so what is he doing here now? From what I can tell from surface searches, he was making quite a name for himself over there. Is he moving to the states now?

I need to do a deep dive on the man. When I next come up for air, it's because my phone buzzes with a text from Davis telling me he's on his way home from work. A thrill zings through me when I see it and I set aside my quest for information on my new target.

Is this what it would be like to be in an actual relationship with him? Would I get excited to see him any time we come back together after we've been apart, even if it's only been for a workday?

Somehow I doubt it. My parents were like that, but I don't think that's the norm. I work for a few more minutes, then shut down my computer and leave my apartment to cross the street to his.

He gave me the door code and a key to his front door before he left this morning. I'm still astonished by the level of trust he's putting in me. But then he seems to know that I'm not the sort to rob his apartment while he's at work.

I perch on the couch to wait, but my eyes are drawn to an elephant on the far side of the room. There's something mounted on the wall that Davis has covered with a sheet. Obviously, he doesn't want just anyone seeing it, so he covered it.

It must be some kind of secret project. Or maybe a case he's working on.

I turn on the television to distract myself, but my eyes are drawn back to the sheet. It was there last night, and I noticed it, but was a bit preoccupied with getting naked and getting him inside me.

This morning, everything was quick, and we were both headed out the door before I thought to ask. Then I got lost in work all day.

Now, curiosity is getting the best of me. Maybe I could take a peek before he gets here. I stand up and pace behind the couch, my fingers itching to lift the cloth.

Just a peek. No one has to know. He gave me a key, didn't he? For all he knows, I've been hanging out here all day, eating Cheetos on his couch and watching TV.

I step close to it. My hand reaches out and is brushing the fabric when the door swings open. I jump back as heat surges into my neck and face.

"Whatcha doin?" he asks, but he has a shit-eating grin on his face because he knows exactly what I was doing. Or was about to do.

I smack his arm. "You can't leave something like that there on the wall and expect people to not be curious."

After he drops his keys in a dish and sets down some bags of food, he pulls me into his arms and smooches loudly on my neck. "You know what they say about curiosity and cats."

I'm equal parts giggly imbecile and turned on as I snake my arms around his neck and press against him. "I missed you today," I admit.

"Missed you, too," he replies with his mouth close to my ear. "It killed me to stay at work all day knowing you were so close."

He kisses me below my ear, making me shiver like it always does. I turn my face to his and kiss him, welcoming him home. Home to me. We don't have long together, so I want to make the most of it.

When we step apart, he reaches out a hand and pulls down the sheet, then steps away to grab the bag of food and take it to the kitchen. While he unpacks containers, I try to contain the shock that courses through my veins like electricity.

I can only assume this is the possible serial killer case he said he's working on. The shock is because several of the incidents are mine. Several aren't, but my work is there, plastered all over the corkboard.

The siblings in North Carolina. The serial rapist in Idaho who started murdering his victims after a near-miss in court when one of his victims identified him.

He had enough money for a hotshot attorney who was able to discredit the victim. Discredit was putting it nicely. He might as well have raped her all over again, right there on the witness stand.

The foster parents in Arizona who pimped out the children they were supposed to be taking care of. South Dakota is there, too.

That was a man who would disable young native women's cars then show up like he was going to rescue them, only to take them out to a field and rape and murder them. He would leave them in the dirt and grass like they were trash. The knife scar on my thigh is from him.

Four other cases are up there, too, but they're not mine, so I study them to see what made him group them together. Does he know I'm responsible for some of these? Is this some sort of test? Is he hoping I'll incriminate myself?

I flinch when he touches my arm and hands me a plate of pasta. When I take it from him, he perches on the arm of the sofa with his own plate. "Sorry. Didn't mean to startle you?"

I wave my fork. "This is the serial killer thing you said you're working on?"

He nods as he puts a fork full of noodles into his mouth. "Yeah," he replies after he swallows.

"Why do you think it's a serial instead of just similar cases?"

CHAPTER TWENTY-NINE

A Fantastic Resource

DAVIS

"I'm not sure it is, but there are enough commonalities that it needs to be investigated."

She takes in the information. There's nothing on the board that couldn't be found by an excellent researcher, so I'm not concerned about her seeing it.

That thought makes me ask, "One of the things that is present in several of them is the use of a hacker. The family or someone close to a victim hires a hacker to help them dig up evidence that can be taken to law enforcement."

Because of who I believe her to be, she might be a fantastic resource for computer related questions. I'm mostly in the dark when it comes to what hackers are capable of these days.

Technology is something I've learned to use in specific ways and don't have a talent for anything beyond that.

"Did they take the information to the cops?"

"Sometimes."

"And did the cops do anything about it?"

I remember the inept, or possibly crooked, Sheriff in North Carolina. And a sigh slides up my throat. "Unfortunately, in all of these cases, no."

She turns and looks at me over her shoulder and raises an eyebrow. I frown and shrug, but don't respond.

Sometimes the ball is fumbled, especially when information is dropped into your lap with no idea of how someone else found what you couldn't. It throws a huge amount of shade over the credibility of the information.

"But someone was killed in all of these cases."

"Yeah." It pops out, but that's not exactly truthful. "No. Well, maybe."

Another questioning look over her shoulder and it's so god-damn sexy I want to go put my hands on her. She must see something in my face because her eyebrows wing up. "Maybe?"

"Several of the alleged perpetrators have disappeared. Their bank accounts are drained and they're just gone with no sign of where they might have disappeared to."

I let her continue to take in the information on the board, but can't let go of the idea of picking her brain, so I dive right in.

"I know hackers are more sophisticated than ever and I have no doubt that one is involved in many of these cases because of the depth of evidence that's been dug up. But draining bank accounts... How hard would something like that be?"

"Very. Banks are tricky because they have increased security. It would take a high level of finesse. Have you been able to trace the money once it leaves the primary account?"

"No. It appears that the individuals withdrew the money, but it's like it just disappears with the people. No ATM withdrawals. No transfers to other accounts. And no one shows up in person to collect it at a bank."

"That would require some extremely savvy hacking. There aren't many who could manage it."

"How many?"

She shrugs. "When I was a kid and just learning how to code, I kept up with lots of the nerds out there. Now, I just do what I do, which is mostly just being a data geek, and don't pay much attention to anyone else. As I'm sure you know, many hackers focus on malicious activities like terrorism or crashing financial systems. Those are mostly located in places like China, Turkey, Russia, and there are even a few here in the states."

She goes quiet and I can almost see the wheels turning in her head as she collates the information stored in that big brain of hers. A hand floats out and motions at the board.

"But this kind of stuff, it's only malicious to the bad guy. And to be a complete ghost, if that's what even happened... Ballpark, I'd say there are maybe a dozen or so worldwide, with forty percent of those being US based. However, it sounds like you're not just looking for a hacker, but a potential killer, too."

"Does that affect your estimate?"

"Yeah. Of those in the US, since they'd have to be here to be able to reach out and lay hands on their target, you're looking at three, maybe four people that I'm aware of who would be capable of killing. Like I said, though, there could be more out there and I just don't know who they are. Also, have you thought about a duo? A brains and brawn kind of thing?"

I take a moment to mull that idea over. It has merit, but my gut is telling me it's not. "Two people leaves more room for error. I don't think it's a duo, but it's a good thought."

With a shrug, she turns away from the board and takes her empty plate to the kitchen.

"So, three or four guys, then." I call after her. "I don't suppose you'd be willing to give me their names..."

A teasing grin spreads across her face as she walks back into the room, so before she can give me some bullshit smart ass answer, I say, "Never mind. Forget I even asked."

She kneels on the sofa behind me, rests her chin on my shoulder, and wraps her arms around my waist. The feel of her body pressed against mine is making me forget all about my hungry stomach.

Her breath is a warm caress on my neck as she says. "I wouldn't know their real names anyway, just hacker names. If you have an in at the NSA, I know they usually track the higher level hackers around the world. Maybe they can give you some insight."

"Nah. If I start finding threads to tie them together, I might, but I don't think there's enough there to say for sure they're all connected."

Soft lips press kisses on my neck, and my dick starts getting hard. Reverting to my days in the service when chow time was limited, I hoover up my food and clear my plate. She reaches up and takes it from me.

"More?"

I shake my head. "I'm good for now, but may get some more later to keep my stamina up if you put me through my paces again like you did last night."

With a smirk, she turns away to take my plate to the kitchen and tosses her comment over her shoulder, "Well, you are getting old."

Yeah, she's gonna pay for that. I thought she'd just go in and leave my plate, but she takes the time to put away the leftover food. When I start to go in and help her, she waves a hand. "I've got this."

It makes me feel good that she's comfortable enough here to just do what she wants. That's what I want. Because if she's comfortable here, she'll be more inclined to stay with me when she's in town.

I don't want any more hide and seek games where she tries to sneak in under the radar. If she's here, I want her with me. Maybe she'll feel the same way when I'm in Oklahoma, even though I don't get home as often as I'd like.

While she is in the kitchen, I cover the board back up because I don't want it to be a distraction for either of us. God knows I've spent enough time staring at it. Even so, I always seem to find something new, but the last thing I want to do with Rae is sit here looking at evidence.

It doesn't take me nearly as long as it does her, so I sit on the couch and let my head fall back against the cushion. I close my eyes, gritty after a day of staring at a computer screen, and wait for her.

Her solid weight settles on my lap as she straddles my legs. A chain reaction ripples through my body, from the smile that spreads on my face to the hardening of my dick to the way my hands automatically go to her hips and pull her close. It feels too good to rest my eyes, though, so I can't bring myself to open them.

"You look tired tonight," she observes as she starts dropping kisses along my jaw.

"Mmm. Someone kept me up half the night making up for lost time, then I spent the day staring at a computer screen."

"Sounds pretty much like my day... but I've heard energy levels and stamina decrease with age."

My hand smacks her luscious ass, and she giggles in response. The minx actually giggles! And it makes my cock strain even harder against the zipper of my jeans.

She rocks her hips against me, the furnace at her core driving me wild, and lets out a small groan. "It seems there's still a little life left in you, after all."

Her breath is hot against my neck when she puts her mouth to my ear and whispers huskily, "You just relax, bodach, and let me take care of you."

"What the hell does bodach mean?" I growl, my hand poised to give my ornery girl another smack on the ass.

"It means handsome..." she kisses the underside of my jaw.

"Sexy..." she slides off my lap and kneels between my legs.

"Hot..." she untucks my shirt, slides her hands underneath and strokes her palms up my torso before dragging her nails all the way back down, making my abs clench in response.

"Super smart..." her fingers land on the waist of my pants and undoes them, then she slips her hand inside and frees my engorged cock.

"Old man." Before I can protest, she swirls her tongue around the head of my cock and all thought vanishes from my mind as even more blood rushes to meet the sensations she's creating.

With her fingers wrapped around the base and her mouth licking and sucking the head and shaft, she works me and it feels fucking amazing. I tangle my fingers in her curls and flex my hips to meet her hot mouth.

Still unable to string together a thought, I urge her on with grunts and groans. Then she gives up playing with me and gets serious. She does that thing where she relaxes her throat and takes me in all the way over and over.

Her hand is stroking as she fucks me with her mouth. When I rock my hips in time with her, she puts her hands on my side to hold on as her head bobs in time with my thrusts. The sting of pain from her nails digging into my skin rockets me to the edge.

A moan crawls up her throat around my cock, creating a sensation of vibration to go with all the other sensations assaulting my senses. I bark out her name in warning before I lose myself.

She lets my cock slide out of her mouth with a pop before she grins up at me. "Might be old meat, but it tastes pretty good to me."

Loving how raw and real she is, I growl and hook my hands under her arms. I pull her onto my lap before I flip her so she's on her back underneath me. My fingers stroke over her ribs, making her laugh, and she squirms to get away from me, but I hold her in place.

Raspberries are blown on her cheeks and neck and then I kiss her neck where I know it makes her go all mushy. I follow that with a nip of my teeth, then lick it to soothe the sting, her dewy skin slightly salty from the workout she just performed on my dick.

There's a powerful need in me to leave my mark on her. I hesitate for the briefest of moments before I fold to the urge and give her a love bite. She gasps in response, which fills me with all kinds of satisfaction.

She likes to play it cool, like nothing matters to her, but I know better. Several times, she's given me a peek behind the façade, letting me see the longing she has for connection.

She thinks she's tough, and no doubt she is, but there's a giant marshmallow inside, too. I just have to figure out how to keep pulling down her walls at a speed that keeps her from running away.

Now that she's staying in one place, her excuse of always being on the road is invalid, but I think the distance between us will work in my favor. I'll make the most of our time together and get that hook set so that when we're apart, I can keep reeling her in bit by bit.

However, I have no clue what I'll do with her once I have her. Long-term relationships have never been my thing, but I just know that there's something there and I want to give it every chance I can to go where it will.

Chapter Thirty

Not the Same Woman

Cam

Rae has been in Boston for two days and I wonder if she's seen whatever it was she was supposed to see. Even if she has, I hope she stays for a few days more. This man she will be spending time with is part of her future, so it's important they have an opportunity to connect more deeply than they have so far.

Exactly what that means, I don't know. It may come to me at a future date, or maybe not at all. My so-called gift can be a real pain in the arse sometimes.

Muscles I didn't know I had are aching after the workout and training regimen Finn has been putting us through. But I have to admit I'm feeling stronger and more confident in my abilities.

I don't think I'm anywhere near to being the badass that Rae is. Yet. A little more training and more real-world experience and I might not be half bad.

Most of my experience in the real world was successful because my stature made them underestimate me. Whatever tools I have in my arsenal, I'll use them even if it's another person's assumptions.

"Think we can make a run to the grocery store this afternoon?" Joelle asks.

I'm toweling off the sweat and still trying to steady my breathing after my round with Finn, but manage an answer. "Sure. I'll just need to shower first."

"Me, too," Tori adds. Her one-on-one with Finn was just before mine, and I notice she's limping a little.

"Maybe you need to take an ice bath instead."

"I can do that when we get back. My sessions online don't start until six."

"Come on," I say and hold out my hand to her. "Let's go get cleaned up."

Jo sighs. "See you in a couple of hours."

"What's that mean?" Tori laughs.

Waggling a finger between us, Joe replies, "You two showering together is going to turn into shower sex, and then I'll still have to wait for you to get ready."

Tori and I look at each other and laugh.

"What's so funny?" Bee asks from where she's across the room, talking to Finn and scowling at us.

"Shower sex," Tori and I reply together, then start laughing again.

When the giggles pass, I add, "We're making a grocery run with Jo in a few hours if you'd like to come with."

She holds my eyes for long moments, then shakes her head. "No, thanks."

I know she doesn't like my relationship with Rae. But she really doesn't like what is going on between Tori and me.

Although I've tried to draw her into interactions with Tori and Jo, she's maintained her distance. I know she believes that soon this will all be over and we'll be headed back to Boston. Once that's done, she'll get on with living her happily ever after and won't need me to keep her entertained anymore.

Rather than wait until she tosses me aside after she's married, I've decided I'm skipping to the part where she doesn't need me and getting on with my own happily ever after. Hopefully, with Tori.

I want to ask her where she sees this going. She might just be having fun and I'm getting all invested in dreaming of something more long term.

It's not that I'm too chicken-hearted to bring it up or anything because I'm afraid of what the answer might be.

Seriously.

It's not.

When her lips meet mine as we let the hot water of the shower run over us, all thoughts of anything but being with her vanish.

An hour and a half later, we're in the car heading into Oklahoma City. Jo has it in mind to make something out of the ordinary, so we're going to a different grocery store in the Asian district to get the ingredients and spices she needs.

I've never been to such a place, so we take our time roaming the aisles and looking at all the interesting items. A young man appears at the end of the aisle and something about him sends a squadron of spider's feet down my spine.

He has a basket in his hand with several items inside, so he appears to be just another shopper. However, I don't like the way he's looking at Jo and Tori.

I want to say something to the others, but I don't want to frighten them so I hold my peace. With ears straining and eyes constantly moving, I follow my charges through the rest of the store.

Since Rae's not here, it's up to me to keep them safe and I will do my damndest to do so. Maybe I'm just reading something that isn't there, but I've learned to trust my instincts and they are screaming at me that danger is lurking.

Nothing else happens in the store and I don't see the guy again. We stop and get a round of boba teas for each of us, and it's uneventful. Finally, we're on our way back to the house and I'm breathing easier.

It was just my imagination. A possibility that could have gone one way or another and it went in our favor for once. I relax back into the seat and join Jo in laughing at a story Tori is telling when she stops speaking.

"What?" I query at the abrupt interruption.

"I think we're being followed."

Twisting around in the back seat, I look out the window. There is a car back there. It's not close, but near enough to track where we're going. The darkling day makes it difficult to get a clear view of the vehicle.

What would Rae do in this situation? She'd lead him into a trap, say something snarky, then either beat him up or kill him, depending on who it turned out to be.

We're approaching our turn and just as Tori is reaching for the blinker, I bark out, "Don't turn. We don't want to lead him to the house. Go straight."

Bee and I have driven the roads around the house about a million times in our driving practice, so I've gotten to know them well. While watching the car out the rear window, I give directions to Tori.

"Um... You really want me to go in here? It's deserted."

"I do, and I want you to drive all the way to the back. There's a cul-de-sac and he will likely pin us in there."

"You *want* him to catch us?" Jo's voice is full of incredulity.

"Yes. There's only one of him and three of us. If we're lucky, he hasn't let anyone know he spotted us."

We found this location on one of our driving outings. It appears to be an abandoned residential development that has been turned into a party place by locals. There is broken glass, empty beer cans, and heaps of trash everywhere.

They look at each other, and some silent communication passes between them. I don't know what they shared, but Tori does as I requested.

We need to find out who he is, what he wants, and who he's working for. We need to know if this is about Rae or something else. Well, I need to know. Tori and Jo probably think I'm insane.

Tori swings into the cul-de-sac and makes it look like she made a mistake. I could kiss her, but now is not the time. As expected, he angles his car so we can't get past.

"Stay calm inside, but act scared on the outside," I tell them.

"Sure. I'm about to pee my pants from fear and you think I can be calm anywhere?" Jo mutters.

"Remember," I tell her. "You're not the same woman you were a couple of weeks ago."

She nods and takes a deep breath just as the lanky Asian man from the grocery store wrenches her door open. Jo screams and swats at the man's reaching hands.

"Get outta tha car, bitch!" he yells. "All you bitches! Out!" He wraps his fingers around Jo's wrist and pulls her out.

"Calm," I hiss at them. "Get him talking."

Tori flings open the driver's door, but instead of being afraid, she is roiling with anger. "Who are you? What do you want?"

The man turns to her and grins evilly, revealing a metal grill over his front teeth. It's not a good one, either. "I'm tha repo man. Gonna return this little bitch to my boss. Then when

I bring him two extra fresh bitches, he's gonna give me a big reward."

He says it like re-ward and I can't help but roll my eyes. Jo pulls against his grip and Tori goes to her aid. She digs her fingernails into the hand around Jo's wrist and starts cursing at him in Spanish while also kicking at his shins.

The two women have his full attention, and I notice when Tori cuts her eyes to me in a silent plea to do something. I think we know what we need to, so I quietly move up behind him. He seems to have dismissed my presence completely, which is fine by me.

I slip my hand beneath my skirt and silently pull the knife out of the sheath on my thigh. He's too tall for me to reach his neck, so I reassess. I could either try to climb him like a monkey up a tree or hit a different vulnerable point.

Climbing trees isn't something I have any experience with, so it's either femoral artery or kidneys. One would be very messy, but the other would require me to get close to make an accurate execution. When he raises a hand to let it fly to hit Tori, my time for debating is over.

I step close, wrap my arm around his waist to get some leverage, and before he can turn to see what's going on, I jab the knife into his kidney. Quick as I can, I pull it out and thrust it into his side, up under his rib cage and into his heart.

"Wha tha...?"

I let him go, and he stumbles a few feet away before falling to his face on the filthy, trash strewn pavement. A dark stain of blood spreads through his shirt and pools on the ground, looking black in the dim light.

"Go to the car." I tell them before going to the fallen man. Now that he's not on his feet, just to be sure he doesn't survive because I botched the job and missed my target, I poke my blade into the side of his neck to pierce the artery.

I take a step back, away from the flow of blood, and bend over to clean my blade on his shirt. Then I turn to the other car and move it enough to allow Tori to get her car out of the cul-de-sac.

After I wipe down everything I touched and give a quick once over for any hairs on the headrest or seat, I get an idea. The car is an old piece of shit and it's full of trash. It could have been a gorgeous classic if the jerk had taken care of it and restored it.

Instead, it's got a primer gray hood and rear quarter panel and several rust spots on other parts of the outside. Inside, there are empty energy drink cans everywhere, as well as empty fast food wrappers and bags in the footwell.

I take one of the paper sacks and twist it a little to make a denser fuse. With the hem of my skirt as a barrier, I push in the cigarette lighter and wait.

Tori rolls down the window. "Come on already!"

I hold up a finger and wait a few breaths more until the lighter pops. Holding it to the paper, I nurture the connection of heat and fuel until the paper flames, then I toss both into the pile of trash on the floorboard of the passenger side.

Leaping out of the car, I slam the door shut and hurriedly wipe away any prints on the outside. After a quick race to Tori's car, I jump inside.

"Go! But no lights." Glancing back over my shoulder, I see the glow of flames licking the interior of the car and growing larger.

She frowns, but does as I say. There's enough ambient light that she's able to navigate fine, her dark car gliding through the night like a wraith.

We don't meet any traffic on the road, so I wait until we're back to the intersection where I told her not to turn and give her the go ahead to turn the headlights on and take us home.

CHAPTER THIRTY-ONE

This Life Isn't For Everyone

CAM

When I wake to find Tori packing her bag the next morning, I'm not surprised. After what happened with the man who followed us to his death, she was quiet. For the first time, we went to bed without making love.

When she slid into bed and turned her back to me without even so much as a kiss, I figured I'd served her more than she could handle when I took that man's life. I'm not sorry I did it. If I were faced with the same situation again, I'd do the same thing.

There's nothing I won't do to keep those I love safe and leading him to our home to cower behind the walls hoping someone else deals with the threat... Well, I've never wanted to be that person.

"You're leaving?" I ask.

"Yeah, I need to go home for a few days."

That doesn't make any sense. If she's just going back to her place, why would she say it's just for a few days? Is she trying to let me down easy? Step away for a few days, then tell me it's over?

"Home? To your apartment?"

"No. Home to my parent's house in Lawton."

She mumbles something about her sister sending a text, and her being needed because of something or other. Her sister didn't give her a clear picture of what exactly was going on.

"I'm so sorry. Is there anything I can do?"

She shakes her head, her silky hair swaying. "No. Like I said, I'm not sure myself what's going on."

"Okay," I say, trying to keep my voice level and not let the ache in my chest bleed through.

I knew it was too good to be true. It's better that she ends things now because I was falling hard for her, but I know this life isn't for everyone.

Most people are either born into it or forced into it. Living the mob life isn't something the majority of people would choose willingly. Not even Rae's cleaner, more righteous version of organized crime.

Her goal isn't to gain power at any cost, but to do away with the worst of humanity to make it a better place. Sometimes only monsters can kill the worst monsters. Rae is willing to become that. And I'm willing to help her.

If Tori doesn't want to be part of it, I totally understand. Her walking away only means that she wasn't the one for me, even if her leaving does feel like a gaping wound is cracking open in my chest.

I get out of bed to dress for the day while she finishes packing everything into the suitcase she'd brought it all here in. Rather than hang around for the dismantling of her presence here, I leave her to it and go downstairs. Watching it is too painful.

Just as I reach the bottom of the stairs, my phone rings. It's early and not a number I recognize, but I answer anyway. When I hang up, I'm glad I did.

The contractor who is slated to do the construction in the basement finished up another job early and has a crew ready to start this afternoon. That's excellent news because, according to Rae, a shipment that will need to be stored in the weapons room is arriving soon, but the room hasn't been built yet and we can't exactly leave multiple weapons just lying around everywhere.

Also, the communications room and additional bedrooms need to be completed ASAP. Rae doesn't think we need to be in any hurry on those items, but I have a feeling we're going to need them sooner than later.

While I talk to the contractor, I make my way to the kitchen where Jo is working on breakfast. Finn is in his usual position at the kitchen island, reading the newspaper. Bee is nowhere in sight, so she's probably still in bed.

Just as I disconnect the call, the clack, clack, clack sound of Tori's suitcase wheels rolling over the stone floor of the foyer echoes down the hall. My throat constricts and I'm glad the call is over because I don't think I'd be able to speak anymore.

She appears in the doorway, so in an attempt to calm my racing heart and disperse the moisture gathering in my eyes, I turn my back and focus on making myself a cup of coffee.

Jo looks up from whatever she's stirring in a bowl for breakfast. Her confusion is obvious when she asks, "Where are you going?"

"I need to go home to help with some family stuff for a few days."

"Oh," Jo replies, but I'm not sure she believes Tori any more than I do. Without another word, she goes back to mixing.

My skin prickles with awareness and I know Tori is standing close. Her hands grip my hips as her warm breath skims across my neck before she whispers in my ear. "I'll call you."

"Mmm hmm."

Her fingers flex tighter, as if she is going to apply pressure to turn me, but after a moment's hesitation, she kisses the side of my neck. The warmth of her touch disappears, and the room turns colder as she leaves it.

"What happened?" Jo asks me when the heavy front door thuds behind Tori.

"I guess me killing that guy last night was more than she could handle."

"What did you say?" Finn snaps.

I turn around and lean back against the counter, still staring into my coffee mug as if it will yield the answer to some great mystery. The coffee doesn't speak to me, so I start talking.

"Yesterday in the grocery store, one of Dang's men spotted Jo, then followed us when we left. Rather than lead him back here, we led him to that abandoned residential development we've used as a turnaround during driving lessons. He tried to take Jo, so while she and Tori distracted him, I snuck up behind him and killed him."

He scowls at me, and I know that's a demand for more information.

"I stabbed him in the kidney and up under his ribs, where I probably hit his heart. Since I wasn't sure I hit my mark, once he fell on the ground, I punched a hole in the side of his neck just to make sure he bled out."

I take a sip of coffee, then remember to add, "Oh, and then I set his car on fire."

Finn sighs and goes back to reading the newspaper.

"Well, I, for one, am glad you did it," Jo says. "Breakfast will be ready in about thirty."

"Thank you, but I'm not hungry."

"Okay..." Just as I reach the door to the hallway, Jo adds, "She'll be back."

"Hmmm..." I respond noncommittally as I take my coffee and go back up to my room.

To prepare for the meeting with the contractor, I want to review the original construction documents Rae approved. What I really want to do is crawl back into bed, but I have work to do.

Under the covers, I could lick my wounds and try to stuff all these feelings into a box deep inside me. But Rae's not here and she needs me to stand in her stead and facilitate the work that needs to be done, so I'll focus on what needs to be done and put off dealing with the hurt until later.

CHAPTER THIRTY-TWO

White Diamonds Tinged with Chili Powder

VICTORIA

After I pull the door closed behind me, I hurry to my car, where I crank up the radio and race away, trying to outrun the chasm opening up in my chest. I know Bridget thinks I'm running away from her, and that's how it might end, but she's done nothing wrong.

Once I get myself sorted, I'll make sure she knows that regardless of where our relationship goes... Or doesn't.

The drive to Lawton is made in record time. My parents aren't expecting me and I didn't call to let them know I was coming, so Mama's exclamation of "Mija!" when I step through the back door isn't a surprise.

If I'd called ahead, it would have only been at half the volume. She hurries over me and wraps me in a hug, the smell of White Diamonds perfume tinged with chili powder washes over me and brings a boatload of nostalgia with it.

Tears well and I can't blink them away before Mama pulls back, puts the palms of her hands to my cheeks, and looks me in the face. Her expression softens. "Ah mija! Qué es esto?"

My fingers wrap around her wrists. "It's nothing, Mama. I was just missing you, so I thought I'd come home for a few days."

Her eyes narrow. She's not buying my lame brush off, but it's all I've got. I can't exactly tell her the truth. After another round of scrutiny, she releases my cheeks from her death grip.

"Are you hungry?"

"No. I got some breakfast on the way here." I got an extra-large coffee, sucked it down on the way here, and was counting it as breakfast. If I'd tried to eat anything, I probably would have had to pull over to throw it up on the side of the road.

She goes back to tending whatever was on the stove. "You need to eat more. You're too skinny." It's like a mantra with her every time she sees me. She says I'm too skinny and spends all my time here trying to stuff food into my mouth.

"Anyway," I say. "I know you've got to get to the office, but I wanted to stop by to let you know I'm in town."

Mama is the Executive Director of a local non-profit that works with at risk youth. Her organization teaches them life skills they don't learn at home.

Their topics cover a variety of topics. They do everything from driving lessons for those that can't afford to pay for it to how to change a tire and balance a checkbook.

Resumes, job interviews, completing paperwork for scholarship applications for college and trade school, and on and on. Essentially, they're the most knowledgeable resource center any kid could ever need.

And that's just the practical life stuff. There are counselors and attorneys that volunteer their time to provide help with even more when needed.

I was extremely lucky to have two loving and devoted parents who did everything they could to help us thrive and prepare us to face the world. They also raised us to understand that not everyone is so lucky. We didn't have a lot of money, but we were rich in love.

"You're not staying here?" Although she's trying to cover it, disappointment rings in her tone.

"Mama, I know how busy you and Papa are, and the last thing you need is me being underfoot. I'm on my way to Esther's but I'll be back for supper tonight."

In an attempt to soothe her wounded ego, I put my arms around her from behind and kiss the side of her head. I'm not staying at my sister's house either because I wouldn't be able to work from either location, and I have several appointments over the next week.

All I get is a grunt in response. She's disappointed, but I'll make good on my promise to be at supper tonight. I'll also starve myself until then, so I have plenty of room to eat enough to make Mama happy.

The drive to my older sister's house only takes ten minutes. She works from home, so I wasn't worried about getting here in time to catch her before she left for the office. Her commute consists of rolling out of bed in her pajamas, walking down the hall to their spare bedroom, and firing up her computer.

She does something with corporate health insurance and spends most of her day fielding calls and emails. Even though she mostly took the job because it allowed her to stay home with her two children, it suits her need to take care of people, something she inherited from Mama.

Her door swings open, and she immediately turns away, walking back toward her office. She has a headset on and is talking to someone, who I can only assume is a client, because she's using words like short-term disability and FMLA that are pretty much Greek to me.

Her crisp lavender button-down shirt tops lime green Scooby Do pajama bottoms and fuzzy bunny slippers. Left with no other choice, I follow her, closing the door behind me.

In my yoga pants, sneakers, and fuzzy sweater, I feel a little overdressed as I sit in a comfy chair in her office and watch as she taps on her keyboard and keeps talking with the person on the line. Ten minutes later, she says her goodbyes, then spins in her chair to face me.

"You have ten minutes before I have to be on a video call. What's wrong?"

I flinch. "Why do you think something's wrong?"

"You haven't been home for months and suddenly, you show up unannounced. Mom says you're not staying with her and as much as I know the kids would love to have you here, the last time you slept on Mari's bed, you said you'd never do it again. That means you're not staying here, either."

"So, again, why does that mean something's wrong? Just because I choose to stay in a hotel, it doesn't mean something's wrong. I was just homesick and wanted to come visit, but if it's going to be some big hoopla when I do, maybe I won't."

She levels her Mom Look at me. "If you came more often, it wouldn't be such a big hoopla. Crap."

That last throws me until she spins in her chair back to face the computer screen on her desk. She must have gotten a call. "I have exactly two minutes before I have to jump on a meeting. What's up?"

The calls last for the entire two minutes before she cuts them off and expertly switches screens from whatever it was on to a new one, then a screen opens with people's faces in squares all over it.

While she's saying good morning to all of them, I rise and leave the room so I don't accidentally overhear something I shouldn't. When working with people's personal health information, there's a lot of private stuff that gets thrown around.

I go across the hall to her daughter, Marianna's room and flop back on the bed. Even though I try to distract myself with my phone, it's too quiet. There's too much time to kill and too much quiet that my mind wants to fill with thoughts of Bridget.

When the room shakes, I startle awake. It's not the entire room, just my sister being an asshole and bouncing her butt on the bed like she's a twelve-year-old at a sleepover, spoiling for a pillow fight. My scowl doesn't intimidate her at all because she grins over at me.

After tossing and turning all night last night, I shouldn't be surprised that I fell asleep. Maybe I will be able to check into my room early and take another nap before I have to work, then come back to face the parents over dinner.

"So," Esther says, her grin gone now, "what's up?"

I throw one of the five hundred and two pillows on Mari's bed at my sister. She catches it and hugs it to her chest.

"I told you, nothing. Classes are stressful. I've been working a lot and just needed a break."

"Bullshit."

Most of the time, I love my family, but at times like these, when they see through me like a pane of glass, I find them extremely irritating. Although I can't exactly tell her the root of what's bothering me, I can tell her some of it.

"I've met someone."

Her face transforms from her attempt at an intimidating scowl to a look of avid expectation. "What's his name?"

"Her name is Bridget." My family believes me to be bi-sexual because I've dated men and women.

She doesn't know that other than losing my virginity to, then fooling around with, Bobby Cooper in high school, my forays with the opposite sex have been primarily financial arrangements. I've told her I'm attracted to women, but those experiences were mostly short and sexual in nature. Until Bridget.

Although our relationship has been both short and sexual, there's more to it under the surface. However, before I can let myself fall all the way down the rabbit hole, I need to make some decisions. Even though I'm halfway to the bottom already.

"Tell me all about her."

This is something I love about my family. They have always accepted me for just who I am.

While my older sister was an athlete, class president, and hardworking in all things, they never viewed me as less than when I was the flighty, artistic dreamer. The fact that I still worked hard and got excellent grades probably helped.

"She's amazing. She's beautiful and smart and funny even though she doesn't try to be and one of those super solid people you can just count on to have your back."

"So, what's the problem?"

I roll my eyes. "Again, with the assumptions! There's no problem."

"If you say so. What does she do?"

Knowing the question would come up, I thought about how to respond. After all, I can't exactly tell them she's the right hand to a wannabe mafia kingpin who goes around making the world a better place and killing anyone who crosses her skewed sense of right and wrong.

I decided it would be best to borrow from what Rae herself told me was her job. "She works in her cousin's business, which is data management and research."

"Ooo...that sounds interesting."

"If you ask Bridget, she'd tell you it's mostly boring." Deciding it's time to change the subject, I ask, "How are Mari and TJ doing?"

Her face goes all soft and glowy like it always does when she talks about her kids. She tells me all about their activities and school performance. TJ is turning into quite the basketball player, even though his dad is hoping he'll switch to baseball at some point.

Her husband Tomas played baseball in college before he joined the Air Force and thinks their son Tomas, Jr., who we all call TJ, is destined to be a star pitcher. So far, he's been encouraging in whatever sport TJ wants to play because if he tried to bully TJ to switch, Esther would eviscerate him.

Esther and her husband met while he was stationed at the base here in Lawton. In short order, they fell in love.

So even though they were young, when he was going to be transferred to a base in England for a cooperative training program, she accepted his offer of marriage and went with him.

They were there for almost a year before returning to Oklahoma with baby TJ, who is now almost thirteen.

Two years later, Marianna was born. When his term of service was up, Tomas left the military and transitioned into civilian life.

He now works out at the base as a civilian employee, so is able to have the best of both worlds. He can be there every day for his family and still be able to serve his country, even though he's no longer enlisted.

We eat lunch together. Well, she eats lunch and I munch on a few carrots, telling her I need to save my calories for dinner with our parents. She just nods in understanding.

When she goes back to her office, I call the hotel to see if I can check in. They have a room ready for me, so I go to my sister's office and wait for her to end her current call to tell her I'm leaving.

"Like I said, I'm going to supper at the rents tonight, but if you can't make it, I'll be around for a few days."

"A few days as in long enough to go to mass on Sunday? If so, we'll have family lunch together then. That means Mama and Papa can have you to themselves tonight, you can come here tomorrow night, and then a family meal with everyone on Sunday."

I let out a put-upon sigh. "Yeah, I can stay until Sunday lunch."

"Perfecto! I'll see you tomorrow night. The kids are going to be ecstatic to see their tia."

Another call comes in, so I blow her an air kiss, which she catches and pulls to her heart before answering. I leave feeling warm all over, but not quite warm enough to dispel the lump of cold lodged around my heart.

It's been a while since I've been home, so I drive around town to see what's changed and what remains the same. Since I'll be here a few days, I swing through the grocery store to pick up a few things.

After an hour-long nap, and almost as long getting ready, I log into the system to have a session with a client. I probably should have skipped the nap because now I'm bleary eyed and have a pillow crease on one cheek, which makeup didn't disguise very well.

My client doesn't seem to notice anything. Like most of them, he was too fixated on my tits to notice much else.

Because of what happened with Jojo, I refused to go back to Cassandra's so buying her out in a few years is off the table. Her place was all I'd known of that type of club, but the realization of just how she runs the place put me off that idea, anyway.

Even if I took over, chances are clients would expect the same laxness in response to their misbehavior. That's not something I want.

I want something different; something better.

CHAPTER THIRTY-THREE

Ruined Me For Anything Else

CAM

The crew with Master's Construction arrived yesterday afternoon and got to work. After a volley of texts between Rae and me, she informed me she was willing to pay extra if the job was done ahead of schedule.

I told her I'd inserted completion bonuses into the contract because I felt she'd want them in and out quickly once they were able to start. She sent me a kissy face emoji, which I took as approval, and that was the end of that.

The emoji made me think of Tori and my heart did a stupid stutter step. I haven't heard from her since she left.

For the last thirty-two hours and eleven minutes, I've been trying to purge her from my mind. Needless to say, I haven't been that successful, even with the construction to focus on.

The construction supervisor, a young Latino man named Alejandro who looks to be only a few years older than me, seems efficient. Best of all, he doesn't ask questions about what the room with all the cabinetry and steel lockers, or the room with the upscale electrical supply, will be used for.

Instead of a dorm with bunk beds, I convinced Rae to build out individual rooms with Jack and Jill bathrooms, each with their own vanity and toilet, and a shared shower. That way, anyone staying overnight will have some privacy for their off time, which will give them space to decompress.

We have the space to put in six bedrooms using that format. I don't know that we'll ever need all of them, but while we're building, we might as well include them. Even with the change in plans, there's room for a small kitchen and break room.

Jo spends the day in the kitchen, avoiding the workers coming and going. They're mostly using the basement entrance from the garage instead of coming through the house, but I also notice that Finn spends most of the day in the kitchen, too.

Even Bee seems to be averse to having any contact with them, but she spends her time in the media room watching movies on the big screen. Of course, she tries to coax me into the room with her, but I'd rather have my mind focused than free to wander and wonder about Tori.

At the end of the day, I send progress photos to Rae and recap the day's activities. For a moment, I feel so lonely and am tempted to call her, but I don't want to take away from her brief respite from having to oversee things here. She's going to be very busy when she gets back, so she needs this break.

I go to my room and ready myself for bed, but I can't bring myself to sleep in it without Tori. Even though I'm exhausted, I go downstairs to the kitchen and find Jo there.

When I enter the room, she looks up and smiles. "Can't sleep?"

"Something like that."

"Me, either. I think it was all the people roaming around here today. Even though I know it's completely ridiculous, some small part of my brain keeps picturing one of them popping out of a closet or from behind a closed door."

"I'm sorry."

She shrugs. "Don't be. It's just part of recovery. I know beyond the shadow of a doubt that I'm safe here and if one of them did try to do something like that, Finn, or you, or Rae would make sure they never did anything like that again. If I keep working with Finn, soon, I'll be able to protect myself like that."

I open the refrigerator door and peer inside, but nothing appeals to me, so I close it and sigh.

"You didn't eat much of your supper. If you're hungry, I can fix you something. Or I was just making myself some hot cocoa to ward off the chill from the cold front moving through."

"Hot cocoa sounds wonderful. Thank you."

She puts some milk on to heat, then takes a bunch of ingredients out of the cabinet. Leave it to Jo to make hot cocoa from scratch instead of using those powder packets like I usually do.

After several glances my way, I say, "If you want to say something, just say it. You don't have to walk on eggshells with me."

She smiles down at the milk she's stirring. "She'll be back, you know."

"Like I said, I think what happened with that guy from the grocery store was too much for her."

"I don't think that's it."

"Even if you're right, she's still gone and I haven't heard a peep from her. It's not much of a relationship if the other person runs away instead of sticking around to talk things out."

Rather than responding right away, she pours the milk into two mugs, taking her time with it.

"Whipped cream?"

I shake my head and take the mug from her.

"I understand you're feeling hurt. But when she comes back, I hope you're willing to hear her out instead of just closing the door in her face."

The cocoa is rich and silky and a million times better than those powder packets. She's ruined me for anything but made from scratch now. When she sets a plate of cookies in front of me, I take one and nibble on it.

"Thanks, Jo. I'll keep that in mind."

"I've seen her with several people over the past year. She was always holding the strings and holding back. There was no holding back with you. I've never seen her so over the moon about someone."

"And yet, she's gone."

Without waiting for her to answer, I take my mug and cookie and head for the stairs. By the time I get back up to my room, the cookie has turned to sawdust in my mouth. If this is what relationships are like, I was better off never having had one.

Instead of getting into bed, I grab a throw blanket and curl up on the chaise lounge in the corner of the room. Maybe I'll move to the room Bee's been using once she goes back to Boston because this one holds too many memories.

CHAPTER THIRTY-FOUR

Go All Mama Bear

VICTORIA

Esther hands me a margarita in a glass the size of my head. I take it from her, trying not to spill as my squirmy niece snuggles against my side.

After supper last night, I was so stuffed with Mama's excellent food, I thought my belly was going to pop. She was happy, though, and seeing her smile was worth the heartburn.

Tonight, Tomas took the helm at the grill, despite it being in the forties outside. Instead of being over stuffed, I'm pleasantly full of a juicy cheeseburger and my sister's infamous potato salad.

Now we're relaxed in their living room and I'm feeling equal parts mildly buzzed and like I'm slipping into a food coma. "If I drink this, I'm not going to be able to drive."

Esther gives me a smug look. "Well, you can always sleep on the couch since you don't like Mari's bed."

"What's wrong with my bed?" Mari pouts.

"Nothing," I say, tapping between her eyebrows to stop her from scowling. "It's perfect for you, but doesn't fit me so well."

"Oh," she replies, and tries to snuggle closer. Her eyes are drooping, so I resume lightly stroking my nails over her arm, a sure-fire way to lull her to sleep.

"How are your classes going?"

"Good. I'm on track to complete the Master's program in May."

"You still going for a Phd next?"

"I'm not sure. It feels as if I've been going to school forever and, frankly, I'm tired. However, I know if I take a break, it's unlikely I'll ever go back, so it is probably now or never."

"Understandable."

Tomas comes toward me and takes a now sleeping Mari from my side. He picks her up like she doesn't weigh any more than a rag doll. She turns into him, resting her head against his shoulder, and I'm struck with such tenderness.

"Come on, TJ, time for bed."

"Aww, Dad."

Tomas gives his son a look. That's all it takes. Just a look and the boy does as he's told.

He rolls his eyes while doing it, but he does it. I hide my smile. At least I thought I did, but when I look up, my nephew is grinning at me.

That one is going to be a handful. He's not even a teenager yet, and he's already as ornery as can be.

When they're out of the room, Esther asks, "So, are you ready to tell me what's up?"

"You are like a dog with a bone."

She sits back in her chair and takes a drink of her margarita. "You say that as if it's something I should be ashamed of."

I sit back, too, determined to be stubborn, and take a drink of my margarita. When she levels her mom look at me, I crack, just a little bit. Staring at my glass, I ask in barely more than a whisper. "How far would you go to protect those you love?"

"All the way," she answers without hesitation.

That shocks me. Of all the things I thought she might say, that wasn't one of them. She must read it in my face because she leans forward and tilts her drink at me, dangerously close to slopping lime green goodness all over her hardwood floors.

"You might think it's just the tequila talking, but it's not. If someone hurts my family, I'll go full on mama bear on them and rip them to shreds. I also know that Tomas would help me hide the body and he's fantastic at that kind of shit."

"Hidden a lot of bodies together, have you?" I tease.

She settles back in her chair again, looking smug. "You have no idea."

I slide onto the pew next to Mama just a few minutes after the start of the early morning mass. She reaches out and takes my hand in hers, squeezing it tight, and I lean my head on her shoulder in response.

While my body goes through the motions ingrained in my muscle memory since childhood, my mind is a hundred miles away.

After Esther's mama bear comment, I did a lot of thinking. Then I did some more thinking yesterday around client appointments and going shopping for something appropriate to wear to mass this morning.

The reason I was late this morning is because I was up until the early morning hours planning. I took out a notebook and started writing out a renewed vision for the future.

I just hope I haven't completely blown it with one of the essential elements for my happily ever after.

After the service, we gather at my parent's house for lunch. This was my favorite part of Sundays when I was growing up. Holding hands around the table while Papa said grace. Breaking bread and sharing our lives.

Papa listens with rapt attention as Mari tells him about her science project and how she got second place by creating a water cycle demonstration in a jar and documenting her observations. He was the same way with Esther and me.

TJ gives a play-by-play of his last basketball game, mostly for my benefit because everyone else at the table was there in the stands cheering him on. There is an abundance of love and acceptance in my parent's home. Always has been.

Sometimes I miss living here, close to my family. But as accepting as they are, I don't think they'd understand what I do for a living.

They think I'm a corporate party planner. Albeit, a well paid one, but planning parties is much preferable to having them know I'm a sex worker, even if it is all online. Having cyber sex with my clients would be just as bad as actual sex for pay. They're accepting, but I think that is one step too far.

When Esther and Tomas make their move to leave later that afternoon, I do, too. It's time for me to go back to the City to see if I have any hope of salvaging things with Bridget.

Thankfully, Esther didn't bring up the topic of Bridget to my parents. It would be a shame to get their hopes up that I'm finally in a serious relationship only to dash them if I can't manage to make things right.

Hugs and kisses are given out liberally, but eventually I make it to my car. And no, I'm not the least bit teary-eyed about leaving home. But I do make a commitment to myself to come home more often.

Part of me is surprised that my gate code still works. Rae must not be home yet to have changed it.

I leave my things in the car. No sense taking everything out, only to have to put it all back in there if I'm not able to convince Bridget to forgive me for taking off the way I did.

Jo is in the kitchen and seems to be the only one home. "Hi there!" she exclaims when she sees me. "About time you got your butt back home."

"Where is everyone?"

"Bridget went with Finn and Bee to pick Rae up at the airport. They should be back any minute."

My throat feels dry, so I get a glass from the cabinet, then fill it with water from the refrigerator door. I drink half of it down before asking what I most want and am afraid to know.

"How is she?"

"Hurt."

A thousand replies jumble in my mind, but they're all excuses. I messed up, but in the moment, I didn't know what else to do. All I knew was that my instant affinity to the darkness scared me and I needed a hot minute to get my head on straight about it.

Chapter Thirty-Five

I Don't Cry

Rae

This little lust bubble Davis and I have had going on for the past several days had to come to an end. We both knew it was temporary, so we tried to make the most of the time we had.

When I told him on Friday that I'd need to fly home Sunday, he seemed to take it in stride, but I could tell he was disappointed. We'd already been sexing it up practically around the clock when we weren't working, but after I gave him that news, it seemed he wanted to pour everything of himself into every interaction.

If I'm honest, I did, too.

Why were things so easy with Davis, the one man who was light years too good for me? Literally. His goodness fed his drive in his work and he excelled.

When I first looked him up, I merely saw that he was an FBI agent and didn't go further. That was damning enough. While I was across the street working and he was in his office, I took another look.

His record is exemplary, and he's received multiple commendations. He could probably request any assignment he wanted, and they'd give it to him. It took some finagling, because I like to stay out of government data bases as much as possible, but I gained access to his military record only to discover another roster of glowing performances.

He was so good at it that I wondered why he left. There was no way for me to ask without divulging how I discovered the information.

Although he knows I'm a hacker, he doesn't know the depth of my skill and I'm fine with leaving him in the dark and letting him go off assumptions. For some reason, the powers that be always seem to think that only someone with a dick would be skilled enough to be the best hackers.

I'm not going to disabuse them of their patriarchal idiocy.

"You sure you can't stay longer?" Davis queries as we pull up to the private terminal where my plane is waiting.

"I wish I could, but there's a lot going on at home that I need to deal with."

Not only is there construction going on, but the first shipment of weapons for distribution is arriving this week. Most of all, this week holds the last date of what the cops are assuming is Dang's plan to rob a bank.

"So, if I come to Oklahoma for Mother's Day next month, do you think we'd be able to see each other?"

With a coy smile, I tease, "I suppose so. It would be a shame to waste the opportunity."

"Brat," he quips as he pulls my hand to his lips and kisses the back. It sends tingles through me, remembering him calling me a brat last night before he swatted my bare ass with one of his strong, calloused hands.

Too quickly, he releases my hand and gets out of the car. I stay in my seat, knowing it pleases him to play the gentleman. Pleasing him pleases me.

When he has released me from the confines of the car, he recovers my luggage from the trunk while I go inside to the desk to check in. Another wonderful thing about flying private is that it only takes a few minutes to get checked in rather than standing in lines several times before being allowed to sit and wait to be boarded.

The plane's staff has already loaded my luggage when I return. Davis pulls me into his arms and squeezes me tight. I squeeze him right back.

He pulls back enough to kiss me deeply. Passionately. I'm a little breathless when a clearing of a throat behind us causes me to pull away.

"I'm sorry, Miss Morrissey, but we need to be on our way."

"Yes, of course."

Davis leans in and gives me one more brush of lips, then another hug. His lips close to my ear, he murmurs, "I'm already missing you."

"Me, too."

There's an unfamiliar ache in my chest. Before I say or do something stupid, I break away. His fingers stay entwined in mine until we're forced to let go.

I don't look back as I climb the steps to board the plane. Can't look back. When I take a seat, I dare a glance out the window to find him staring right at me.

There's a thump as the outer door is closed and the pilot comes over the speaker, telling me we're ready to go. I put the palm of my hand to the window as the plane begins to taxi and Davis raises his in return, looking more miserable than I've ever seen him.

As he disappears from sight, I'm startled by someone touching my arm. It's the attendant handing me some tissues. Only then do I become aware of the dampness on my cheeks.

What the hell? I don't cry. Haven't cried since I was a kid.

There's no reason to be crying over Davis. It's a good thing he lives too far away. Otherwise, he'd be too close and seeing him more often would mean he'd be more likely to discover my secrets and that wouldn't be good for either of us.

It would be horrible if I had to choose between killing him and avoiding prison time. I don't know that I could do it, but going to prison for the rest of my life isn't an option, either. Maybe I need to have an escape hatch in place.

Next the attendant hands me is a double shot of very fine whiskey. One sip tells me it's a brand I like. I guess they pay attention to the questionnaire you're required to complete before your first flight. Yeah, I think I'll enjoy flying private from now on.

When the plane touches down, I jolt awake. It's unlike me to fall asleep around strangers, even if it is just the one attendant. I guess several days of little sleep are catching up with me.

Cam, Finn, and Bee are waiting to pick me up. Cam hugs me. Finn gives me a nod and takes my luggage. Bee never gets out of the SUV.

It's funny that I used to think we were close. Since she's been in Oklahoma, it has become clear our relationship wasn't what I thought it was.

Perhaps she's just used to being the queen bee, pun intended, and isn't sure what to do when she's not. Also, I can tell she's not oblivious to the changes in Cam, but I can't figure out why it bothers her so much.

Soon, she'll be married to Geno. Surely she's not foolish enough to think that nothing would change when that happens. As if they'd live in her father's house where she's the cherished princess and still have Cam at her beck and call whenever she gets bored.

As we pull up the driveway, the front of the house comes into view. Cam stiffens next to me and the temperature coming off her drops by a dozen degrees.

"Hey, looks like Tori's back," Bee observes.

"Back?"

"Yes," Cam bites out. "She left."

Confused, I ask for an explanation and Cam tells me about the encounter with the man, her subsequent taking of his life, and Tori's departure.

"Well, fuck me."

Whatever happened between the two women is their business and I won't get in the middle of it. I like Tori, but I don't want her dicking around with Cam's emotions.

"Listen," I continue, "your relationship is your business, but whatever you decide, I'll respect and support you."

Wanting to give them their privacy to deal with whatever their issues are, I go straight up to my room. Because I promised I would, I take out my phone and text Davis.

Me: *Home.*

Bodach: *Glad you made it home safe. Was the house still standing?*

Me: *Still standing and full of drama. Speaking of drama, kept forgetting to tell you the guy with my uncle is an Albanian named Ilia Starova. Haven't gotten the audio back from my guy yet. May take a while.*

Bodach: *Interesting. I'll see what I can dig up on him.*

We text back and forth for a while longer. It seems as if we're both trying to hold on to our connection and not say goodbye. That would mean our time together was officially over.

Me: *I don't want to say good night.*

My phone buzzes with his call. I answer and put the phone to my ear.

"Me, either," he says. "If everything works out, it'll just be a few weeks before I can see you again."

"K. Just let me know."

"Will do. Good night, Rae."

"Night, Bodach."

His chuckle rattles through the speaker as I disconnect the call. For a minute I lay there and hold the phone to my chest, reveling in the puddle of warm goo that has taken up residence in the vicinity of my heart.

CHAPTER THIRTY-SIX

More Communication Than Fucking

CAM

When I walk into the house, Tori is there waiting for me. "Hi," she says.

I tried to make myself cold, willing my heart to turn to ice, but at the sound of her voice, I flinch. However, as much as I want to run to her and wrap my arms around her, I manage to keep the soles of my shoes where they are glued to the stone entry floor along with everyone else's apparently.

"What do you want?"

There. That's better. My tone isn't exactly frigid, but it isn't friendly, either.

"I'd like to talk, please."

I narrow my eyes and wish I was quick with an acerbic retort, but I've never been good at that type of thing. Three days from now, one will come to me when I'm in the shower and no one else is around.

Instead of telling her to go away, my stupid tender heart wants a reason for its suffering, so I turn on my heel and bite out, "Fine. Rae, I'm going to use your office for a moment."

"Mkay, but it's not really my office, so maybe we should call it something else."

I look at her and frown.

"Never mind," she says, waving a hand. "You two go talk."

When I start to move, everyone else does, too. Rae takes her luggage upstairs, presumably to her room. Bee goes toward the media room and Finn goes toward the kitchen.

I don't look to see if she's following me. Instead, I walk purposefully to the large room down the hall styled as an office. There are shelves along three of the walls, so maybe we should restyle it as a library.

Stop it. You need to focus or you'll probably do something stupid.

Feeling the need for a barrier between us, I sit behind the desk, leaving her no choice but to sit in one of the chairs on the other side of the humongous wooden furniture shield. It shocks the crap out of me when, instead of sitting in a chair, she perches on the corner of the desk.

Within touching distance.

I'm not going to make it easy for her, so I keep my mouth shut and wait for her to talk. After all, she's the one who wanted the opportunity to talk, not me.

She reaches her hand out toward mine, but I roll the chair away, denying her. After she draws in a deep breath, she lets it out and says, "I'm sorry."

I look away.

"Relationships aren't something I'm very good at. The ones I've had with men have been primarily contractual and my experiences with women have been driven by sexual need. In all of them, I held the power and controlled the direction. But with you, it was different. Is different."

Now I look up at her, and her gaze on me is tender.

"I never saw you coming. There was that instant attraction and chemistry and from there, things only got better. For once, I felt like I was on equal footing with someone. I didn't have to pretend, but I could just be myself and you liked me. It was amazing and, oh, so, freeing."

She gives me a shy smile.

"I was falling hard for you. Then you killed someone..."

"And you ran away because it horrified you. I understand."

She drops off the desk and kneels on the floor before the chair. Before me.

"No," she replies vehemently. This time, when she reaches for my hand, I let her take it.

After she draws in another breath and lets it out, her voice is calmer. "No. That's not what happened. Since I left home for college, I've been on my own. Because I can't tell my parents what I do to make money, every struggle, every challenge, every setback, I've been on my own."

She's squeezing my hand so tight my fingers are tingling.

"Then there's you. Letting me be who I am and then, when trouble comes knocking, you step right up and slay the dragon for me to keep me safe. And I liked it. I liked it so much that it scared me. My Catholic upbringing said I should be appalled by what happened, but I wasn't."

Her eyes are searching mine, but I'm too shocked to react.

"I was already falling for you, but when you did that, I did a swan dive right over the edge."

Is she saying what I think she's saying? Wild horses begin to gallop through my chest.

"I know I hurt you and for that, I am so utterly sorry. But I know words aren't going to cut it. So I'm asking if there's even still a chance for us, for you and me. Whatever you want me to do to prove myself to you, I'll do it."

My heart is pounding in my chest, moving beyond pounding hooves to a symphony of base drums. For a moment, I think I might pass out.

"So..." I lick my lips because they're so dry I think they'll crack if I say another word. "Um... Well, I think we moved a little fast. As you know, I've never had any kind of relationship. None. So when you just left without saying anything, I didn't know what to do and yeah, it hurt. It hurt a lot. I didn't think you were coming back."

She bows her head against my hand. "My biggest wish is that I could go back and do that morning over, but I can't."

Although Tori seems earnest, her leaving has me second guessing my instincts with her. I'm not sure I'll ever be able to trust myself again where she's concerned. But I also can't stand the prospect of cutting her out of my life completely.

She made a mistake. If I'd been in her shoes, would I have done anything differently? I mean, of course I would have because I was raised in a life where violence and murder are the norm.

This world is new to her. But to know that she didn't leave because she was afraid, that's something altogether different. It means I wouldn't have to hide that part of myself from her or cushion it to calm her fears.

"Okay," I finally say, wanting to be as honest with her as she's been with me. "I can see where you're coming from, but I can't just set aside the hurt. As much as my body wants to drag you upstairs and touch you, my heart isn't so forgiving."

"I understand."

Holding up a hand, I go on. "For now, I think it would be a good idea for you to move back to your apartment and we can start over, taking things a little slower. It's going to take me a while to be able to trust my instincts with you, but I believe we had something special that's worth seeing if we can restore it."

Her smile is beautiful, and I have to fight the desire to kiss her. "We need to get to know each other better. To create a stronger foundation with a lot more communication than fucking this time around."

She laughs at that. "I agree and I'm so thankful you're willing to give me, to give us, another chance."

CHAPTER THIRTY-SEVEN

Someone's Learning

RAE

After I hung up with Davis, I took a shower and dressed, divided on checking in with my wee beasties or calling it quits for the day. I fall back on my bed and stare at the ceiling.

I'm still laying there, spread eagle, when someone knocks on my door. Thankfully, I still have my clothes on because I'd debated putting them on after I showered and about taking them off again to just go to bed.

"Come in," I say to the ceiling.

The door cracks open and Tori comes in, followed by Cam. "Do you have a minute? I'd like to talk to you about something."

I glance at Cam, but she shrugs. Apparently, whatever they talked about alone, this wasn't included. With a sigh, I sit up.

"Lay it on me."

"First of all, how was your trip?"

My insides go all mushy. "It was wonderful."

"I'm really glad for you," she says with a smile. "I'd love to catch up with you and hear all about it, but I know you've probably got a million things to deal with and that the last thing you need is a touchy feely round of chitchat."

"That's appreciated." It's majorly appreciated because until Cam tells me where they stand, I'm not going to be sure how to respond to anything she tells me.

"Also, I'm sure you'll need to find out exactly what went on between Bridget and me before you can comment on anything I'm going to talk to you about. However, while I'm here, I wanted to run it by you."

Okay...so someone's learning. I nod.

"While I was gone, I did a lot of thinking. Not only about our relationship," she says, holding out a hand toward Cam, "but also about the future. When we first met, I told you I wanted to buy Cassandra out and take over her club. However, after what happened with Jo and seeing how she reacted and tried to sweep it under the rug...well, I don't want that anymore."

"Okay."

"The women in that club are merely commodities, and Cassandra turns a blind eye when the members break the rules and it has always pissed me off, but I can't stomach it anymore. So, I had an idea."

"You want to create your own club," I guess.

"Yes, but not like Cassandra's. I have something else in mind."

Then she lays out her idea to me, and it's a good one. Instead of an overt BDSM club, she wants to create a fitness center. However, the fitness center would be its cover story.

It would be a legit operation with all the amenities any high-level fitness center would have. But much like Cassandra's, it would cater to the patron's carnal desires, too.

Unlike Cassandra's, the workers would hold the power. Consent would be required and no one would be forced into doing anything they didn't want to do.

Membership would be by invitation only, and applicants would be vetted up to their eyeballs. They would also sign very specific contracts and if they violate those contracts, the price exacted would be steep.

Through her work at Cassandra's and the dating life she's led for several years, she has plenty of contacts for both clients and staff. Her plan is so thorough, I wonder why she's telling me.

"I know you're wanting to change the landscape of criminal activity in the state, so I wanted to submit my idea to you for approval."

Yep. She's learning for real.

"Also, I have quite a bit in savings, but not enough to do things right, so I wanted to see if you'd be willing to partner with me. Aaand, you have vastly more experience than I have in setting up layers of corporations to shield actual ownership."

The idea intrigues me. Although I'm vehemently opposed to trafficking, unlike most of the puritanical population of this state, I don't have a problem with sex workers. For some women, they're just using what they have to make a living and doing it in a safe environment is all the better.

"I'll consider it, but it's a big ask, particularly considering recent events between the two of you," I say, waggling a finger between her and Cam. "If I do this and partner with you, that puts you into my inner circle. We're taught this from birth, but it's new to you. If you want in, you have to be all in. Once you are, there's no walking away. No changing your mind. In the inner circle, you know secrets that aren't yours to share, and if you do, I'll put you in the ground."

Surprisingly, she doesn't run away screaming or even backtrack. Not even a little bit. Instead, she shocks the shit out of me when she nods.

"Understood. If I try to leave or betray you or yours, I'm dead. I would expect nothing less."

We stare at each other for long moments. When I don't say anything else, she turns to Cam. "If you're okay with it, I'd still like to come in the mornings for training, but if you're not, I'll understand."

"Yes. That's okay for now. I'm going to tell Rae what happened between us."

Tori nods. "Of course you should. She needs all the information to weigh in her decision."

Again, I'm surprised at her calm demeanor. Then she gets a little too eager and steps closer to Cam. "Do you think you'd be able to give me a hug before I go?"

Cam steps back. "I don't think I'm ready for that."

Although she's nodding, the disappointment is written all over Tori. She has a good poker face, but her body deflates with the rounding of her shoulders and dropping of her head and arms. "I understand. I'll see you tomorrow. Is it okay if I stop by the kitchen to say goodbye to Jo?"

Cam nods and stands there like a statue as Tori leaves the room. We're both quiet until the door clicks shut behind her. "Alright. Spill what happened between you two."

She tells me everything, as I knew she would. It's a little daunting that she trusts me so implicitly. I just hope I can live up to that trust.

"How do you feel about what she said?" I query when she finishes her story.

"I'm scared because I've never done anything like this before. But does it make me stupid if I believe her?"

"Nope. I believe her, too. Like you said, we grew up with this shit, so it's old hat to us, but it's all new to her. It's better than her running away screaming in terror."

"Did you see what you needed to see in Boston?"

I tell her about seeing the two men together and what I discovered about the newcomer. She asks several questions about the purpose of the meeting and where they went, but I have to admit that I don't know.

"Albanian? You're sure?"

"Yep."

"That's interesting."

"Agreed."

"So, how was the crow?"

I can't help the grin that stretches my lips, and she laughs at me when my face grows hot. For fuck's sake, why am I blushing? Great sex with a gorgeous, sexy man is nothing to be embarrassed about.

Crying at the airport. Blushing now. What's next?

"That good, huh?" she asks with a low chuckle.

"Yeah. He says he might be coming to Oklahoma next month for mother's day and wants to see me."

"I hope I get to meet him someday. Now, let me take you downstairs and show you what's been accomplished."

CHAPTER THIRTY-EIGHT

It's Nice to be Back Home

RAE

C am is an excellent right-hand woman. Of everything that
has come up, I can't say there is a single issue that I would
have handled differently. From the construction progress to the
killing of the asshat that followed them from the grocery store,
I wouldn't change a thing.

As she shows me around the construction area, I discuss with
her the idea of setting up an office somewhere other than at the
house. Dealing with more people means meeting with them in
person, and I don't want people coming and going from the
house and making it a target.

"Depending upon where you fall on Tori's ideas, perhaps we could find a space that could house both. With the downturn in the office market, we should be able to find a good deal."

"That's a good idea," I tell her. "I like her proposal and I'd much rather see a situation like what she's proposing where the women are empowered and protected. The men might grumble a bit in the beginning, but they're always going to do whatever gets them the attention of beautiful women."

"If they're trained to behave differently, that becomes their new normal."

"Exactly. If they fall in line, they can have their cake and eat it, too."

Cam giggles at that comment.

"Okay, so maybe it won't be cake that's getting eaten," I reply with a laugh. "Your changes to the construction plans were the right move."

Her neck turns pink, and she gives me a nod. In her time here, Cam has really started to come into her own. I'm proud of the woman she's becoming and am selfishly ecstatic. With her, everything is easier.

"Let's go upstairs and talk," she says. "You can tell me what you saw on your trip and we can discuss next steps."

"Okay. Then I'm going to sleep. I didn't get much rest while I was away and need to get some sack time. This next week is shaping up to be a big one."

On my way back to my room, I swing by the kitchen, where Jo sets a plate in front of me. The first bite makes me groan with pleasure. "Damn, I've missed your cooking. You are a goddess in the kitchen."

She smiles at me like I'm some amusing child. "It's nice to have you back home."

"It's nice to be back home."

Before I go to bed, I check Dang's accounts. They're no longer locked down by the bank and he has moved a significant portion of his cash. Again, he's broken it up and spread it across three banks.

With a grin, I rub my palms together like a diabolical villain and let my fingers fly over the keyboard. One of the banks he chose has security so lax that it's like using an ATM without needing a pin code.

This week is the last date on the list of three the pretty doctor gave to the cops after Dang attacked her. He kidnapped her from work, took her to his lair, and did vile things.

I read the police report, and it was brutal. It didn't take a genius to read between the lines and understand that it was much more than just a beating.

It's incredible that she had the presence of mind to observe her surroundings and decipher information posted on the wall of Dang's office. He had photos, including some of the interior and exterior of a bank and three dates circled on a calendar.

The first two dates for what they believed to be his bank robbery options were a bust, so fingers crossed that this one proves true. If his ass is locked up, I won't have to get physical in my goal of pushing him out of the state. The last thing I want is a bloody war.

Once I set my clever little code beasties to work, I unpack my suitcases, then curl up in bed. It feels weird to be in this big old bed alone. So weird that I can't sleep and end up tossing and turning.

Finally, I give up and change clothes, deciding to go downstairs to wear out my body in the gym. Maybe Finn will be up for a spar. That would be sure to wear me out faster than anything.

He is in the kitchen, as usual. Instead of sitting there reading the paper and drinking his morning coffee, he has his notebook. I still don't know what's in it, but he deserves his privacy. He probably has more here than he has anywhere else.

"Hey," I say when I enter the room. "I'm wired and need to get some sleep. Wanna go spar?"

Jo looks back at me from where she's stirring a pot on the stove. "Oh! You're talking to Finn. For a sec, I thought you meant me."

"They've been training," Finn adds.

"Is that so? Well, if you want to go a round with me, Jojo, let's go."

She chuckles and turns her attention back to her pot. "Unh uh. I'm getting better, but I'm not that brave yet. However, if you're going to spar, I want to watch."

Finn just hitches his chin a millimeter.

"Well, it looks like it's on, Jo, so lower your burner and let's go."

"Excellent!" she whispers.

I head downstairs and Finn goes to his room to change. As soon as Jo hits the foyer, she calls out in a voice louder than I imagined a tiny body like hers could muster. "Battle of the Titans part two is on in the basement!"

Bee appears from down the hall and Cam looks over the railing from the second floor. "What?" they both ask.

She's practically giddy when she replies. "They're going to spar again."

The bout with Finn does the trick. A half hour with him and I'm ready to shower off the sweat and fall into bed.

After a quick hose down, I stop by my computer to check the progress. In this short amount of time, the majority of the account in the bank with the lax security is bouncing around the world. I think I'll hold off on the other accounts until I see what happens this week.

The bed still feels empty when I return to it, but this is my reality. Snuggling up with Davis is the fantasy. I know he thinks there should be some way for us to be together, but I just can't see it.

Going into something with him without him knowing everything is a recipe for disaster. But then I can't exactly tell him everything, can I? Especially not now when I'm positioning myself to take control of the criminal underground in the entire state of Oklahoma.

Once Dang's out of the way, the other active groups are small fish and easily brought to heel or eliminated if they don't want to play by my rules. Thinking about that side of things reminds me I need to reach out to Bernardo Cruz to give him an update.

My phone buzzes on the nightstand.

Bodach: *You've ruined me for sleeping alone. Miss you.*

I smile at the screen. Although I'd been itching to send him a text message, I had forced myself to resist. Davis is like a drug to me and the more I have of him, the more I want, so like an addict, I need to exercise self-control.

Me: *Miss you, too. Had to go spar with one of my housemates just to wear myself out enough to be able to even think about sleeping.*

Bodach: *Bet that was something to see.*

CHAPTER THIRTY-NINE

This is My Home

CAM

When I go downstairs for training and find Tori there warming up, my heart squeezes. I've missed her so much and all I want to do is race over to her, wrap my arms around her, and ask her to move back in. Permanently.

But that would be stupid. It might take her watching me kill someone again and her not running away before my trust is restored. It's not like I go around killing people all the time, so that could take a while.

Finn puts us through our warm up. While we're going through the motions, he goes over and sits with Rae, who has come down to watch. When he returns, Rae comes, too.

They demonstrate a complicated defense move over and over, then pair us up to practice. Usually, I'm paired with Jo since we're of a size. Also, I have a bit more training because of my upbringing whereas, Jo has none.

For the same reasons, Bee is usually paired with Tori. Today, they mix it up and I'm paired with Bee. Rae had explained that the move is particularly effective when used by a smaller opponent against a larger one.

Bee snorts as if she thinks there is no way I'll be able to use the maneuver on her. She is probably thinking of all the times we used to spar back when we were teenagers and being trained to defend ourselves.

What she doesn't realize is that I always let her win because it was just easier. However, there's no need to help her save face as the daughter of Keegan Morrissey here. And I won't be going back to Boston, so I don't give a flying fuck, as Rae would say, about maintaining our relationship.

We stand to the side and watch as Tori plays the aggressor and Jo practices the move. After the first attempt, Rae steps in to coach Jo and they go again. This time, she gets it right and puts Tori on her ass.

She gives a little hop and pumps her arm in the air with a whoop. Then she quickly reverts to sweet Jojo and apologizes to Tori, offering her a hand up, which makes me laugh.

Finn takes over the offensive role with Tori and lets her complete the move. There's no way she would have been able to pull it off if he hadn't let her, but she acts as if she did it for real.

When I become aware of the grin on my face at her accomplishment, I squash it and replace it with a stoic façade. Next, it's our turn.

Bee's look is haughty, as if she believes there's no way I'll be able to pull it off without her letting me. I can tell she has no intention of doing that.

We circle and she lunges. I dodge and use her momentum against her, executing the move flawlessly and putting her on her ass. As she's swinging past me, she lets out a squeak of shock, making me grin.

When she stands at her full height, her face is red with embarrassment. Finn steps up to take on the role he did with Tori, but I put a hand up. It's time she realizes I'm not the same girl she knew in Boston.

Finn raises an eyebrow and steps back. Bee leans in and hisses, "You're gonna get it. I won't hold back."

I shrug. "Better that you don't."

When I lunge at her, she botches the move, but catches herself quickly and tries to correct course. It's too late because if she wants to change things up, I can, too, and counter her correction with one of my own.

She ends up on her ass again, and she's furious. "What was that?" she shrieks.

With another shrug, I reply, "You missed the move and improvised, so I improvised, too."

"Bitch!" She lunges at me and I use the move we're supposed to be practicing on her and she ends up on her ass again. Although I want to laugh, I don't because that will only make her madder.

When I start to walk away, she grabs my arm and swings me around and gets in my face. "What is your problem? Ever since we got here, you've been a right cunt to me."

Fine. She wants to know what's going on, I'll tell her. It's about time she had a reality check. I get right back in her face, too.

"No. I just quit demurring to your every whim. In Boston, it was easier to just go along with what you wanted, but I don't have to do that here."

"So when we get back to Boston, which Bridget are you going to be?"

I should really keep my mouth shut and let it go. But there's no telling how much longer we're going to be here.

Uncle Keegan could call us home next week, or it might be another month. The sooner she understands that her world is going to change when it comes to me, the better. Does she really not understand what it's going to be like when she's back in Boston and married to Geno?

"I'm going to be Cam, the same person I am here, because I'm not going back to Boston. This is my home from now on."

She staggers back, flinching as if I've slapped her. When I look around, my gaze snags on Rae, who just raises an eyebrow at me. Next to her, Finn is giving me an inscrutable look, but it seems to hold much more than his usual stoic, blank expression.

I yank my arm out of Bee's grip and stalk away. Halfway up the stairs, Rae catches up to me, her phone in hand. As she passes me, she says, "Delivery's almost here."

She takes the steps two at a time. I hurry after her. Christ, how does she do that? If I tried, I'd fall on my face.

"Which delivery?" I ask when I reach the first floor, huffing and puffing.

My break from cardio on the treadmill is catching up with me. Once I got used to running outside, I hated the thought of running like a hamster on a wheel again, so I haven't done it since we moved.

Since my workout today was cut short, I'll make myself spend some time running this afternoon. And I'll hate every minute of it.

"Our crate of weapons is just a few miles out and should be here soon. Since the room downstairs isn't finished, we'll leave them crated in the garage, then move them once the construction is complete."

"Really? That was quick."

She pauses to open the gate, setting it to remain open, then goes out onto the front terrace. "Yeah. Things went so smoothly, it's astonishing. The main shipment has already been offloaded at the port in Muskogee, broken up and loaded onto trucks for transport to contacts all over the US."

"Wow. That's excellent news."

Her excitement has her unable to stand still, so she paces back and forth over the stone patio. "It is. Turns out that

Whiskey...do you remember Whiskey? The big guy that was in Yona's crew? Well, his cousin is the operations director for the port. He smoothed the way for us."

"That is an extremely fortuitous development."

"Yeah. And putting him on retainer wasn't nearly as expensive as I expected it to be."

A panel truck pulls into the driveway and stops. We can see the top of the truck, but I doubt they can see us here on the porch. Rae pulls her phone out of her pocket and puts it to her ear.

CHAPTER FORTY

Stop Calling Me Ma'am

RAE

"Yes, you're in the right place, you big lummox." The truck begins to lumber forward again. "As soon as you top the hill, you'll see me and Cam out front."

I can imagine after seeing my rental house in Tahlequah and Dad's cabin, this place is a shock. The truck moves slowly up the drive as if he's still not sure he's in the right place. But when he tops the small rise and sees me, he picks up the pace.

He stops at the top of the circle drive, and I hurry down the steps. As excited as a kid on Christmas morning, I practically bounce in place, waiting for him to disembark.

He takes his time stepping down out of the truck. I think the jerk is torturing me on purpose. When he finally puts his feet on the ground, I wrap my arms around him and give him a hug.

Somewhere along the way of having all these people around all the time, my anti-social walls started to crumble. Davis is probably due a portion of the blame, too. I never thought it was possible, but I have become a goddamn hugger. The insanity seems to be permanent.

"Hey," Whiskey says and gives me an awkward pat on the back, but there's so much more in that one word than just a greeting.

"I've missed you, too, big guy."

"Nice place. Where you want your box?"

"Let's take it around to the garage."

He climbs back into the cab, and instead of giving him directions, I hop up on the step and hang onto the side mirror. With a scowl, he rolls down the window. "That's dangerous."

"Don't get your panties into a twist. We're not going that far." With a look over my shoulder, I call out, "Cam, will you please go around and open the door for the empty garage space?"

She nods and hurries into the house. I turn back to him and, for the first time, realize Whiskey isn't alone. "Who's this?"

"Nephew. Name's Kanati, but we call him Nate."

I grin over at the boy? Man? He's big like Whiskey, but his face still has the smoothness of youth.

"Osiyo Nate, I'm Rae."

The man-boy is looking at me as if I'm some sort of strange new species of bug. After a half dozen heartbeats, he gives me a nod. I guess he's just as much of a talker as his uncle.

"Go back around the drive to the offshoot that went to the right when you were coming up. It'll be on the left now."

Just then, Tori's car pulls out onto the driveway from the back of the house. She lifts a hand and I lift one back. I wonder if she and Cam had time to say goodbye.

Whiskey slides his eyes to me, and there's an almost imperceptible quirk to the corners of his mouth. Damn...I've got the man laughing.

"That's it. Where the car came out a second ago." I say as we near the turnoff. "Follow it around to the back of the house. That's where the garages open."

He follows the drive around and we find Cam waiting just inside one of the open garage doors. Once he clears the screen of trees and catches sight of the expanse of property, his eyes slide to me again.

"Big place."

"Yep," is all I say before I hop off the step and head to the back of the truck, guiding Whiskey to back up so it's easier to transfer it into the garage.

Nate gets out first, moving faster than his uncle. Yeah, he's more boy than man, but big enough that most people probably don't realize it. He's got the clumsy agility of a large-breed puppy that hasn't grown into his paws yet.

At the back of the truck, Nate operates a steel plate that pivots down to be level with the bed of the truck and parallel to the ground. He climbs up, unlocks the roller door on the back, and pushes it up.

Inside is a large wooden crate on a pallet, which is sitting on a dolly with casters. The whole thing is strapped to the wall to keep it from moving around. Nate releases the straps and maneuvers the crate onto the lift gate.

I'm practically giddy as it lowers to the ground. Whiskey has finally made it to the back of the truck. He helps Nate shift the crate off the lift.

Suddenly, Finn is there with a pallet jack which he slides into place, lifting the crate off the dolly. He pulls it into the garage, his muscles bunching with strain until Nate helps push the burden into the center of the empty garage space.

"Do you remember my cousin Cam and our friend Finn?"

Cam smiles and nods at him. Whiskey nods, then holds out his hand to Finn, who shakes it with a nod in return.

"The young gentleman is Whiskey's nephew, Nate. You guys want to stay for lunch before you head back?"

Nate looks hopefully at his uncle. A kid his age is probably hungry all the time.

"You cookin'?" Whiskey asks with a smirk.

I feint a punch to his stomach and laugh. He doesn't move. "Nope. I have a pro fixing the meals, so I'm eating a lot better these days."

He raises an eyebrow, but doesn't say anything.

"I know, I know, it's a far sight different from what I had in Tahlequah. Come on, let's go see what Jo's whipping up."

I hook an arm in his and lead him into the house, leaving the other three to follow. The whir of the garage door sounds behind us. Probably thanks to Finn, who is always paying attention to the details.

It's so nice to have him here. When he goes back to Boston with Bee, I'm going to miss him. His solid, stoic presence is a comfort at my back.

Jo looks up as we enter the kitchen and I can tell she's evaluating the potential threat. Something about Whiskey radiates that he's no danger to her, so she relaxes and goes back to doing whatever black magic she does in here that produces excellent food.

"Jojo, this is my friend Whiskey and his nephew Nate. Do you think we have enough for them to stay for lunch?"

"Of course we do," she answers, as if I've just asked her the most ridiculous question in the world. "I have a lasagna in the oven and a salad ready to be dressed. Everything will be ready in about thirty minutes."

"Perfect. Thanks Jo."

She nods and I hitch my chin at Whiskey. "Come on, I'll show you around."

The grand tour only comprises the first floor and basement. I don't feel the need to show him the second and third floors that are just bedrooms. That's private space, and it's better to leave a little mystery.

"Quite a step up," Whiskey says as we go up the stairs to return to the main floor.

"Yeah. Did a favor for the previous owner and convinced her to sell me the house. It was a shocker when she let me have it for a helluva price."

My timing is good, because as soon as we step onto the first floor, Cam is there waiting. "Jo says lunch is ready. I've set the dining table since there are guests."

"Thank you, Cam. I appreciate that."

Cam, Finn, Jo, and I sit down at the table with our guests. When Bee comes into the room, she stops as soon as she sees the two newcomers and frowns. She takes a seat only long enough to fix her plate, then takes it back to the media room to eat alone in front of the enormous television.

It's so strange how she's chosen to distance herself. When I lived with them in Boston, I thought we were friends. Apparently, her friendship is only offered on her terms and only when she's in the position of power.

Instead of seeing me as an equal, she's building walls. At least, that's what it appears to be from my side of things. Perhaps I need to sit down and have a conversation with her because I don't want us to be enemies regardless of who her father is.

Nate eats two large helpings of the meal. He probably would have had a third, but Whiskey gave him a quelling look after the second. When Jo goes to the kitchen to get the tiramisu she made for dessert, Whiskey drops some news into my lap.

"Yona's running for a new position."

"What position is that?"

"Council member."

I nod. Am I petty enough to attempt to torpedo his campaign? Yeah, I think I just might be.

Being a council member would position him to run for deputy chief or even chief in a few years. He and his forked tongue need to stay out of my nation's leadership. I make a mental note to see who's running against him.

We chat some more. Mostly I chat with Cam, and Whiskey occasionally tosses out a monosyllabic response. Jo is quieter than usual and Finn, well, he never contributes much to any conversation. I never thought I'd be the chatty one.

When the meal is finished, Jo starts clearing the table and I'm surprised when Finn rises to help her. Those two are spending an awful lot of time together. Could there be something blossoming there?

It's probably a ludicrous thought. When Bee goes back to Boston, Finn will have to go with her. For Cam to balk at going back is one thing, but Finn is a made man and a trusted one to be give the duty of guarding the boss's daughter. He can't just walk away from that.

"Can I talk to you for a minute?" Whiskey asks, surprising me.

"Um, yeah. Let's go down to the office."

"Wait here," he tells Nate. The boy looks away, but not before I catch the cast of resignation.

Jo smiles at him and asks, "There's still plenty of dessert left. Would you like some more? I remember when my brother was your age; he was always hungry."

Nate nods and speaks for the first time. "Yes, please. Thank you."

As soon as I close the door behind us, Whiskey says, "Need you to do me a favor."

I turn to face him and raise an eyebrow. "How much do you need?"

His lips quirk on one side. "Not that. My nephew..."

Oh no. The last thing I need is another person to take care of. It's not that I can't afford it because I can. But I'm already fucking up with Bee and don't need someone else to fuck up with.

"Nope. I have enough people to look after."

"Just hear me out."

With a sigh, I roll my hand in the air, signaling for him to continue.

"He's a good kid, but his mom, my sister, has a new beau. The man is a scrawny white dude who likes to drink a little too much. He's scared of Nate because he's a big kid, so when he drinks, he's on Nate's ass."

Whiskey stops talking and moves to stare out the window overlooking the expanse of lawn.

"Last week, he shoved Nate, not for the first time, but this time Nate shoved back. When he tried to tell his mom about it...well, she's blinded by her hormones. Thinks she's in love.

Understandably, Nate's been spending a lot more time with his friends, a pair of brothers who fancy themselves gangsters but don't have two brain cells between them."

"So, what do you expect me to do?"

"If he could stay here a few days, out of the dude's way and away from his idiot friends..."

"Days won't do it. You mean weeks, don't you?"

He has the decency to look chagrined. I shake my head and pace.

"Damn, Whiskey, you don't ask for much, do you?"

Can I take on another person? Whiskey is putting a lot of trust in me. He's also an integral part of my operations at the port. One fuck up by him or his cousin and the entire operation could go to shit.

"Fine. But I need to talk to him first."

Whiskey nods and goes to the door. When he opens it, he sticks his head out and says the boy's name. It's louder than I've heard him speak before and apparently, Nate was listening for his uncle's call.

He shuffles into the room, looking down at his boots.

"Nate, look at me."

He lifts his eyes to mine. "Your uncle has asked me if you can stay here for a little while. Is that something you want?"

He lifts one meaty shoulder and looks back down.

I bark at him. "Look at me when I'm talking to you."

His eyes snap back to mine.

"That's better. I might be a woman and smaller than you, but make no mistake, I'm in charge here. You do as I say, when I say. Got it?"

He nods.

"You're going to hear things and see things here that are nobody's business but mine. I need you to give me your word that you'll keep your mouth shut about it."

He nods again.

"I need your words, Nate."

"Yes, ma'am."

I let my voice go icy so he knows I'm not playing.

"Good. Now you need to know this is serious, so I'm going to let you know where I stand. If you don't keep your mouth shut and talk about my business to anyone else, I'll put you in the ground, or drop you into a strip pit. Understand?"

He glances at his uncle, who nods back.

"Yes, ma'am."

"In return, I'll let you stay here. You'll have a place to sleep and plenty of food to fill your belly. You'll take part however I need you to, but it will mostly be things like driving me around, or stuff like what you did today. I will treat you as an adult and with respect and the same is expected of you. If you need something, ask me."

"Yes, ma'am."

"Lastly, there are three other women here besides me, and none of them, and I do mean none of them, are here for your sexual advances. If you lay a hand on any of them without invitation, you will be dealt with harshly. Understand?"

"Yes..."

"And stop calling me ma'am. My name is Rae."

CHAPTER FORTY-ONE

Trying to Open a Dialogue

RAE

Nate gets his bag from the cab of the truck. He, Cam, and I watch as the truck lumbers down the driveway. When it disappears from sight, I pat Nate on the back.

"Let's go inside and I'll show you your room. When there's downtime, you're free to do what you want, but if you want to go somewhere, you'll need to ask for keys and I prefer that no one go anywhere alone for safety reasons."

He nods and follows me into the house along with Cam.

"There's a television in your room, books in the office, and a gym in the basement. Speaking of the basement, I am going to require you to participate in training every morning after breakfast at ten downstairs. I want everyone to be able to defend themselves."

He grunts as if he's amused. That's okay. He'll learn soon enough that there's a reason I want everyone to be capable.

By the time we're on the third floor, I can tell he's a little winded, even though he's trying to hide it.

"You and Jo are the only ones up here. Her room is at the other end of the hall. I'm putting you here in front of the stairwell, because if anyone comes in and makes it up here, while you're here, you're the line of defense on this floor."

He casts a glance down the hall. "Miss Jo's the one who cooks, right?"

"Yes."

"K."

"You're up here because this is where the empty bedrooms are, but in a couple of weeks, the rooms in the basement will be finished and, if you're still here, you can move down there if you're tired of doing the stairs."

He glances down the hall. When the time comes, I have a feeling he'll stay where he is based on the way his shoulders went back and his chest puffed a little when I told him he was watching out for Jo.

"I expect you to keep your room reasonably clean because there's not a designated maid in the house. There are a couple of washers and dryers in the basement. If you need help with knowing what to do, just ask Cam, me, or Jo. Before you eat anything in the fridge, touch base with Jo and she'll tell you what's up for grabs and what's being set aside for a meal. Otherwise, we're pretty easy peasy."

I open the door to the room.

"This is it. I'll leave you to get settled in. If you have questions, talk to Cam or me. If you can't find us, ask Finn and he'll tell you where we are."

He steps inside the bedroom.

"This is my room?"

"Yep."

"No one else will share it?"

"Nope. All yours. That door there is to your bathroom."

He stands there and stares at the door to the bathroom and it makes me wonder about his living situation at home. Maybe he's always had to share, so having his own private space is a novel experience.

Cam and I leave the room and I close the door behind us. I can't believe how gooey my heart is getting, forcing me to take on another person. Finn can take care of himself. Cam is getting close to being able to take care of herself. But the rest of them are my responsibility and it weighs heavily on my shoulders.

We're on the second floor landing when Cam says, "I guess it's a good thing I stocked all the rooms up there with toiletries. He'll probably need some razors and shaving cream, though. I'll put it on Jo's grocery list."

"There's probably no rush. From his smooth face, I'd say he's like a lot of full blood native men and doesn't have a lot of facial hair."

When we reach the first floor, I turn toward the media room. There's no reason to put off having a talk with Bee.

The room is dark except for the glow of the screen, and the volume of the television is up too loud. I pause in the doorway, waiting for my eyes to adjust to the low light. Finally, I spot her in a seat close to the wall on one side. She's curled up in a ball and covered with a throw blanket.

I make my way to her row and slide in. The seat next to hers has her lunch dishes stacked on top, so I move them one seat down before curling up next to her. She gives me a sideways look and doesn't say anything.

The show she's watching is one of those sappy romances she enjoys. Personally, they make me want to gag, but I'll keep that to myself since I'm trying to open a dialogue with her. If I come in bashing her choices, I probably won't get very far.

I slide my arm over and link it with hers, snuggling closer. We used to watch television and movies this way when I stayed with them in Boston. For several minutes, I just sit there watching with her, letting her get used to someone invading her hidey hole.

"What do you want?" she queries in a tone that's assertive, but not aggressive.

"Are you okay? You've been shutting yourself in here every day for a while."

"I'm surprised you noticed. You've been so busy with Bridget and Victoria and Jo that it seemed like you didn't miss me."

Is she jealous? I guess she's so used to being the Princess at the center of Geno and Bridget's attention when she's at home that she's not sure how to take it when she's not.

"I'm sorry you feel that way, but I've mostly been busy with business. Cam has been helping me with it, but it's not like I've tried to leave you out of anything."

"You haven't tried to include me in anything, either."

Yeah, I can see why she'd think that, because it's true. I haven't kept her in the loop with things like I have Cam because I don't want her running back to Boston telling tales to her daddy. The last thing I need is him turning his eye to Oklahoma.

"Well, soon you'll be going back to Boston and getting married to Geno. I figured the last thing you'd want to do while you're here is work."

"And Bridget will be staying here."

"Yes."

"But I need her in Boston with me."

I frown because that seems so selfish of her. Instead of being impatient, I decide to appeal to her love for Bridget. Surely Bridget's more to her than just a companion who is supposed to be available when wanted and forgotten the rest of the time.

"If Bridget goes back to Boston, what's she supposed to do after you're married to Geno? Your time will be spent being a wife. And soon you'll be having children and they'll need your attention, too."

She doesn't answer, but just shrugs. It looks like she's pouting.

Seriously?

"Also, I think it's pretty clear Bridget is gay. If she goes back to Boston, your father will force her into a marriage with one of his cronies. Do you really wish that for her?"

"She's just fooling around," Bee says with a huff. "Fucking that whore is just her being rebellious. Dah would give her to someone like Geno, young and handsome, and she'd learn to love him."

I'm shocked. Not only at how she talks about Tori, but how can she believe that about how her dad would treat Cam? It's like she's oblivious to everything but the parts she wants to see.

Fuck that shit. I'm more determined than ever to do whatever it takes to keep Cam here, where she's safe and able to be who she is.

"Yeah, I don't see that happening. I'm glad you have Geno and you love him and are looking forward to your life with him, but history contradicts you. Your father will do what all family leaders have done since the beginning of organized crime. Bridget is a pawn to be used to his advantage and he'll use her, however he sees fit regardless of what she wants."

"You don't know what you're talking about," she snaps. "I know you've been encouraging her to be with that... that... prostitute because it makes her want to stay here. You're trying to steal her away from me."

I do know what I'm talking about, but she's not going to hear me, so I let it go. Also, I'm not even going to dignify that last part with a response. Bee has convinced herself of some pretty fucked up stuff.

"So, has Geno said when you're likely to get married?"

"No. He thinks Dah is going to let him come down here for a visit and then we'll go back to Boston together, but he's not sure when."

"That's exciting. Perhaps it will be soon."

Hopefully.

Bee has officially worn out her welcome as far as I'm concerned. When I stayed at her house, I was always on my best behavior, not only because I thought I might have found a connection with family... Yeah, looking back, that's laughable. But that's how my mama taught me to be.

Maybe I can send her back without waiting for Geno's visit. If not, she can just keep hiding in here watching the television. I've got things to do.

CHAPTER FORTY-TWO

Never Been On a Date

VICTORIA

Hoping to talk to Cam, I arrive early for our training session with Finn. I hold my breath as I punch in the code and only let it out when the large iron gate begins to swing open.

Every time I come here, I half expect my code for the gate will no longer work and Rae will tell me to leave and never come back. But then, the gate will swing open and I count my blessings that I still have a chance to win Cam back.

If I'd been smarter, I would have never lost her. But in the moment, my mind was reeling so much that the thought of just talking it out with her never occurred to me.

It was a situation completely different from anything I'd ever experienced. I mean, who sees their girlfriend, or boyfriend, for that matter, kill someone to keep you safe?

And if you did see your significant other kill someone to keep you safe, how many of them would react like I did? I wasn't disgusted or frightened. No, it was a primal thrill of satisfaction that ran through me because someone wanted to hurt me and the ones I love, but they're the one who ended up dead.

There isn't a doubt in my mind that if she hadn't killed that guy, all three of us would be in some shitty brothel, like the one we rescued Jojo from, being used in deplorable ways. That Tai Dang asshole was one who thought women were disposable, to be thrown away when they were broken beyond repair.

Hell, he probably thought that about everyone. If you were no longer of use to him, he'd put a bullet in your brain and get someone else to use up and throw away.

I enter the house through the back door, which is right off the kitchen. I'm greeted by the aroma of excellent coffee and Jo's humming. She's always here and seems to love just being able to cook all day for people who love her food.

Finn is there, too, an ever-present fixture in the mornings as he pours over the newspaper. "Good morning, Jo," I say in greeting, then give a nod to her companion. "Finn."

He nods back but doesn't say anything, as usual.

"Mornin' Tori."

I'm about to ask where I can find Cam when a very large, young Native American man, or maybe a boy, shuffles into the room, looking as if he just woke up. He looks me up and down, but it's more appraising than sexual.

"Hi," I say.

He simply nods like Finn. Geez, another non-talker. I've never seen someone gather people to her like Rae does.

"Tori, this is Nate. He's going to be staying here for a while. Nate, this is Victoria. Would you like some coffee, or maybe some milk? And breakfast? I've got some breakfast casserole keeping warm in the oven."

"Yes, ma'am, milk and some casserole, please," he mumbles and takes a stool at the counter.

"Did someone say breakfast casserole?" Rae queries as she enters the room.

I swear, I've never known another woman who can eat like she does and stay so skinny.

"Hey, Tori," she greets, sitting between the two men. "You're here early."

"Yeah, I was hoping to get a word with Cam. Do you know where she is?"

"She had breakfast earlier, so I think she went to her room to change," Rae answers just as Jo places a cup of coffee in front of her. Rae picks it up and takes a drink. "Jo, you're the best."

Jo turns away, but I don't miss the pleased smile that crosses her face.

"Great. Thanks!"

I turn and leave the room, hurrying up the stairs to Cam's room. Just as I start to turn the doorknob, I stop myself. This isn't my room anymore, so I knock instead of walking right in.

A pain squeezes my chest, but as soon as I hear her call for me to come in, it lightens just from hearing her voice. She looks up when I step inside and for a moment, one of her brilliant smiles begins to bloom.

Then, as if she is just remembering she's supposed to be mad at me, the smile falls apart and her face goes blank and I hate it. I hate that she has to gauge her reactions to me and that it's all my fault.

She's sitting at the small desk in the corner working on her laptop, already dressed for training. That's just like her to be working away, but ready for what comes next. It seems she's always prepared for what comes next, except when it comes to me.

"Hi," I say, breaking the silence that fell between us.

"Hi."

I have something to ask her and the answer will let me know where I stand. Let me know if there's any chance for us as a couple.

Moving closer, I decide to leap off the cliff and lay my cards on the table. "I wanted to see if you would like to go to an art show with me tonight. Maybe we could get dinner before..."

She frowns. "Are you asking me on a date?"

I smile, feeling a little silly. Maybe this was a bad idea, but in for a penny, in for a pound. "Yes. I would like to take you out on a date."

She blinks at me, looks away, then returns her gaze to mine before whispering, "I've never been on a date."

"Well, if you'll let me, I would be honored to take you on your first one."

Her head dips forward and her hair shifts to cast her face in shadow. She looks coyly up at me through her lashes and says, "Yeah. Okay."

Holy shit, she said yes. I want to race over to her and kiss that beautiful face, but I keep my feet planted for fear that I'll scare her into changing her mind.

"Thank you. I'll pick you up at seven, and we'll have dinner before. Dress code is cocktail attire."

She nods. "Okay. I have some things that will work."

"Great." I check my watch and grin. "We'd better get our butts downstairs or Rae will send Finn up to get us."

A gorgeous grin spreads on her face in return and I'm back to wanting to race over and kiss her. "We can't have that now, can we?"

When I return to the house that evening, I'm feeling nervous. I wanted to give Cam some space, which I feel I did, but now it's time to start turning things around.

When I enter the house, she's waiting for me in the kitchen, talking to Jo as she preps supper for the house. "Ooo, you look pretty," Jo says when she sees me. "Both of you are gorgeous. Where are you going tonight?"

I answer Jo, but my eyes are only for Cam. "To dinner and an art show." Cam squirms under my stare. "You look beautiful," I tell her.

The dress she's wearing is form fitting and leaves one shoulder bare. It's a vibrant turquoise in a fabric that has a sheen to it.

Her hair is down, a sheet of silky darkness pulled over her bare shoulder. The color of the dress and her inky hair make her skin look even more like moonlight personified than ever.

Spots of color appear on her cheeks and she looks away. "Thank you."

"Are you ready?"

"Yes," she replies with a nod.

I take her to my favorite Thai restaurant because I remember her telling me she had tried the cuisine once and liked it, but hadn't had it since. We get way too much food, but I want her to be able to sample a variety of dishes.

With an unsteady hand, she attempts to use chopsticks to pick up a dumpling. It's almost to her mouth when her fingers slip, the sticks twist, and the dumpling goes flying. The young man with quick reflexes at the table next to ours catches it before it can land in his lap.

Cam's face flames for a moment, and her hand swings up to cover her mouth in shock. Then we both burst out in laughter. The tension and insecurity break and we relax in our seats.

Everything after that is easier. It almost feels like we're back to being how we were before. Almost.

I'm still leery of touching her. Even though it's difficult, I know that if I try to rush things, I'll lose her.

When we leave the restaurant, we're still laughing and re-laxed. The gallery having the showing isn't far, so it only takes a few minutes to get there. Once we're out of the car and headed inside, she reaches over and takes my hand in hers.

I know there are a lot of things she hasn't been allowed to do, and I want to do everything with her. We can experience the great wide world together.

"What do you think of this one?" I ask Cam of an enormous canvas painted peach except for a small brown circle offset from center.

She leans forward and looks at the tiny placard listing the name of the piece and price and reads, "The Existentialism of Evacuation for forty-five hundred dollars. I wonder if it's some-one trying to evacuate their bowels, because that's what it looks like to me."

A laugh barks out of me before I can stop it, but I rein it in, looking around. "I think you might be right," I murmur to her.

"It might make a wonderful Christmas present for Rae. I mean, what else do you get for the woman that has everything?"

We're both giggling like schoolgirls when a cool voice just behind me says, "Don't I know you?"

Thinking it might be a former client, I blank my face. When I turn around, I come face to face with Tai Dang, a tight smile on his face. He's dressed in an impeccable charcoal gray suit and on his arm is a young girl who might not even be a teenager yet.

She's pretty, but wearing a dress and makeup inappropriate for someone that young. When she inspects me right back, I can see that her pupils are blown. She's high as a kite.

Cam's arm links with mine, and she's holding tight. "I don't think you do," I say.

He leans in, no longer cordial. "Yes. You do. You're Joelle's friend from Cassandra's, but I haven't seen you there recently. Do you know where Joelle has gotten off to?"

I let my own face go hard and reply, "Last I heard, an evil man kidnapped her after work and then some angel came and rescued her from that devil."

"If you know where she is, you'd better tell me."

As I'm trying to think of something cutting to say in return, a man's voice cuts in. "Is there a problem here?"

He's tall and stocky and looks like a man who knows how to handle himself. His suit is off the rack, but decent, and looks a lot like the suits a few other men around the room are wearing. Security, I realize. That explains his intervention.

"No," I reply. "Mr. Dang thought he knew me, but he doesn't. Not at all." I take Cam's hand and move away. "Come on, Cam. I don't think I like this painting after all."

She resists for a moment, narrowing her eyes at Dang. He gives her an aggressive, toothy smile in response. Finally, she relents and follows me.

Behind us, Dang snorts. "I like 'em feisty. We'll be seeing each other again."

"Maybe it's time to go," I say to Cam.

"Agreed."

When we're in the car, Cam is practically vibrating with anger. "Are you okay?"

She looks back toward the door of the gallery. "That girl with him, that was Kimmy."

"Kimmy?" Then, I remember the girl she'd met in the mall. "But she's..."

"Only thirteen." She finishes for me.

"That son of a bitch."

"Agreed."

On the way home, we stop by an ice cream shop and linger inside in our fancy dresses, eating a scoop each. I think both of us would love to go back to take Dang down a peg, but instead we talk about everything but him.

When we're finished, we get some ice cream to take to the house and make our way home. To Cam's home.

I'm still staying in my apartment with my annoying cousin, but I have my sights set on the goal of spending every night with her. Whether that means me moving back into Rae's house or Cam coming to live with me remains to be seen. It doesn't matter to me as long as I'm with her.

The house is quiet when we go inside. We store the ice cream in the freezer, then stand there awkwardly. Neither of us knowing what to do.

I know what I'd like to do, so I go with that. "Can I kiss you goodnight?"

Her bottom lip is pulled between her teeth as she mulls it over. After what seems like an eternity, she nods.

Stepping close, I cup her face between my palms and lean down to kiss her. Mustering the entirety of my self-control, I pull back after a moment and put my forehead to hers. She reaches up and grips my wrists.

"Thank you for going with me tonight."

"Thank you for taking me. It was a good first date."

"You're welcome. Turned out to be more of a visit to the zoo than an art show, though."

She chuckles. "I still think I might get that painting for Rae."

CHAPTER FORTY-THREE

The Nerve of That Guy

RAE

After our training session yesterday, I asked Nate if he'd be willing to drive me to Tahlequah today. I figured it might be good for him to get out of the house. When he looked over at Jo, I reassured him.

"Finn and the others will be here, so everyone will be safe."

He's taking his protector duties seriously. In a way, it's good to see. They are the youngest and closest in age, so it's understandable that he'd be drawn to her, but I don't want him developing an unhealthy attachment to her.

When I told him and Cam what I was going back to Tahlequah for, she insisted he needed to dress the part of my driver. She couldn't talk him into a suit, but Jo went with them to get him some slacks and dress shirts.

Can't say that I blame him, because as soon as Cam informed Nate that they were going shopping, she told me I needed to dress the part, too. That means that instead of jeans and my beat up leather boots, I'm in the passenger seat dressed like I'm some kind of high-class businesswoman.

"I can't believe she made me wear this," I grouse for the millionth time.

"For someone so small, she's kind of intimidating," Nate agrees.

"Yes, she is."

He parks in front of the restaurant and we both sit there, eyeing it for a moment. This is a new situation for me, but it's a role I knew I'd want to take on eventually, so I suck in a breath and tell him I'm ready to go.

While they were out shopping, Cam drilled him on what his duties would be as my driver, and he said he was fine with it. True to his word, he gets out of the car, comes around, and opens my door, his eyes scanning the parking lot.

Staying close behind me, we make our way inside. I have a reservation for me and my guest with a table for Nate close by. Rather than make him stand by like security would do for someone like my uncle, I'm not about to make him stand there and watch me eat.

But then, I'm not a complete asshole like Keegan.

We're a little early so I'm sitting there drinking a whiskey until my guest arrives. Sasha Shotpouch is in her early thirties and of a height with me. Her black hair is cut into a short, stylish bob, and she wears minimal makeup.

When she approaches my table, she's got her game face on. It's a good thing, because this is a quasi interview. I'm not looking to hire her, but if things go well today, I'll be making a sizeable donation to her campaign fund.

She's running against Yona for the council seat he wants.

I'm not petty. Usually. But someone like him who uses his charm and lies through his teeth to manipulate people is not someone I want on my nation's council guiding the organization on behalf of its people.

He knows all the right things to say, but Yona is all about Yona and he doesn't give a shit about anyone else. If he wants this position, it's because it will give him more power and the ability to figure out a way to line his own pockets.

No sooner does her butt hit the seat across from me than I ask, "So, Ms. Shotpouch, why do you want to be a council representative for your district?"

She smiles, so I guess she appreciates the direct approach. A woman after my own heart.

"Please, call me Sasha."

With that request, she launches into her thoughts on the direction of the nation and how, if elected, she'd be one of the younger members of the council. When she starts talking about how she intends to use her position to draw in other young tribal members to help uphold and expand language programs and cultural understanding, her passion is clear.

The woman is on a mission to perpetuate and expand the customs of our people so they're not lost to time. Her enthusiasm is contagious.

She also wants to work to draw in those who are tribal members who might have felt overlooked because the blood in their veins wasn't one hundred percent native. I tell her about my experiences growing up half Cherokee and half Irish. She's attentive and taking to heart the challenges I faced, asking questions as if she's cataloging each one.

By the time our meals are delivered, I'm sold and wishing I'd left the check blank instead of pre-filling an amount because I'd double it. When we settle in to eat, our conversation turns casual, and she tells me about her husband and children. I tell her about growing up just south of Tahlequah, but leave out the whole mobster thing about Dad and give her an extremely sanitized version of my work.

I keep the conversation going until I'm sure Nate is finished with his meal. That boy can put away some food. Once the check is paid, I hand over the donation, for which she gushes her appreciation.

I'm walking to the exit with Sasha, Nate following close behind when the front door opens. Yona walks through the door, his eyes scanning the restaurant.

"The nerve of that guy," Sasha mumbles at my side. "I'll bet someone told him I was meeting with a potential donor and he had to come see for himself."

When Yona's eyes land on me walking next to Sasha, he frowns. Then his frown turns to a scowl. "Rae?"

"Yona," I respond, his name rolling off my tongue as cold as an Arctic breeze.

"You two know each other?" Sasha asks.

"We're acquainted." I don't stop to speak further to Yona, but just keep on going. When we're outside, Sasha thanks me again and gives me a hug before she heads to her car, eager to get back to work on time.

Yona bursts through the door behind me. "What the hell, Rae?"

Nate steps between us, putting a hand up for Yona to stop.

"Who is this?" Yona continues to bluster. "What's going on Rae? Did you donate to her campaign?"

Yep. The snake is worried about the competition and had to slither his way down here to...what? Did he hope to discover who it was only to approach them about donating to him?

Too slow, bucko. The check is already in her hot little hand and I'm glad for it.

When I'm almost to the car, I call back to Nate. "Come on, Nate. He won't do anything. He knows better."

Yona is still yammering. "So this is how it's going to be? You said I should stay in politics, but now you're funding my opponent?"

I'm far enough away that he's raised his voice and people are starting to pay attention. A smile tilts the corners of my mouth.

Let him make a spectacle of himself in public. If he keeps that up, I won't have to work very hard to keep him out of any position of significance; he'll do it for me.

Once we're closed in the car, Nate says, "Never did like that guy. Always acted like he was too good."

I bark out a laugh. "You hit the nail on the head."

Nate gives me a rare grin, puts the car in gear, and turns us toward home.

CHAPTER FORTY-FOUR

Not So Untouchable

RAE

Today's the day.

Hopefully.

If it's not, I might have to take matters into my own hands.

Cam told me about the encounter with Tai Dang last night and the threat he made. After all these months of monitoring his activity, I know he'll make good on it if given the opportunity. The man seems to think he's untouchable.

Today is the third and final day the Feds think might be Dang's bank robbery day. Early this morning, I found a building a couple of blocks away that was abandoned and tall enough to give me a view of the bank.

His typical MO, or modus operandi, is to hit the bank right after they open or right before they close. I perched up here with a pair of binoculars this morning and waited until a couple of hours after opening. When nothing happened, I climbed down and went home for lunch.

Once my belly was full, I returned and climbed back up here. The sun is high in the sky and the day is warm, so I'm lying here in a pool of my own sweat watching the bank and the various cops and their cars positioned all around.

A check of the time on my phone lets me know my ordeal is almost over. Through the binoculars, I watch as a young man shuffles down the block and goes into the bank. A few minutes later, he comes back out and when he's about a half block away, he takes his cap off and puts it on backward.

The clock continues to wind down and I'm just about to give up when an enormous black sedan roars down the street and screeches to a stop in front of the bank. People in black hoodies and kabuki masks rush out and into the bank.

The exterior is swarmed and surrounded by cops and cop cars. I can see the trap close as the thieves hurry back out of the building, only to have the door slammed shut and locked behind them. Like many banks, it's probably made of some sort of bulletproof material.

The cacophony of shouts is so loud, it carries to me. Like the idiot he is, Dang...at least, I figure it's Dang because he's flanked on both sides by the other robbers and he's the only one wearing a red devil mask. The others are in similar masks, but they're significantly plainer.

The Devil raises his hand with the gun, pointing it at one of the cops. In horror, I watch as the slight form on his right dives in front of him when the officers open fire. The smaller person, who appears to be about the same size as Kimmy, falls to the ground. Then Dang is perforated by several hits.

I guess he wasn't so untouchable, after all.

The other robber goes down, too, having raised his weapon when Dang did. Wisely, the driver of the getaway car puts his hands out the window and I keep watching until he's yanked out of the car and slammed to the ground.

I never wished Dang dead, just behind bars. However, I can't say that I'm sad about how things turned out for him. Kimmy, if that's who the protective robber was, is another matter altogether.

After that last message she sent Cam, she never responded again, despite Cam reaching out to her over and over. Cam hoped to break through to the girl and help her get away from Dang's influence.

If I'm correct, and that was Kimmy that tried to shield Dang from the consequences of raising a gun at the cops in an already heated exchange, it's going to tear Cam up. She already feels like she failed Kimmy, but this is going to make it even worse.

I hate that for her, but she needs to realize you can't save everyone. Kimmy was a kid. The only one responsible for her possible death is the asshole who was grooming her, Tai Dang. Call me harsh, but the world is better off without him in it.

I'm about to pull out of the alley on my bike, but stop short to avoid being plowed down by the first of the news vans. They need to pay attention before they make some news of their own by creating a hit and run.

"Vultures," I mumble and look both ways before I hit the gas.

When I get home, the house seems empty until I hear the television. They must have left the door open because normally, there's no noise at all, even if the thing is turned up to full volume. I make my way down the hall.

The entire household, except Nate, is there, watching the breaking news flash across the screen. With all the police presence, it looks like they were able to set up a perimeter to keep the press at a distance. When the reporter whines about not being able to get close, I smile.

Good on the cops for keeping them at arm's length. I'm not opposed to the news in general; when I was a kid, it could be relied upon to actually be news. These days, it seems like they're only interested in sensationalism and half-truths and it only gets worse every year.

"So, you think that was the guy? What was his name?" Bee queries.

I go in and sit next to Jo. "Tai Dang." As soon as the name crosses my lips, she begins to shiver. Linking my arm with hers, I scoot close. She leans into me and puts her head on my shoulder.

This is more evidence that something weird is happening to me. I've never been touchy feely like this and certainly never tried to comfort someone. Although it's unusual, it's starting to happen more and more and I have to admit, I kind of like it.

"Where's Nate?"

"Downstairs." Cam turns around and grins at me. "You missed the training session this morning. I guess he has decided to beef up on the weights after Bee put him on his butt."

"Way to go, Bee!" When she turns around to smile at me, accepting the praise, I put my fist out. She just looks at it for a moment, then bumps my fist with hers.

"Do you know for sure it was him?"

It's barely a whisper, so I reply to Jo just as quietly. "Pretty sure, but not one hundred percent. Sure enough, though, that I'd be willing to bet money on it."

CHAPTER FORTY-FIVE

Blowing Off Some Steam

VICTORIA

Every day, I come to Rae's house. I say it's so that I can train and workout with the crew, but really, it's so I can be close to Cam. However, I'm not hating the payoff from the training. It's only been a few weeks since we started and I already feel stronger and more in control of my body.

In the two weeks since Tai Dang's death, Rae has been busier than ever. Cam and I have both offered to help, but she has put us off time and again. It's understandable that she wants everything to go perfectly, but if she keeps this pace up, she's going to burn out.

We're wiping away the post-workout sweat when Rae says, "Y'all have been hounding me, so I think we'll go out tonight and have some fun. You know, blow off some steam if you're up for it."

Bee does a little hop and claps her hands. "Really?"

"Yeah, there's a club I want to check out."

Cam stares at Rae for a long time, then cocks her head. "Check out..." she echoes.

The way she says it clues me into the fact that there's more to it than just going out and having fun. That's all right. I'm learning it pays to be prepared when going places with Rae.

"Want to run to my apartment with me so I can get some clothes for tonight?"

"Sure," Cam replies. "I need to shower first, though."

I grin at her. "What a coincidence, I do, too."

She grins back and holds out her hand to me. We've slowly worked our way back into intimacy. I stayed close to her and after a while, when I reached out to hold her hand, she didn't pull away.

Then there was the kissing and the touching and...well, we haven't had sex yet, but we're getting closer. Two nights ago, we fell asleep in each other's arms and I slept through the night for the first time since I left.

It was me who fucked up, so I've left everything up to her. She needs to get comfortable with trusting me again, so I'm sticking close but letting her set the pace for how quickly we move forward.

We take another step when we enter her room. She strips off her clothes and when I don't, figuring I'll shower after she does, she looks at me, confused. "Aren't you coming?"

"I...uh...wasn't sure."

Understanding dawns and turns tender. "We might as well shower together. After all, it's better for the environment."

I smirk. "The environment, huh?"

She sashays her fine ass toward the bathroom. "Absolutely."

We're under the warmth of the shower spray, hands slick with body wash roaming everywhere, and hope blooms in my chest as heat pools in my core. My hope is dashed when I slip my hand between her thighs to cup her sex and she eases it away.

Instead of letting my disappointment show, I turn her so her hair is out of the spray. I squirt some of her shampoo into the palm of my hand and take my time washing her hair. Slowly, she relaxes under my ministrations until she lets out a long sigh.

"I'm sorry..."

"Don't be. If you're not ready, you're not ready. I don't want you to feel pressured."

She leans back against me. "Thank you. I do want you and I'm close. It's just with everything..."

When she trails off and doesn't say more, I respond. "I understand. Let's get rinsed off and dressed and go run errands."

We spend the rest of the morning making several stops and decide to have lunch while we're out. The hostess seats us at a restaurant I picked at random based on where we were in town.

A few moments later, a man is led into the room and something about him draws my attention.

Perhaps it's the way his bespoke suit fits him. Or maybe it is the black ink that peeks out from the collar and cuffs of his crisp white shirt. The minute I laid eyes on him, the hair on the back of my neck stood on end.

I'm surprised when my response is different from how I would have reacted a few months ago. If he had walked into Cassandra's club back then, I would have steered clear and cautioned the other girls to stay away from him. I would have reacted like prey.

Now, I simply track him, noting his presence and location. Cam's palm smooths over my thigh. "Do you know him?"

Turning to her, I notice she's watching the same man. "No, but I don't like him."

"Same."

We don't dawdle at lunch, but don't rush, either. I refuse to let some man intimidate me into changing my behavior. That's the old Tori, but the new Tori is letting the swagger of Rae Morrissey rub off on her and is learning to live in her power.

For the rest of the day, I keep one eye on the rearview mirror, especially on the way back to the house. I'm glancing toward the mirror yet again when Cam says, "I think we need to be prepared for tonight to be more than just an opportunity to have some fun."

"Is that why you looked the way you did when she mentioned tonight's little outing?"

Her only response is a shrug.

"So, nothing specific," I guess, "just a feeling."

With a nod, she turns to look out the window.

I reach over and squeeze her thigh. "I trust your feelings, so we'll be prepared."

Her hand covers mine and squeezes back. My phone buzzes and when I check it at a stoplight, I'm surprised to see Cassandra's name on the screen. I pull over into a parking lot to read the text.

Cassandra: *There are some of your things here you need to pick up.*

Me: *Not sure what could still be there.*

Cassandra: *You need to come pick them up and we need to talk.*

Me: *Fine. I'll come by this evening.*

I figure we can stop by on the way to the club. If Rae doesn't want to, we can take two cars, but I really hope she wants to.

Something about this doesn't feel right, but maybe I'm just on edge because of the man at lunch. However, anything I might have left at the club is inconsequential and could have been thrown away, and I'd never have known the difference.

Thankfully, Rae is agreeable to take just the SUV and make the additional stop. It's early evening and there are only a few cars in the parking lot. Most of them I recognize as belonging to other employees.

Cassandra's car is also there, as well as a Porsche SUV I don't recognize. Perhaps it belongs to a client despite it being earlier than they usually arrive.

Rae, Cam, and I go through the front door. There's not the usual security slash bouncer there, which has me feeling doubly cautious. We don't see anyone all the way to Cassandra's office, which is up a flight of stairs and toward the back of the building.

I knock on her office door. "Come," she calls out.

It's the same way she's always given entry to her office, and it never bothered me before, but for some reason, it grates on my nerves now. With a twist of the knob, I push the door open and we step inside.

Surprise flickers across her face that I'm not alone, but she recovers quickly, schooling her face into a mask of stoic indifference. Rather than linger, I get right down to business. "You said you have some of my things?"

She waves a hand at a small bag on the corner of her desk. "Yes, those are the things there. However, I also wanted to speak with you."

"About?"

Her hand waves again at the chairs on this side of her desk. "Please, won't you sit?"

"That's okay. I can't imagine this will take long."

I've never felt so uncomfortable in this building, but since we stepped out of the car, it feels...off. Like something has changed.

"All right then. A few years ago, you had proposed an eventual buy out of my shares in the company..."

I cut her off. "After what happened with Joelle, that is no longer my desire. It seems clear there has been an ever-growing tolerance for behavior that I cannot condone. With it being so pervasive in your operations, I doubt I would be able to overcome and redirect that behavior, and it's not something I could or even would allow to continue."

Her face turns to stone. "You have no idea what it's like to run a business like this. Expenses outran income and investors were needed."

"Investors like Tai Dang?"

When she flinches, I know I've hit the mark. "Is that why you wanted to speak to me? You were hoping I'd want to invest with you now that Tai Dang is dead, which means his money has dried up? Do you even realize what he did to Joelle?"

Remembering how Jo looked and acted that morning when we rescued her from the brothel where he'd taken her clogs my throat with emotion.

Rae steps forward, speaking for the first time. "She's not going to give you any money. In fact, I suggest you close up shop and leave town."

Cassandra straightens her spine and levels her eyes on Rae. "Who are you to suggest any such thing to me?"

Unfazed, Rae replies, "I'm the one who knows all your dirty little secrets, including, as I've told you before, the fact that Joelle isn't the first employee to be kidnapped from your parking lot. Unlike Joelle, no one was there to rescue her. What was her name again? Samara? She was found dead, wasn't she? Guess you didn't cover that up as well as you thought you had."

Rae roams around the office looking at the art on the walls, blatantly turning her back on Cassandra as if she's of no importance. "Like I said, close up and get out. If you don't, I'll make sure everyone knows your dirty little secrets."

"You should be careful about whom you threaten," Cassandra hisses.

Rae shrugs. "Not too worried about it. Take your chances and ignore me if you like. Come on ladies, this has grown tedious."

She opens the door and allows Cam and me to go through first. It isn't until we get in the car again that I realize I left the bag of stuff on her desk. Somehow, I doubt it was even my stuff, just crap she gathered under the pretense of drawing me to her office.

When we walk into the nightclub Rae chose, I'm glad the behemoth bouncer at the front door is unaware of the weapons he allowed to walk into the door because the place has a strange vibe. He checked Finn, but didn't give a second glance at anyone with breasts.

I'm starting to enjoy being an incognito badass. Not that I'm a badass exactly. Not yet, but I'm getting there.

The location of the club is great and the exterior screams upscale. Inside, it has some good bones, but has been neglected until it's become kind of dodgy. The aesthetics are okay, but the vibe it's putting off makes me glad I have people here to watch my back.

Maybe Cam's clairvoyance is starting to rub off on me, too. I think I would dig being a badass clairvoyant. Again, I'm not there quite yet, but...well, you know.

Cam, Bee, and I dance and have a good time. Unsuprisingly, Jo stayed home, so Nate stayed home, too, to watch over her. It seems as if Rae and Finn are watching over us while we play and laugh, hyper-aware, despite their relaxed slouches on stools by the bar.

However, I think Bee is the only one totally relaxed and unaware of the pervasive sense of threat bouncing around the room to the beat of the bass vibrating the floor. My eyes occasionally snag on Cam's and she seems to be as aware as I am.

We take a break and get drinks. Rae nods at Finn, who nods back. She goes over to talk to a bouncer. The conversation appears to become heated because he leans down, putting his face near hers, and says something.

Based on his scowl, it's not something nice. She jabs a finger into his chest and snarls right back. Then she turns on her heel and stalks away. Her trajectory doesn't bring her back to us, but she goes to a young woman toward the end of the bar who is talking with a man.

The man looks smarmy, his cheap pants a little too tight, pulling and bunching, his shirt unbuttoned a little too far. When the woman picks up her drink, Rae takes it from her and puts it out of reach. The woman looks as if she's going to object, but Rae says something to her.

Instead of being upset with Rae, the woman turns a look of disgust onto the man, grabs the drink and tosses it into his face. In moments, she gathers her things and heads for the exit. Cam touches my arm and we follow her out the front door.

The woman is clearly frightened. She jumps when I tell her, "We'll watch over you to your car."

When she whirls around and sees two women instead of another predator, she relaxes. "Thank you. I can't believe... What could have... If it hadn't been for her..."

"But it didn't happen. You're safe," Cam assures her.

The woman nods and hurries to her car. Once her lights fade from sight, we go back inside the club.

The predator is holding his throat, and Rae is leaned over the bar talking to the bartender. Although the conversation is heated, I can't make out what's being said, but those near them, especially the women, are gathering their things and headed toward the door.

Once the women leave, the men follow suit soon after. Only our group and a few stragglers remain. Finally, Rae returns to us.

"What did you do?" Bee hisses angrily.

"Nothing you need to worry about. In fact, Finn, why don't you take Bee home and send Nate back with the SUV? Have him text me when he gets close."

He frowns at Rae, but she doesn't flinch. Eventually, he gives in with a nod.

CHAPTER FORTY-SIX

You Belong To Me Now

RAE

"Y'all can go with Finn, if you want," I tell Cam and Tori.

Cam hitches her chin and glares at me as if I've just asked her to drown a puppy.

"I'm not saying you have to, just giving you the option. Sheesh!"

"You should know better than to even think that I'd leave you alone in a place like this."

"So you like it?"

"This place feels gross," Tori says.

"I don't know. A little sprucing up, a good sageing, and it might not be half bad."

Cam frowns and cocks her head at me. I almost laugh, but she doesn't know what I know, so I don't. The bartender called the owner about thirty minutes ago, so he should be showing up any time now.

"Dave," I call to the bartender, "why don't you pull down that bottle of Teeling for me?"

Now I have another person frowning at me. I'm about to explain to him why he should give me what I want when the front door bursts open and a short, round man comes puffing into the room.

Puffing. Both from a lack of fitness and the nasty smelling cheap cigar clenched between his teeth.

The man is wearing a tracksuit, for fuck's sake. Instead of sneakers, he's wearing a pair of scuffed loafers. Christ, it's like he's out of some bad nineties sitcom and his character would be described as greaseball.

"Turn off the goddamn music!" he shouts.

Abruptly, the room goes quiet. I can hear him breathing all the way across the room. This is probably more cardio than he's done in his entire life. I just hope he doesn't have a heart attack before we can complete our business.

"Which one of you fuckers is Rae?"

I push myself up from where I've been leaning on my elbows on the bar. "That would be me."

He flinches back. I'll bet the last thing he expected was for a woman to command his presence. Once he recovers, he looks me up and down.

"What the hell is some bitch…"

That's enough. I'm already sick of this asshole, so I raise my voice and interrupt. "You might want to think before you finish that sentence." When he shuts up, I add, "And if you call me a bitch again, I won't waste my time doing this the nice way."

"What the fuck are you talking about?"

"I'm here to discuss a few things with you. Most notably, I have news from some gentlemen in Vegas."

I'd received a request to dig up information regarding Mr. Randall Butts - seriously, that's really his last name – and discovered he has been a very bad boy. After living in Vegas for a time and experiencing some of the worst luck ever, he fled the state to Oklahoma.

He owed some folks of the loan shark variety a crap ton of money. The gentlemen he owed had their hands full enough that they weren't motivated to chase Butts across the country for a few hundred grand.

I don't care anything about someone welching on their debts as long as it's not me they owe, but when they come here, to my state, and open a club that becomes a hunting ground for sexual predators, that I do care about. Based on his texts, he's aware of the problem and turns a blind eye.

There have been reports of the use of date rape drugs, but all have been regarding different men. Just because a club doesn't watch out for it's patrons doesn't make them legally liable. Although it should, in my opinion.

I'd always thought I'd like to follow in my dad's footsteps and own a bar and buying Butts' debts is going to make it easy. And cheap by comparison.

Butts blanches at the mention of his little problem in Vegas. Little does he know his problem has come home to roost.

"Everybody out! We're closed!"

The few remaining patrons down their drinks and shuffle toward the exit. While we wait for the place to clear, I turn and give Dave a pointed look. Wisely, he gets the bottle I want and pours me a shot.

My phone buzzes in my pocket. When I check it, I see Nate has arrived. I send him a text and tell him to wait and that we'll be out in a minute.

A man sitting at the back of the room in a gloomy corner catches my eye. He rises slowly, purposefully, taking a moment to toss some bills onto the table.

His clothes are quality, way too good for this place, which is my first clue. He also has black ink peeking out from under his collar and on the bare forearms revealed by his rolled-up sleeves.

Tattoos don't bother me and these days are more likely to adorn some zero threat hipster than to signify a badass. But it's his confident swagger, more of a prowl, really, that has me keeping an eye on him all the way to the door.

He doesn't look at me, but I can feel his awareness stroking over my skin. Cam sucks in a breath next to me. When I look at her, I see she's watching the man, too.

"What's wrong?" I whisper.

"There was another man like him at lunch today. They might not look exactly alike, but they're the same."

I raise an eyebrow, unsure what to make of her declaration, but otherwise, I don't respond. When the customers are gone, I throw back my shot, stand, and face my target.

Waving a hand around to indicate the staff still present, I ask, "Are you sure you want your employees to know your business?"

He simply glares at me, so I go on. While I speak, I walk in slow circles around him.

"As I said, there are some gentlemen in Vegas to whom you owed a shit ton of money. I say owed, in the past tense, because now you owe it to me. So, today's your lucky day, Buttsy, because instead of giving you a beat down and targeting those you care about like they would, I have a different plan. You belong to me now."

I stop in front of him and turn to face him.

"Instead of being unalived, you're going to sign this club over to me and leave the state. I don't want your kind here. You've turned a blind eye to multiple women being slipped drugs in their drinks in this shitty establishment and being raped when their date hustles them out to their car or the back alley."

I step into his personal space and pull papers out of my back pocket.

"This is the transfer of ownership documentation. You have twelve hours to comply. If you fail to present me with these documents signed and fail to leave the state within twenty-four hours after that, I'll come find you and you won't like what happens."

He sneers at me and snaps his fingers. The big bouncer who failed to react when I told him the woman's drink had been drugged lumbers forward.

I step back and tilt my neck to one side and then the other to loosen the muscles. Tiny pops sound as my neck stretches. A hand appears on my arm. It's Cam.

"Let me."

"You sure?"

"Absolutely. This arsehole needs to know who he's dealing with."

The lummox puts a meaty hand on Cam's shoulder and shoves her. "Whachoo gon do little girl."

Cam grins at me. "You saw that, right?"

"Yep, a room full of witnesses saw him assault you first."

Calm, reserved Cam becomes a flurry of motion, her scrap of a club dress throwing sparkles across the room as it catches the light. She doesn't have the size or strength to take him on fist to fist, but thanks to her training, she knows all the points of vulnerability on a man.

A well-placed kick lands in his groin. When he sags forward holding his balls, she grabs his watermelon head in both hands and yanks it down so that when it connects with her rising knee, a satisfying crunch reverberates through the quiet room.

Big boy howls and grabs his nose while Cam swings around and roundhouse kicks him hard in the kidney. He rolls over and holds his hands up, palms out, in surrender. It took all of about forty-five seconds. Why is it that so many big men go down so easily?

"Who's the little girl now, you wanker?" Cam snarls, her Irish accent on display.

"Who the fuck are you guys?" Butts growls.

I cock my head. "The Morrigan. This is our town now, and you're not welcome here." I slap my hand against his chest, holding the paperwork there. "Twelve hours, Randall. If you think about running before you take care of our business, I'll find you, and it won't be pretty."

"So, if I sign this, my Vegas debts are done?"

"Only the ones you owed to the Blumfeld brothers. If you owe others, that's still in play. Considering the amount you owed them, you're getting one hell of a deal."

"You got a pen?"

Tori opens her purse and hands him an ink pen. Randall signs the paperwork and hands it back to me. "You have…"

He turns on his heel and waves a hand at me as he waddles toward the door. "Yeah, yeah, twenty-four hours to get out of town."

The employees watch him leave with looks of confusion. Can't say that I blame them.

"All right folks, this place is officially under new ownership…"

CHAPTER FORTY-SEVEN

Like a Couple of Teenagers

CAM

After collecting building keys and visiting the office with the manager, Rae sent everyone home with a request to meet each of them face to face over the next few days. Employees would be paid their normal wages with extra for the servers to cover their missed tips until everyone had their meeting.

"So, what's the plan?" Tori asks when we're in the SUV with Nate driving us home.

Rae shrugs. "Thought it would be nice to own a bar. When I got the research request on this place and Butts, it seemed like a simple path. Two positives with one buy out. We get a bar and any predators that come here from now on will have to deal with me."

"With us," I say.

"With us," Tori and Rae agree.

Tori nuzzles my neck. "By the way, watching you kick that guy's ass was boiling hot."

Warmth flushes through me and settles between my thighs. I snuggle closer to her, still feeling jittery from the adrenaline burn off.

When I stepped up to take on that ogre, I was feeling strong. But then that meaty hand shoved me and my confidence flew away like a startled flock of birds. There was no way I could back out, though.

If I did, it would have reflected poorly on not only me, but on Rae, and she needs to know I can fight my own battles and even some of hers. We're in this together, and I want to be an asset, not a liability.

Then I did it. I kicked that numpty's arse faster than I thought possible. Sometimes it pays to be underestimated. Sometimes being underestimated and coming out on top leaves you feeling powerful.

And horny. My libido is in overdrive and I can't wait to get Tori home and naked.

"What?" I ask, realizing Rae was talking to me while I was thinking of burying my head between Tori's legs.

"I said, I'm thinking you should manage the businesses, Cam. You're much better at that organizational stuff than I am. We'll have the bar for now, but I want more legit businesses. If things get to be too much to handle, you can hire anyone you think you need."

"People will come along when we need them. Of that, I'm sure. Just like Nate did."

Although it's probably not apparent to anyone else yet, Nate is part of the family now and won't be going back to Tahlequah. There are others coming, but I'm not sure when they'll be here, so that's all I say on the topic.

Instead, I turn to Tori and lean up to kiss her. I don't miss the surprise that flickers across her face, but it's gone in an instant and she returns my kiss. My arms slip around her and she embraces me back.

For a moment, we're making out in the back seat like a couple of teenagers in no hurry to make it home in time for curfew. But I remember we're not alone and pull back. However, I remain in her embrace, not wanting to let her get too far away.

Finally, we arrive at the house and, with Tori's hand in mine, I head straight for my room. I am still so aroused, blood pumping through my veins so hot that I can hardly wait to get out of these clothes.

With the door closed behind us, we are a flurry of hands and fingers pulling at buttons and pushing at anything loose. We fall into bed with arms and legs tangled, both of us trying to swallow the other with kisses.

There's a bit of a wrestling match to see who is going to take the lead, but Tori relaxes and lets me take the reins. I push her down, flat on her back and nuzzle her neck, her scent making me think of a garden of night blooming jasmine with hints of earthy musk.

While my lips taste her neck and shoulders salty from dried sweat created on the dance floor, my hands are fondling her full breasts. Her taste is like nectar to me.

It feels as if I've been starving, and she is the only satisfaction I can find. I blaze a trail with kisses, licks, and nips until I reach one plump nipple, peaked with arousal and suck it between my lips.

She whimpers as I draw hard upon it and tweak her other nipple between forefinger and thumb at the same time. I shift my weight and she spreads her legs for me, my hips settling between her thighs.

Because she's taller than me, my pelvic bone snugs up against her sex and I can feel how wet she is for me. "Put one leg over mine," she rasps.

I frown, because it seems odd, but when I do, it aligns our soaking wet cunts and a zing of pleasure surges through me. "Oh!" I gasp and begin to move.

When I lean forward to increase the contact and friction, my nipple is the one being sucked. Our hips rock, and as our pussies slip and slide against each other, my orgasm builds.

Why on earth did I push her away for so long? My emotions soar along with the physical sensations, and I feel so full everywhere that my eyes prickle with tears. Before they can spill, my swollen clit strokes just right against Tori's and the orgasm crashes over me.

Every muscle in my body tenses as if I've been hit with an electrical charge, then I go limp, sensations rolling through me with the waves of aftershocks. My shaking is echoed in Tori's body pressed to mine.

We stay there in each other's arms until the trembling fades. When it finally does, she turns to face me and pecks me on the lips.

"I have something to tell you."

When my lips part to speak, Tori puts a finger gently over them to stop me.

"Please, just let me get this out. I love you Bridget. I've never felt this way before. If you don't love me back, that's okay. I can wait because I never want to be with anyone else. You're my life and I'll wait for you forever if that's what it takes."

The tears return because I feel the same way about her. But me saying so right now, she would question whether I was just saying it because she had, so instead of speaking, I snuggle closer.

With a sigh, I close my eyes and fall asleep in the arms of the woman I love.

CHAPTER FORTY-EIGHT

Once I Get My Breath Back

CAM

The building we pull up to looks quite different from the photos online. When we went downstairs for breakfast this morning, Rae told me we'd gotten a call from the realtor for one of the properties. There was time available today to view the property, so she booked it.

As with most dating profiles online, the photos appear to have been taken years ago. The actual building direly needs a facelift. That would explain the price.

Hopefully, the inside is better than the outside because the location is fantastic for our purposes, including being near to our new bar. Already, I can envision updating the exterior to make it more modern. Sleeker, more in keeping with Rae's aesthetic. It could work.

"She's no beauty," Rae says when she steps out of the SUV and surveys the front of the building.

"But there's potential," I reply, following her onto the sidewalk. "I already have some ideas. If the interior checks out, I don't think it would take much to refurb it for our purposes."

"I agree. This place could be kinda cool," Tori says as she joins me on the sidewalk and links her arm with mine.

"Y'all have a better eye for such things than I do," Rae replies. "I'm no interior decorator."

A Masters Construction truck pulls up, and Alejandro gets out. Although he's not a structural engineer, he's got a ton of experience with commercial construction. Rae paid the company a hefty consulting fee to have him here today.

"Hello, ladies," he says when he joins us on the sidewalk and starts shaking hands.

"Good to see you again, Alejandro," I say. "You know what we are looking at doing, so feel free to do your thing and check out the building to see if it will work. Also, your eyes are much more experienced than ours, so just let us know if you notice any big red flags floating about."

"Can do."

A BMW pulls to the curb and a tall thin woman gets out. She's dressed stylishly and her blond hair is coifed to perfection in a close-cropped pixie. "Hello! I'm Amy Dillon."

Her voice is loud and her smile broad, but her handshake is dead fish limp and I have to school my face from reacting. "Hello Amy, I'm Cam, and these are my associates." I purposely don't give out Rae and Tori's names. "Alejandro is with our construction company and will be performing a preliminary evaluation to assess whether the building will fit our needs."

She smiles brilliantly. "Let's get started, then."

The building is an ideal location. Literally, last week I chose the key areas of the city and marked them on a map. Then I drew a circle around them and chose a few locations toward the center of the grouping.

Of the three options, this one is in the middle of the group as far as price, but I like the location the best. The less expensive one is quite a bit smaller and the more expensive one is overpriced based on my research.

It's a six-story building with frontage on a busy thoroughfare, and the bottom floor would be ideal for retail spaces and an upscale restaurant. The top two floors would be Rae's to do with as she will.

Tori's space would be somewhere in the middle. A building like this gives us plenty of room to work with.

Alejandro goes off with a tablet in hand to give each of the floors his critical review. Rae and the realtor go to the top floor because those are the floors she most cares about. Tori and I start moving up from the first floor.

I take my phone out and start videoing as we walk through spaces. Tori is taking pictures with hers, too. We're on the third floor trying to figure out what a large open space was used for when the stairwell door clatters shut.

"Rae? Is that you?" I frown when there's no answer.

Clipped footsteps approach across the linoleum floor and the length of the stride makes it clear that it's not Rae or the realtor. The realtor is tall, but this is a man's stride, and Alejandro is wearing rubber-soled boots.

Leaving my phone in record mode, I hiss at Tori. "Dial Rae."

She quickly finds Rae's contact and just as she presses the button, a man I don't recognize steps into the large office space where we're standing. He reminds me of the strange men we've seen in recent days.

Like the others, he's not a twin in looks, but is in dress, demeanor, and hints of black ink under his clothes. Unlike the other men, he's not playing it cool. His face is full of malice when his gaze falls upon us.

"Who are you?"

The man gives me a wolfish grin. A predator's grin. As if he's positive he's the only threat in the room.

Tori and I glance at each other.

"I'm here to deliver a message to the bitches that think they can tell people what to do." One hand slides behind his back and he pulls out a knife as long as my forearm. Light from the windows glares off the polished blade as he brandishes it.

"What are you talking about?" Tori asks.

"Don't play dumb. You know exactly what I'm talking about."

Actually, we don't. We've told a couple of people to leave town recently. Is he talking about Cassandra or Butts?

Although he's doing a fair job of keeping up an Americanized accent, it slips occasionally. Unfortunately, it doesn't slip often enough for me to identify the underlying linguistic influences.

There is a red and black tattoo on the back of his hand. Between him moving his hand around in what I'm guessing he thinks is a threatening manner and the poor lighting as it moves in and out of beams of light from the windows, I can't identify it. It might be a family crest, or a flag, or nothing of significance at all.

Damn it, I can't tell.

My focus is so intent on trying to identify something about him that there's no fear in me. I can see Tori analyzing and watching his moves, ready to counter if he comes at her just as I am. Although my mind is tied up, my body is ready to react.

"I'm not playing dumb," Tori spits back. "You're not making any sense."

He stalks toward her, but she doesn't move. Confusion registers on his face because he's not getting the reactions he expected. We're supposed to be scared, but we're not and he's not sure what to do about it.

Just then, Rae races through the door and shoves him off balance. Tori grabs one of his arms, which distracts him as I step into place.

With a grip on a pressure point in his wrist, I numb his hand. Then I twist it around so the pointy end of his knife turns back toward him as he pitches forward.

My attempt to get out of the way fails because if I let go, the knife won't hit its mark. We both fall to the floor with him half on top of me. I hit hard, all the breath leaving my lungs. The realtor comes into the room and screams when she sees the blood spreading on the carpet.

"Call 911," Rae barks at her.

"Yes, yes, of course," the realtor stammers.

Tori rolls the man off me, then pulls me to my feet. Her hands roam over me, checking to make sure I'm not injured. When she doesn't find any gaping wounds, she puts her palms to my cheeks and turns my face to hers.

"Are you okay?"

I put my hands over hers and wheeze. "Once I get my breath back, I'll be fine." I look down at myself and see the man's blood has gotten all over my clothes. "Damn. This was one of my favorite blouses."

Rae guides the realtor to the lone desk and chair remaining in the enormous room behind us and has her sit. She's clearly in shock. I'm not sure why, though, it's not like anything happened to her. Maybe she has a problem with all the blood.

When Rae returns to the room, she is looking at the man's hand that held the knife. I'm not sure why, but she takes several photos of him and of his hand. I move closer and see that whatever the markings on the back of his hand were, they're smudged now.

"What's that?" I query.

"A feint or a disguise of some sort. It seems like he wanted us to think he was someone other than who he is." She runs her hands over his pockets. "No wallet, so no ID. That's a shame."

Despite the rundown aspect of the building, it's in an upper class area of town, so police response is swift. Within ten minutes, several police cars surround the building. Alejandro has given a statement – he was in the basement at the time and didn't see anything – and been allowed to leave.

The rest of us aren't so lucky. We've given statements separately several times. Then, when two men in suits arrive and identify themselves as homicide detectives, we start all over again.

I voluntarily send them the video I kept running after the man burst into the room. With their heads together, they watch it on one of their phones through to the end. Once Rae dashes into the room, my phone falls and gives a beautiful view of the stained ceiling tiles and audio of me crying out when I hit the floor and the man groaning.

The sounds of Tori asking me if I'm okay cut off just as Rae's face appears and she stops the video.

"Who's Rae?" asks one detective, a middle-aged man with smooth dark skin, silver at his temples and laugh lines around his eyes. He told me his name, but I can't remember it. Only that his first name was something to do with cars.

"I'm Rae," my cousin volunteers.

"Why did you want to call her?"

Without hesitation, I reply. "She was elsewhere in the building, so I thought if she heard what was going on, she would either come help or call for help or both. We're just lucky things turned out the way they did. I only meant to trip him as he fell forward."

Over and over, we tell the same story. They question us separately and together, changing up the configuration multiple times. An eternity later, we're allowed to leave.

CHAPTER FORTY-NINE

More Than Ready

VICTORIA

O nce we're back in the SUV, I pull Cam into my arms and kiss her. While we were facing down that man, my adrenaline was pumping, and all I wanted to do was jump her bones right then and there.

I don't know what it is about violence that always leaves me so turned on. At first she tenses, but only for a moment, then she goes soft in my arms and kisses me back.

Ever since I made my declaration of love, everything has been different. She hasn't told me she loves me back, but things are even better than they were before my crisis of conscience when I stepped away for a few days.

I mean, I felt like we were getting there, but now, I'm sure. What does it say about us that bloody violence solidified our future with each other?

She's unlike anyone I've ever known. With her I feel freer and more myself than ever before. Being with Bridget makes me believe that anything is possible, and the future is limitless.

It's all kinds of fucked up, but when someone is willing to kill for you, kill *with* you, nothing can hold you back. Feeling the energy drain after the rush of adrenaline, we doze off in the back seat, tangled up in each other's arms.

Rae wakes us when she parks the SUV in the garage and it seems our little nap did the trick of diffusing the aftereffects of the adrenaline burn off. I wake feeling fresh and energized, and it seems as if Bridget is feeling it, too.

She practically bounces out of the car and into the house. Jo is in the kitchen preparing supper and looks up when we come in from the garage.

"It took you all a while to look at a building."

Rae snitches a piece of carrot from where Jo is chopping them for a salad. "Ran into some trouble and had to wait to be questioned by the cops."

Jo gasps. "What?"

"How long before dinner is ready?" I ask before Rae gets rolling on the story.

"About thirty minutes."

I give Bridget a wicked look. She grins back, takes my hand, and we race up the stairs.

When we're both sated with a myriad of orgasms, we're lying in bed. The sun has set, and the room is layered with shadows and mystery. Her head rests on my chest as my fingertips languidly stroke over her shoulder.

"I'd like you to move back in here, if you're ready for that," she whispers into the dark, as if she's sharing a secret.

"I am more than ready. Sleeping without you has proven difficult. Not only that, but I'm ready to start our forever together."

"Me, too," she replies. "I love you, Victoria. I've never felt for anyone what I feel for you. You are my one, my forever, and I didn't realize just how cold and dead I felt inside knowing what my uncle had in store for me. My life started when I met you."

"I love you, too," I rasp, my throat choked with emotion. She takes me by the hand and leans in to place a soft kiss on my lips, then pulls back and grins. Despite the smile, I don't miss the emotions shining in her eyes because they're shining in mine, too.

"Come on. Jo will kill us if we don't go down for supper."

We roll out of bed and throw on casual clothes. When we enter the kitchen, everyone is already eating. "Sorry, not sorry," Rae says with a smirk. "I was starving and couldn't wait for you two to stop orgasming each other."

Bridget's face turns pink, as she rebuffs, "Shite, Rae! No one wants to hear that!"

I'm not bothered by Rae's teasing.

"I wouldn't mind hearing more," Nate mumbles, but the slight tilt of his mouth lets me know he's teasing.

Rae smacks him playfully on the back of the head and laughs. "No. Just no."

We all join in laughing, too. With full plates, we take a seat at the island with her, Nate, and Finn while Jo hovers, making sure everyone gets their fill. We eat in here so often that we added a couple of barstools so we could all eat together.

When she is settled in her seat, Bridget announces, "Tori is going to be moving in here permanently."

"Bout time," Rae retorts. "I trust you two will be able to coordinate everything. Just let me know when you need me to carry stuff."

She is so nonchalant about it, as if she knew me moving in here was a foregone conclusion. Warmth spreads in my chest to know that she accepts me as one of the family and trusts me with her dearest friend and family member.

I'm going to do my best to live up to her trust and spend the rest of my days living and loving and proving myself worthy of her trust and Bridget's love.

With the serious stuff out of the way, we talk about plans for the building and the club. Cam talks about playing up the hints of art nouveau architecture on the exterior and creating a speakeasy bluesy type atmosphere in the bar she'll be running.

What she wants will be expensive, but based on Rae's non-chalant agreement, we're well funded. I can't wait to add my earnings into the mix because I know the fitness club I want to open is also going to be a hit. Once it's up and running in the black, I'll open another one in Tulsa.

If Rae is intent on making this state hers and building an empire, I'm going to help make that happen. This is my family now, too, and I want to contribute.

We also talk about plans for the fitness center. I've already reached out to some of my former co-workers and most of them are highly interested in making a change from Cassandra's.

Apparently, they aren't happy with the way things are there, either. Cassandra is stepping away from the club, but someone new is taking over.

Rae perks up at that. "I'll have to see who it is. They didn't ask for my permission to be in our town."

That comment goes all over me. Not her town, but our town. I never imagined this kind of future for myself, but now that it's looming large, I'm excited because it's bigger, brighter, and more amazing than I ever thought possible.

Best of all, every step of the way, Cam and I will be side-by-side to face the dangers and challenges and take out anyone who tries to stand in our way.

Cam's cousin bursts into the room. "Oh my gosh, you guys! I'm so excited! Geno's coming to visit!"

The End

Get a **FREE** copy of a bonus that occurs right after Bee's announcement that Geno is coming to visit.

https://dl.bookfunnel.com/ddqzumwxmt

If you enjoyed Coup, do me a solid and leave a review! It's not a
book report; it's okay to keep it short. Have fun! Be honest!

https://mybook.to/CoupKitMcKenna

Thank you loves!

XOXO

Kit

About the Author

Kit McKenna writes romance books that are dreamy, dirty, and sometimes have a splash of darkness and danger set against the backdrop of Oklahoma.

Kit is a born and raised Oklahoma gal who has lived here her whole life except for a brief detour to hang out in the mountains for four years. She is an artist and free spirit who loves roaming around in the woods and finds great joy in the unusually and sometimes darkly beautiful. Kit has worn a lot of hats in her life, a server, a factory worker, nightclub manager, office administrator, state drone, and business owner.

A bit of a dichotomy, she loves all things positivity and light, but still loves to play in the dark. Her favorite book offerings range from authors like Eckhart Tolle to Stephen King. Her favorite movies are horror and holiday is Samhain (Halloween) but she still loves a good romance. She's a huge sucker for a story where the underdog comes out on top.

If the bar doesn't have a good cider, she'll opt for a fine whisky.

She comes to writing later in life after tiring of reading books that seem to only focus on perfect, perky, barely legal heroines. Her stories are about real people who have their own demons, drama, and challenges to overcome.

You can find her on online at:

Website – www.kitmckenna.com

Facebook – @authorkitmckenna

Instagram - @kitmckennaauthor

TikTok – @kitmckennaauthor